TROUBLE
IN THE
EVERGLADES

TROUBLE
IN THE
EVERGLADES

LEE GRAMLING

Palm Beach, Florida

An imprint of The Rowman & Littlefield Publishing Group, Inc.
4501 Forbes Blvd., Ste. 200
Lanham, MD 20706
www.rowman.com

Distributed by NATIONAL BOOK NETWORK

Copyright © 2020 by Lee Gramling

British Library Cataloguing in Publication Information Available

Library of Congress Cataloging-in-Publication Data

Names: Gramling, Lee, 1942- author.
Title: Trouble in the Everglades / Lee Gramling.
Description: Palm Beach, Florida : Pineapple Press ; Lanham, MD : Rowman & Littlefield, [2020] | Summary: "When Tate Barkley meet[s] up with a man who calls himself "Gator" he doesn't know he's the boss of a gang of "plumers" - men who kill thousands of birds in the Everglades so their [plumes] can adorn fashionable ladies' hats. In fact, he doesn't even know what a "plumer" is. But he learns quick enough, and more about the rough and dangerous bunch than he ever wanted to know. When he joins up with a rich Yankee detective who's hunting a friend that's gone missing in the vast and watery wilderness you can be sure there's going to be trouble in the Everglades"—Provided by publisher.
Identifiers: LCCN 2019048589 (print) | LCCN 2019048590 (ebook) | ISBN 9781683340805 (paperback) | ISBN 9781683340812 (epub)
Subjects: LCSH: Everglades (Fla.)--Fiction.
Classification: LCC PS3557.R228 T76 2020 (print) | LCC PS3557.R228 (ebook) | DDC 813/.54—dc23
LC record available at https://lccn.loc.gov/2019048589
LC ebook record available at https://lccn.loc.gov/2019048590

For Jeremy Frank

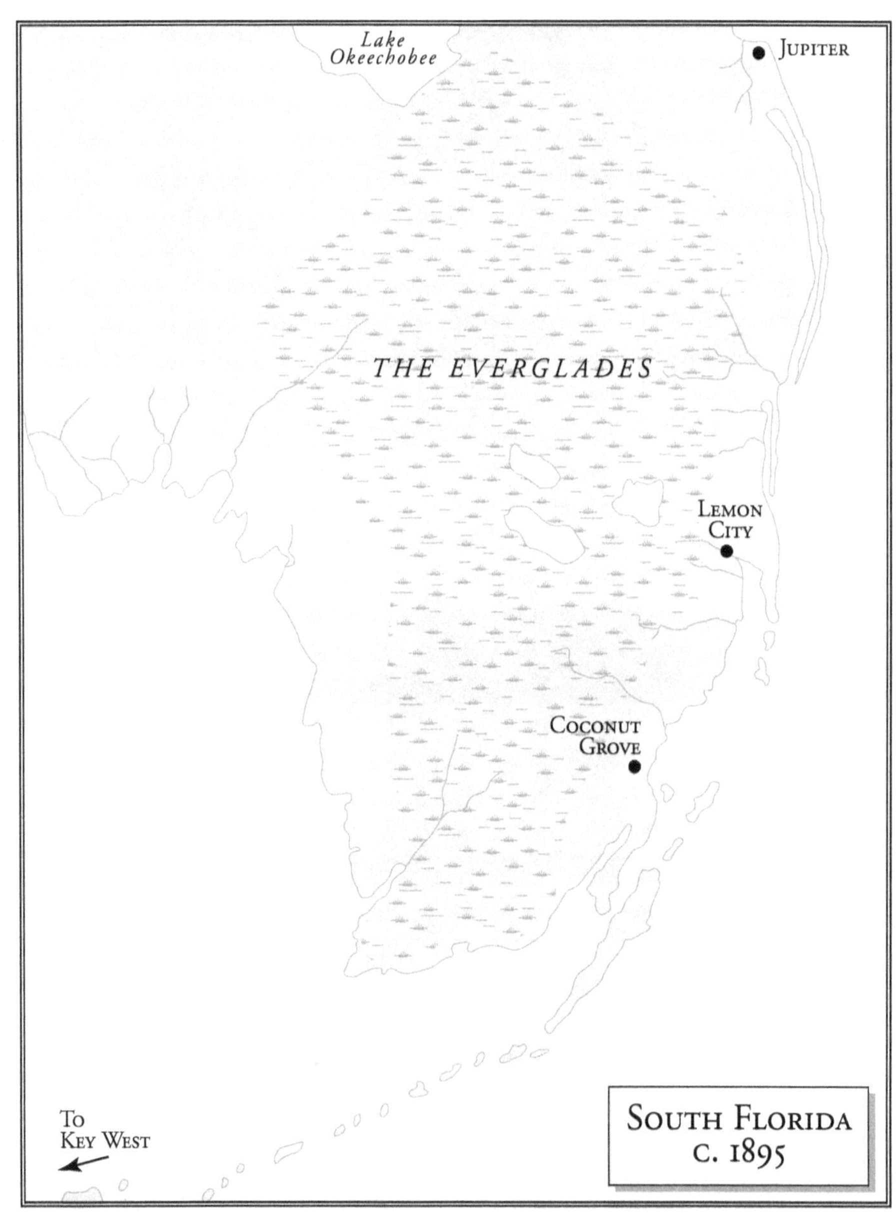

Lake Okeechobee
JUPITER
THE EVERGLADES
LEMON CITY
COCONUT GROVE
To KEY WEST
SOUTH FLORIDA
C. 1895

❧ 1 ❧

I COULD OF SWORE THAT FELLER WAS DEAD. HE WAS LAYIN' HALF IN AN' HALF out the water of that li'l creek runs from the Everglades down into Biscayne Bay. Weren't stirrin' a-tall. It was gettin' on towards dark an' what little I could see of his face an' hands 'peared kind of grayish-white. Like some other corpses I seen time to time.

It didn't hardly seem decent to leave him all sprawled out like that with the water flowin' 'round him. For one thing, they was folks downstream what prob'ly depended on that creek for washin' and drinkin' and such.

So I swung down from the leather an' looped my reins over the saddle horn, meanin' to fetch him up onto drier ground where somebody could come along an' bury him proper. When I bent down an' took hold of his shoulders to roll him over, that's when he let out a kind of a low, shudderin' moan.

I mean it give me a turn. I felt the hairs on the back of my neck rise up an' I stumbled back a step so's that I almost dropped him right back in the creek.

'T ain't that I'm afeared of h'aints an' such. I seen a sight of dead men in my time, and nary one of 'em ever come back later on to trouble the livin'. But the thing of it was, the light was kind of bad right there an' that sound just come out of him all sudden an' unexpected-like.

I knew right away that feller was still alive, though maybe only barely an' maybe not for a whole lot longer. I dragged him up onto the bank and laid him out so's I could have me a better look.

When I'd got him situated on his back an' pulled open his coat it didn't take no dee-tective to figure out what was his problem. He'd been shot twice, once in the shoulder an' once in the leg. Bullets passed clean through both times, leavin' the flesh all tore up where they come out the far side. That was good news, 'cause it seemed no bones was broke nor nothin' important inside him had got hit.

But it was bad news too. 'Cause he'd been bleedin' from four places for what 'peared to be a while. I tugged off his jacket an' slit his trousers with my Bowie, then tore off pieces from his shirt to plug up all the holes. It were a right fancy shirt when I started in on it, with ruffles down the front an' at the ends of the sleeves. Didn't leave him too much of it by the time I was done. But I figured he weren't liable to object.

That jacket was a real fine one too: light-colored leather near-'bout soft as felt. 'Course it had a couple bloodstained holes in it now that didn't do much for its looks. He'd had him a tooled leather holster belted on underneath it, well-oiled an' showin' plenty of use. But when I pushed the coat back so's I could see it, it was empty as a church on payday night. Whilst I was settin' to work on his leg, I noticed his boots was of that Boston kind, shiny black an' coming almost up to his knees.

Any way you looked at it this feller 'peared to be some kind of real for-sure gent. Rich Yankee tourist maybe, come down here into Florida for his health.

Which hadn't worked out too good for him so far. I was right curious to know what it was led to him gettin' all shot up like he was. An' I hoped he'd live long enough to tell me more about it.

Whilst I was pluggin' up them bullet holes he'd moaned off an' on but never onct opened his eyes. I figured he was out for the count an' likely to stay that way for a spell. Considerin' all the blood he'd lost, it weren't no great surprise.

When I was done I listened to him breathe for li'l bit. Seemed regular enough but shallow. I reckoned I might's well try movin' him. Couldn't leave him out here all alone with it comin' on dark and nobody else to do for him.

I had me a li'l cabin a mile or two away, built tight against the weather an' with food an' fixin's an' such. Even a rope bed I hadn't got real used to yet an' what I reckoned I could do without for a spell.

So I brung my horse over an' manhandled him up into the saddle. He was a good-sized gent, but I ain't 'zactly no midget my ownself. An' when Tate Barkley takes hold of somethin' it most generally moves.

That mare was a Cracker horse with a level coon-rack gait an' a naturally gentle nature. Onct I'd got the feller up on top of her I could see he was a rider from the way he held on with his knees an' kept his seat without never 'pearin' to wake up. Which made the job a heap easier under the circumstances. I worked his toes into the stirrups an' started off walkin' alongside, holdin' on to his good arm to keep him from slewin' sideways.

When we got up to the cabin I lit a coal-oil lantern over the front stoop to give us a tad of light. Then I lifted him down an' kind of frog-walked him up the steps an' in through the door. He showed a few signs of life durin' that, but not enough to be much help.

When we got next to the bed I pulled back the covers an' helped him lie down; then I laid a couple blankets over him 'gainst the chills an' fever I reckoned would come. Afterwards, I stood catchin' my breath an' just watchin' him for a couple minutes. Even after all that ridin' an' movin' about he still 'peared to be breathin' pretty regular, which I took to be a hopeful sign.

I went out on the porch an' fetched the lantern to lead my mare 'round back to where I'd got a log corral with a shed at one end that was roofed over by palmetto fans. My Ole Roan horse let out a snort when he seen me, ornery as always an' jealous to boot. We'd covered a heap of country together when it was just him an' me. But he was gettin' a mite long in the tooth now, and I'd took to ridin' the mare more frequent lately.

After I'd hung up the lantern I unsaddled an' started to give the mare a rubdown, thinkin' whilst I did it how I didn't have no food in the house that wouldn't need a bit of fixin'. It bein' plumb dark now and me some tired after a day's ride follered by manhandlin' that gent hither an' yon, I figured I'd just put off supper 'til it got to be time for breakfast.

But I knew the horses wouldn't of seen things that way, so I forked out hay for 'em both. Then to keep peace in the family so to speak, I set about givin' Ole Roan a rubdown of his own whilst he nipped at my legs more for form than out of any real meanness.

Time I'd made it back into the cabin that gent in my bed 'peared to be sleepin' peaceful, only mutterin' to hisself a li'l now an' again. Come daylight I'd try an' find somethin' to bind his wounds up more proper. But for now it seemed like a better idea to just let him sleep.

I fetched my ole bedroll from the corner where I'd throwed it some time back, an' spread it out on the wood floor not too far from the bed. I had another look at my visitor 'fore I blew out the light and stretched myself out for the night. He was a right sturdy feller, an' I'd a notion he might manage to live if the corruption didn't set in.

Next mornin' I was up with the chickens, which I could hear cut-cuttin' 'round underneath my window. It weren't full light yet, but they was a rosy streak of sky away off to the east. I rolled up my bedroll, slung on my gun belt, an' stamped into my boots.

The gent in my bed still 'peared to be sleepin', or anyhow he was still breathin'. I knew 'cause I bent over him to check.

I picked up the lantern off the floor an' set it on the table, not botherin' to light it an' waste oil when day was right on the horizon. Then I went outside to tell the horses good mornin' an' put out a li'l dried corn for their breakfast.

Speakin' of which, my stomach had started to growl by now an' get my attention. I took a basket an' rousted 'round on my knees till I come up with a half-dozen brown yard eggs the hens had left here an' there. Then I went back inside an' cut a mess of thick slices off the side of bacon that was hangin' from a rafter. I set my ole iron skillet up on the wood stove an' bent down to light the fire.

Whilst that was gettin' started good, I went over to take another look at my visitor. He was stirrin' an' mutterin in his sleep a tad now, but he still didn't look near ready to wake up. I put the bacon in the pan an' then rummaged 'round in a cracker box I was usin' for a chest till I found a ole sheet I could tear up for bandages. Took that an' a pint bottle of turpentine to put by the bed for when I got 'round to doin' a mite of doctorin'.

But breakfast come first. Whilst the bacon was sizzlin' an' poppin' I dipped out water from the li'l tank in the stove an' put it in a pot with a handful of grounds to boil up some coffee. Then I whipped together a batch of cornbread batter to fry in the grease after I'd scrambled them eggs.

Time I sat myself down at my ole deal table, I'd fixed me a reg'lar early mornin' feast.

I reckon it showed I was doin' pretty good for myself these days. I had a cabin with a honest-to-God wood stove on several acres of scrub land, two horses, chickens, an' a half-dozen hogs rootin' round in the woods that I laid claim to. Only thing I might still use was a ox or a mule to make this homestead a goin' concern.

'Course none of it had come easy. I'd rode into Florida on Ole Roan a heap of years ago with nothin' else to my name but a pistol, a Winchester rifle, an' some mighty high hopes. Did whatever I could to make a dollar, which in those early days had more to do with them guns than too much else: a li'l deputy sheriffin', a li'l private hirin' out for this an' that. But I'd turned my hand to cow huntin' too, and lumberin', an' anything else that called for a feller with a strong back an' a weak mind.

I'd lived poor an' saved up. Li'l under a month ago I was able to make a deal with a Yankee an' his wife who'd got sick an' plumb tired of the skeeters an' the gators an' the once-in-a-while hurricanes at this here south end of the Unitey States. They'd left out for Ohio in what would of been a cloud of dust. 'Cept it happened to be the rainy season just then.

Myself, I'd 'bout had my fill of wanderin' from pillar to post without no place I could call my own. I'd never had no ambitions to be a dirt farmer, and I weren't real sure it was in my plans for the future. But I reckoned I could manage to dig coontie roots for a spell, an' maybe even put in a crop of pineapples. Heard they was folks in this part of the country made a fair livin' doin' that.

I figured after while somethin' better might turn up. It often did, an' I weren't a man that planned too far in the future.

When I'd got done eatin' I dipped more water into a pan on the stove an' shaved some beef jerky into it that I'd had left over from a trip up the country. Figured that shot-up gent might take a li'l broth when he finally woke up.

By now they was aplenty of sunshine comin' in through the window facin' towards the east, so I pulled a chair over next to the bed an' rolled back the covers, fixin' to have a more careful look at all that gent's hurts.

But 'fore I could get started good I heard voices outside by my front porch. They was men's voices an' they didn't sound real cheerful.

It's a kind of a custom wherever I been, both here in Florida an' in the western lands, to call out from a distance 'fore comin' up to somebody's house or campsite. Lets 'em know you're friendly an' don't mean to take 'em unawares.

If they don't do it there's generally only one of two reasons for it: either they're just plain ignorant, or they ain't so friendly as a feller might want or expect.

I'd no way of knowin' which it was right then. But my momma didn't raise no careless children. I got up an' went to fetch my Winchester from where I'd leaned it up against the wall. Then I stepped over to the side of the door an' cracked it open just a tad so's I could take a peek outside.

✿ 2 ✿

THEY WAS FOUR OF 'EM, ALL LOOKIN' SO SHAGGY AN' ROUGH THAT I RECK-
oned they could of wore their clothes out from the inside. An' all of 'em
was totin' guns: three shotguns an' a rifle.

I cocked the Winchester, which I knew would sound real sharp in the
still mornin' air, an' maybe it'd give 'em somethin' to consider upon. Then I
pushed the door open with my left hand an' stepped out on the porch.

"Somethin' I can do for you gents?"

"Well, I reckon that depends." The feller with the rifle was talkin', an'
he eyed me careful-like without 'pearin' too concerned since I was one against
their four. His three companions each took a li'l step to one side, the shotguns
under their arms not quite pointin' at me but not 'zactly pointed towards the
ground neither. My Winchester kind of followed 'em accidental-like whilst I
kept my eyes on the man who was speakin'.

'Sides the rifle he carried he had the only hand gun that I could see—an
ole Army Colt shoved down into his belt. He was sportin' a big wide slouch
hat with a egret plume stuck in the band, an' wore a scruffy droopin' mustache
stained yellow from tobacco juice. He spit on the ground by my front steps
an' squinted up at me. "You happen to see any strangers hereabout in the last
couple days?"

I met his look without answerin' for a second or two. Then I said, "Who
is it that's wantin' to know?"

"Me an' my three friends here, together with a bunch of other hard men
back yonder in the Glades."

If he was hopin' to impress me with those numbers he'd gone an' suggested he was talkin' to the wrong Cracker boy. I had me seventeen shots in
that Winchester of mine, an' five more in the Smith an' Wesson on my hip.

All of it without reloadin'. Which ought to be aplenty considerin' I ain't too much in the habit of missin' whatever I shoot at.

"You got a name?" I asked.

"Gator." He spit some more tobacco juice there by my steps. "Just Gator's enough. Most folks 'round these parts has heard of me."

"Well Mister Gator, I reckon I ain't one of 'em. Haven't been livin' here so awful long."

"Well if you 'spect to keep on *livin'* here . . ." He put a little extra stress on that word *livin'*. ". . . you'll come to know it soon enough. In the meantime you ain't give me a answer to that question I asked you earlier."

"You mean 'bout whoever it is you-all are huntin'?" He hadn't said they was huntin' nobody, but it didn't take no genius to figure it out. Folks don't go 'round armed to the teeth like that to greet some visitin' friend or relative.

I frowned kind of thoughtful-like. "Don't rightly know how to answer that. You got any kind of a description?" I'd a pretty good notion what was goin' to say 'fore he ever got 'round to sayin' it.

"Tall, good-lookin' Yankee dude, maybe your height or a little under. Clean-shaved with black hair a li'l bit gray over the ears. All dressed up in fancy eastern duds."

I shook my head. "Feller like that ought to stand out like a red flag in this country. Don't 'call seein' anybody a-tall like that since I first got down here."

The man who'd called hisself Gator kind of scowled like he weren't sure if I was tellin' the truth or not. Which o' course I wasn't. But it ain't real smart to call a feller a liar when he's holdin' a cocked an' loaded Winchester in his hands.

"Well," he said after a minute, "you see any sign of that gent you pass along the word. Tell anybody hereabouts that Gator is lookin' for him an' I'll know 'bout it."

I nodded without sayin' nothin' an' the four of 'em turned to leave.

"Oh, just by the by," I called out when they'd taken a couple steps. "Might be a good idea if you all pass this way again, to call out kind of loud an' friendly-like 'fore comin' on up to the cabin. Wouldn't want no kind of a accident to happen 'cause I didn't know who you was."

That Gator give me a real hard look over his shoulder. But then he an' the others kept on stridin' off west towards the Glades without another word.

I watched from the porch till they'd got completely out of sight. Then I went inside an' bolted the door. Kept my Winchester in easy reach when I sat down again to look after that Yankee feller's wounds.

He hadn't made nary sound whilst I was out there talkin' to them men, an' I weren't real sure at first if he was still asleep or not. But then he opened his eyes an' studied me kind of thoughtful whilst I set about uncoverin' him an' pullin' off his bloody bandages.

When I went to clean his bullet holes with a cloth soaked in turpentine he cussed an' started to rise up off the bed. But I pushed him back down an' held him there with my free hand. "You just settle down an' try to stay quiet. There's some fellers out yonder been huntin' you, an' I've a idea they're wantin' to finish the job they started."

I slid a bullet out from my belt an' put it between his teeth. "Bite down on that for a spell. I won't take no longer 'bout this than I have to. But if we don't keep the corruption away it'll kill you a sight quicker'n anything else 'bout them flesh wounds you got."

He done like I said an' I got on with the job. When I'd finished tyin' on the clean bandages an' was kind of lookin' him over, he handed the bullet back to me. His eyes was wide open now an' I reckon he was kind of lookin' me over too.

"Thanks," he said kind of quiet-like. "I guess I owe you my life."

I shrugged. It were prob'ly true, but I hadn't done nothin' any decent feller wouldn't of done. Done the same for a hurt dog or a mule.

He kind of gritted his teeth an' pushed hisself up with his good arm to take a look around. I could see the effort pained him but he was tryin' not to let on. "You live here?" he asked.

"I reckon."

"Have you lived here long?"

Now that seemed a kind of a odd question under the circumstances, but I'd no reason not to answer it. "In this here cabin? Not more'n a couple-three weeks. Made a deal for it with some Yankee folks that didn't care for the country."

"And in this area? Between Biscayne Bay and the Everglades?'

"No longer'n that. Passed by here a time or two in my travels."

"And since you moved here have you come to know many of your neighbors?"

"Met a couple. Folks in these parts don't 'zactly take to strangers right off."

I was eyin' him pretty curious by now. He was askin' things 'bout me an' my life I figured weren't rightly none of his business. An' for a gent who'd just been a whisker away from never learnin' nothin' more a-tall, his serious way of askin' made it 'pear he weren't only passin' the time of day.

Well, they was plenty I wanted to know 'bout him too. Maybe that weren't none of my business neither. 'Cept I figured keepin' Gator an' his friends offen him earlier might give me some cards in the game.

But I could tell the gent was startin' to run out of steam so I reckoned all that would keep. He weren't goin' no place real soon.

"I got some beef broth simmerin' on the stove," I said. "Think you might take a li'l nourishment?"

He nodded weakly. "And some water too if you don't mind. I've had a raging thirst ever since I woke up."

"Losin' blood'll do that to a feller." I got up an' fetched the water bucket over by the bed an' helped him to drink from the dipper. Then I went an' poured broth into a tin cup an' brought it over to where he was layin'. Usin' one hand to help him up a li'l straighter I held the cup to his lips with the other.

He managed to get the most part of it down 'fore his head started in to nod. I put the cup by an' helped him down on his back again. No sooner'n I'd got finished doin' that than he was sleepin' quiet as a baby.

He kept on sleepin' for 'most the rest of that day. Me, I hung 'round the cabin attendin' to this an' that. Carried my Winchester under my arm whenever I went outside. But I didn't see no more of that Gator an' his pals. Maybe they was out yonder someplace watchin' from a distance. Or maybe they'd bought my story an' went on to lookin' elsewhere.

Didn't matter a awful lot to me. I hoped they'd take to heart my message 'bout comin' up on my place unawares. But if they didn't I figured to remind 'em of it quick enough.

Weren't no way they could see or hear my visitor inside the cabin from any kind of a distance. An' as for trailin' him here, that path from the creek was all loose sand an' the only tracks on it anyhow was mine an' them of my Cracker horse. Back where I'd found him was right sandy too, and they'd been a tad of rain durin' the night to help wash out the sign.

It seemed likely enough to me that Gator an' them was who'd done gone an' shot this gent. They must of lost sight of him after he fell down amongst the trees. Could of 'peared like they'd done for him, but they'd wanted to be sure. And he'd prob'ly made it hard for 'em by crawlin' 'long in that creek bed for a ways. With it comin' on dark an' all they'd finally had to give it up an' wait for daylight to seek him.

'Least that's the way I made it out from what little bit I knew or could guess. Whatever might lay behind it I had no notion a-tall. Hell, I didn't even know who the gent was. Nor Gator an' his mean-lookin' tag-alongs neither 'cept for what he'd gone an' told me. Which weren't much.

Why they'd shoot a man down in cold blood without even a how-d'-you-do was more'n I could figure, though killin's in this country didn't always need a heap of reasons. I'd cause enough to know that for myself after all the years I'd spent here an' abouts.

However you wanted to look at it I 'peared to of got myself smack in the middle of somethin' that was just liable to end up in the smoke. An' I reckoned it was time an' past time I went about learnin' the why an' the wherefore of it.

But 'fore nightfall that gent in my bed come on feverish and weren't in no shape for any kind of talkin'. Alls I could do was watch over him an' keep him covered up against the chills whilst he tossed an' turned an' muttered things I couldn't make no head nor tail of.

Next day the fever finally broke an' he started in to sweat. I mopped his face an' give him three, four dippers of water. But still I couldn't ask him no questions. He was so weak an' tired by then he just rolled over on his side an' went right on back to sleepin'.

❧ 3 ☙

WHEN I SAW HIS EYES WAS OPEN AGAIN IT WAS COMIN' ON TOWARDS night an' I'd just lit the lantern on the table. He 'peared to finally know where he was an' who he was, but he didn't say nothin'. Just laid there watchin' me with that curious look I'd noticed on his face earlier.

I went over to the bed an' looked down at him. "How you feelin' ole son?"

"Better I guess. Weak as a kitten from the loss of blood and still pretty thirsty." He smiled "And hungry."

"Good signs. Dyin' men don't hardly drink nor eat nothin' towards the end."

"Dying has no place in my plans. Not now, and not for some time to come I hope. There are things I need to do."

What those things was is just what I'd been wonderin'. But he got quiet again an' didn't 'pear moved to explain. I just shrugged an' knelt down to fetch some water from the bucket an' held the dipper whilst he drank. Then I stood an' went to set the rest of that broth I'd made over the fire.

Whilst it was heatin' I come back an' took a seat in the chair alongside the bed. We studied each other for a minute or two. Then I asked kind of quiet-like, "You happen to know a feller 'round these parts that calls hisself Gator?"

His brow knit up like he was tryin' to recall, an' then he shook his head. "No. Why?"

"Well, it 'peared to me like he knows you. Or somethin' 'bout you anyway. Him an' three other hard cases was 'round here yesterday lookin' for a gent that sounded like you. An' I got the notion they wasn't 'zactly interested in your welfare."

I reckon I'd finally got his whole attention. He tried to sit up straight an' near 'bout made it. From the way his face twisted up I could see it pained him considerable.

"What . . ." He kind of swallered a groan. "What did you tell them?"

I shrugged a mite. "Tole 'em I never seed hide nor hair of nobody in these parts looked close to the feller they was describin'."

That didn't 'pear to calm him a awful lot. He started to throw back the covers an' make a stab at gettin' up. If he weren't careful he'd open up them wounds again an' bleed all over my bed. I laid a hand on his chest and eased him back down.

"You just settle a mite. You ain't goin' no place in the shape you're in, an' if you did you wouldn't be so safe as you are right here. Me an' them four reached a kind of a understandin'. They won't come up close to this cabin no more. And 'long as they don't, I'll refrain from weightin' their hides down with lead."

The gent stopped his strugglin' an' just laid there, breathin' hard and eyin' me mighty careful. I let him do it whilst I went to get a spoon an' fetch the broth from the stove.

When I come back I helped him up on one elbow. Then I sat down in the chair an' started in to feed him.

'Course he couldn't talk much whilst he was eatin' an' I was willin' to wait. He finished off the rest of that broth without neither of us sayin' a word. When he was done I wiped his mouth with my kerchief an' went to put the pan an' spoon on the table.

Time I'd got back an' sat down again I figured he'd had long enough to mull things over. I leaned forward an' looked him in the eye.

"I figure I done my part," I said. "I hauled you outen that crick an' brung you in an' patched up your hurts. Then I lied through my teeth to keep those men who was huntin' you from finishin' what they'd started.

"But the trouble of it is," I went on, "I got no earthly idea what-all I was doin' it for. Helpin' out a hurt man ain't no more'n just Christian charity. But facin' down four men totin' rifles an' shotguns is somethin' else again." I paused an' shrugged. "Ain't 'zactly the first time I ever done such a thing. But generally, whenever I did I had me a pretty good notion of what it was about an' why it was I was doin' it."

I paused again, still meetin' his eyes. "You reckon you might just fill me in a li'l bit on that last part?"

He didn't say nothin' for a right long spell, lookin' at me in the face kind of thoughtful-like. Prob'ly calc'latin' how much or how little he'd ought to tell me. Or maybe to keep his affairs to hisself an' just leave me wonderin'.

I leaned back in the chair. "I reckon you don't got to explain nothin' if you ain't a mind to. But 'pears to me you done got yourself into a sort of a fix here. You're laid up in bed without no horse an' no gun, an' they's four hard-case killers out yonder seekin' your hide. From what you asked me yesterday, my guess is you're new in this country an' prob'ly ain't got no friends or relations you can look to for help."

I figured I weren't tellin' him nothin' he hadn't already thought of. An' he'd likely been wonderin' 'bout what he or anybody else could do to get him shut of his troubles.

"Looks to me," I said, "like you ain't got a awful lot of choice but to trust me a li'l bit. I reckon you might do worse. I ain't been in this here place too long, but I've covered a sight of country in my time. An' I've had more'n a couple whiffs of gunsmoke along the way. You got my word that nothin' you choose to tell me needs to go outside this room. An' Tate Barkley's word is a thing nobody's ever questioned."

His eyes narrowed a tad. "Barkley?"

"That's the name. First part of it's Tate."

"I think I may have heard of you. Weren't you involved in that affair up in the Green Swamp several years ago?"

"I been there."

"I knew some other people who were there. They said they thought you were some kind of western gunfighter."

"I been out west. But actual truth of the matter is I'm a Florida Cracker, born an' bred."

"And a gunfighter?"

I shrugged. "Not 'zactly what I'd like to claim as a perfession. Never been one to go 'round seekin' trouble. But ever now an' then it's managed to find me. An' if a feller comes 'long with trouble on his mind, I'd purely hate to let him go off disappointed."

The gent kind of half-smiled. "Those people I spoke with said you were a pretty rough customer. I think they were a little afraid of you. But they also said they were awfully glad you came along when you did. You helped them get out of a very bad spot."

I didn't have nothin' partic'lar to say 'bout that, so I just nodded an' held my peace.

He was thoughtful for a second or two. Then he asked, "You didn't know any of those men who came here looking for me?"

"Never set eyes on ary one of 'em." Damn. I ask this gent for answers an' all I keep gettin' is more questions. "But I reckon I know their kind."

"Killers, you mean?"

"Uh-huh. Figure it was them four that bushwhacked you back yonder in the woods."

"But you'd never seen or heard about any of them until yesterday?"

"Nope. 'Course I ain't been livin' here too long. An' that Gator feller did say if I told the locals I seen you the word would get back to him. Give me the idea he was a knowed man in these parts."

"Hm. So some of your neighbors may know where to find him."

"They might. Or maybe everbody just knows somebody who knows somebody who's heard somethin'. An' if anybody does know I don't imagine they'd be too anxious to let on 'bout it to strangers."

"Yes, you're probably right. And there's not much I can do about it anyway until I'm back on my feet again. That's the first order of business."

"Uh-huh." I was gettin' right tired of this gent just askin' questions an' not tellin' me nothin' useful. Figured it was high time we got down to the meat of the matter.

"Be some days 'fore you're able to be up an' about," I said. "Reckon you could spend 'em here with me. Only that Gator an' his friends is still out there somewheres, an' I don't 'spect they'll of forgot why they was askin' here 'bout you. 'Spite of what I told 'em, I'd a notion they was still a mite doubtful. Time's liable to come when they let their curiosity get the better of their good sense.

"Now, so far," I went on, lookin' at him kind of sharp, "you ain't give me a single good reason why I shouldn't just ask 'em inside an' save myself a heap of trouble. Might be you're some outlaw or killer your ownself. Could be I'd be doin' the public a service by lettin' 'em get their hands on you."

I didn't much believe in what it was I'd just said, but I needed this gent to start thinkin' 'bout my part in all this. Figured I'd got a reason an' a right to know what kind of a situation I was gettin' into. 'Tain't 'zactly the way to put your best foot forward amongst new neighbors by right off havin' a shootin' scrape with a bunch all the locals know.

When I'd said my say I just waited, an' the gent didn't speak for a couple long minutes. Then he nodded.

"There was a wallet in the inner pocket of the coat I was wearing when you found me. Do you still have it?"

"Uh-huh." I'd kept the coat an' felt the bulge of the wallet inside it, but I hadn't took it out nor thought to open it. Feller's private things should ought to stay private. Same thing went for the money belt I'd took offen him after I'd put him in bed.

"Could you get the wallet and bring it to me?"

"Sure." I shrugged, wonderin' what this had to do with the questions I'd asked him. Maybe he thought Gator an' them had meant to rob him. Or maybe he suspicioned that I had.

I got up an' went to where I'd hung the coat on a nail in the wall, then fished out the wallet an' brung it to him without openin' it. It had got a good bit of blood on it from where he'd been shot. But he managed to find a card inside that weren't smeared with it too bad. He took it out an' handed it to me.

I started readin', an' I done it out loud: "Major Briand Cameron, USA, Retired." They was smaller print underneath that caused me a mite of trouble. But I managed to sound the words out: "Con-fi-den-tial En— Enquiries an' Con-sul-tations." When I looked up I could see he was smilin'. But I reckoned I'd got the gist of it.

"This mean you're some kind of a dee-tective?"

"Something like that," he said. "I could provide character references too, if you still think I might be a criminal. But they'd have to come from people a long way from here."

"You a policeman of some kind? Or a Pink?" I meant Pinkerton, but I reckon he understood me.

"Neither one. And for the most part now I'm retired."

"Lots of retired folks in Florida these days, though you 'pear a bit young for it. But I'm guessin' whatever it was brought you down to this place has somethin' to do with the part that ain't retired."

"That's true." I waited while he was quiet for a moment. "It's kind of a long story."

"I ain't goin' no place," I said. "An' neither are you. You feel up to talkin' about it?"

He took in a deep breath an' then he nodded. "I think so. At least enough to give you some idea of what I'm doing in South Florida."

4

"A little over a month ago," he said kind of quiet-like, "I received a letter at my home in Savannah from an old friend, Doctor Richard Summerfield. He's a naturalist I met some years earlier in New York, and he's one of the few who know that I've conducted private investigations. He asked if I'd undertake something of the kind in this area near the Everglades. He made the matter sound rather urgent and hinted there could be large amounts of money involved.

"As I said, I'm mostly retired now. But his letter piqued my interest and I wrote him back for further details. There was no reply. Then my wife and daughter went off for an extended visit with friends in the North and left me feeling at loose ends. So I decided to travel down to where Doctor Summerfield was staying in Coconut Grove and talk to him face-to-face. Only when I arrived he was no longer there.

"I asked some of the residents, and they said they thought he'd gone to Lemon City. One believed he'd heard mention of a trip into the Everglades. Doctor Summerfield's current passion is the rich and varied bird life of South Florida, and he's been anxious to observe them in their natural setting."

Cameron paused to take in a breath or two whilst I mulled that over. Lemon City was a couple miles down that creek where I'd found him all shot up. Weren't much of a town, settin' right there on the edge of Biscayne Bay. I'd been in an' out of it a time or two but didn't stay no longer'n it took to stock up on a few things at the general store.

"It seemed nobody in Lemon City remembered my friend ever being there," Cameron went on. "At least that's what they said, though the way some of them acted when I questioned them made me wonder. They avoided my eyes and seemed anxious not to let any of their neighbors see me talking to them."

"Lots of folks in these parts is a mite stand-offish 'round strangers," I said, not lettin' my voice show if I agreed with his suspicions or not.

"I guess that's true. But their behavior made me curious enough to ride on west toward the Glades in hopes of finding someone else I could ask. I hadn't gone more than a few miles when those shots came at me out of the forest." His voice kind of tapered off for a minute an' his eyes closed. Then he opened 'em again an' looked at me. "The rest of it's mostly a blur, so you probably know as much about it as I do."

"Well, what I figured was it must of been gettin' on towards dark 'bout then, an' you managed to keep on movin' long enough to give 'em all the slip."

He nodded an' kind of half-shrugged with his good shoulder. "That sounds about right."

"So what you plan to do now? I mean after you've done got your strength back an' can be stirrin' 'round?"

I didn't get no answer to my question, 'cause that gent's eyes had gone shut again an' he'd plumb drifted off into sleep.

Next mornin' he 'peared some livelier than before, so I figured maybe he'd be able to take some solid food. After I'd seen to the horses an' had me a look 'round the property, I fried up some eggs, bacon, an' cornbread for the both of us.

He did justice to it, even managin' to feed hisself after I'd propped him up into a sittin' position. When we was done an' I was puttin' the plates away, he asked if I'd noticed any signs of people comin' near the cabin lately or maybe watchin' it from a distance.

"Nope," I told him. I come back an' sat down next to the bed. "If they're watchin' they're doin' it mighty careful. An' from a good long ways off too. Them horses of mine would of surely let on if they'd been anybody sneakin' 'round in the vicinity."

He nodded an' we both was silent for a minute or two. Then I said, "You reckon you could stand for me to change out them dressin's an' have another look your hurts?"

"I guess." He grinned a li'l bit. "You're the doctor."

So I done it, swabbin' his wounds with the terps just like I done before. He didn't need no bullet to bite on this time, though he did screw up his face an' swaller a yelp or two. When I was through an' he was restin' comfortable, I finally got 'round to askin' that question I hadn't got no answer to earlier.

"'Pears you're healin' up real fine. Prob'ly be able to be on your feet in another day or two. 'Course it'll take a mite longer to get all your strength back." I paused, watchin' him. "So what you got in mind to do then? 'Bout that problem of yours I mean?"

"Well," he said, "there are a couple of problems I've been thinking about. One of them is what's happened to Doctor Summerfield and whether or not he's safe and well. Then there's the matter of that ambush, which left me in my present condition." His eyes narrowed an' he give me a hard look. "I've heard enough about Tate Barkley that I think I might be able to respond to that by asking, What would you do?"

Well, it didn't need no serious ponderin' to know the answer to that. I don't take kindly to bein' shot at from hidin'. Mightn't be the smartest thing, but I'd go lookin' for them as done it an' I'd read 'em from the Book. This here Cameron though, he didn't 'pear as dumb an' plain bull-headed as me. Was he really figurin' to go after Gator an' all them others by his lonesome?

I reckon the next thing he said didn't leave me in too much doubt. "Do you think you can find me a good pistol in the next day or two? With a good balance and plenty of ammunition?" I told him I'd already got a spare one like that stowed away, what I'd took off a feller didn't have no use for it no more.

"Good," he said. "Then that's the only thing I'll ask of you once I'm up and around. You've already done more than I'd any right to expect, and as far as I'm concerned the rest is a private matter." He thought for a second. "I'm afraid you may still have some problems of your own though, after I'm gone."

Well, I reckon he'd got that right, although some of them problems was likely to be with the same men he'd a mind to be huntin'. I hadn't 'zactly made me no friends by the way I'd faced 'em down a couple days ago. What I needed to consider was how I meant to deal with them an' all the others they claimed was out yonder in the Glades. That was a-plenty to concern me without involvin' myself with none of this gent's other doin's.

But then he said somethin' that put a entirely different complexion on the matter.

"You know," he said, his voice was real slow an' thoughtful, "in spite of what I just said, there may be a more sensible way to approach my two problems. And yours."

His fingers felt 'round till they come to that wallet of his I'd left layin' in the bed next to him. "I'm not exactly without resources. In fact, over the years my profession has earned me quite a substantial income. More than enough to pay for services rendered."

I was lookin' at him right curious now, an' he was meetin' my eyes. "Do you think you might be available for a period of employment at present?"

"You mean a job? You're thinkin' to hire me to do somethin'?"

"That's the idea. As you said, it'll be a while yet until I can get around well enough to pursue my investigation . . . and other things. Even then I couldn't move about this country without calling attention to myself, which seems already to have proven costly. But you live here and you could call on some of the locals, very possibly finding out things they'd never tell me. What do you think?"

"Well . . ."

"How about for, say, fifty dollars a week?

"That's a heap of money. You sure just goin' round askin' questions is all you got in mind? I been knowed to rent my gun out here an' there. But I sure ain't no hired killer. Whatever you're thinkin' to do 'bout them men that put lead into you is purely 'tween you an' them."

"Fair enough. I wouldn't have it any other way. But while I'm laid up I'll also be hiring you for personal protection. And you deserve some compensation for saving my life, not to mention providing room and board during my convalescence."

"Well, when you put it that way . . ."

"Then you agree?"

Fifty dollars was more'n I'd made in a month at any other job I'd ever had, even them that involved totin' a gun. I was already figurin' to look after this gent till he was able to fend for hisself. An' I was likely goin' to have to deal with Gator an' his friends whether I took the man's money or not.

"I reckon," I said, offerin' my hand. "You just done hired yourself a 'prentice dee-tective!"

It weren't till a mite later that I started to wonderin' what other kinds of trouble I might be gettin' myself into.

❦ 5 ❧

IT WERE A COUPLE DAYS LONGER 'FORE I COULD GO OUT AN' ABOUT ASKIN' questions of anybody. We both of us wanted to wait till Cameron was on his feet 'fore I left him alone there at the cabin. Then, if that Gator bunch showed up unexpected-like, he could decide whether to use that pistol I give him or make a stab at runnin' an' hidin'.

He was a mite wobbly there at the first, usin' a chair as a kind of a crutch an' not takin' more'n a step or two at a time from bed to table an' back again. But he 'peared to get his bearin's quick enough, an' I'd already seen from my doctorin' that he'd got him a right smart set of muscles under them fancy duds he'd been wearin'.

An' damn if the first thing he wanted to do onct he'd climbed outen that bed weren't to borrow my ole straight razor so's he could have a go at that crop of whiskers he'd been cultivatin'. I found him a hickory shirt he could put on over the bandage on his shoulder, an' fished out a ole hat of mine with a bullet hole in it 'case he'd a need to go outdoors.

Then I dug out that spare six-shooter I'd told him 'bout an' he took to it like a new-borned calf takes to its momma. He unloaded it first thing to check out the action, then tested the balance an' the grip like a man who'd had occasion to do a mite of shootin' now an' again. When he sat down at the table to wipe off the bullets 'fore reloadin', I filled up the loops in the holster the pistol come in an' laid it down beside him. Figured it would be some handier'n for a big '44 than that li'l hide-out rig he's been wearing' earlier.

An' onct he'd stood up an' belted it on he 'peared a heap more comfortable than he'd been till now, game leg or no.

He was eatin' pretty good by this time too, almost good as me. I reckoned whenever I did leave this place I'd best stock up on some more supplies down to Lemon City 'fore I did a awful lot else. He figured that out his

23

ownself an' give me some cash money I could use for the purpose when I got the chanct. It was the foldin' kind, 'cause he hadn't had too many coins on him the day I found him.

Which could get me a curious look or two down to the general store. But they was enough well-heeled Yankees travelin' the country nowadays that it weren't so uncommon as it would of been earlier. An' I just had a way about me that sort of discouraged any nosy questions I didn't want to answer.

So finally one mornin' I saddled up the Cracker horse an' set out down that trail 'longside the creek to do a mite of buyin' and try to find out what I could 'bout ole Gator an' that missin' naturalist friend of Cameron's.

By that time he was gettin' about right sprightly, usin' a crutch he'd fashioned outen a young saplin' I'd cut down for him. An' he'd been practicin' some fast draws with that six-shooter I give him. Couldn't risk shootin' it off o'course, what with no way of guessin' who might be close enough to hear it. But I reckoned if his aim was anywhere near good as he 'peared to think it was he'd give any unwanted visitors a mite of difficulty if they come 'round to trouble him.

I rode on down to Lemon City, tied my horse up 'front of the general store an' went inside. Picked out a ham an' a couple sea bass they'd just got in that mornin', 'long with corn meal, lard, an' coffee. Then I poked 'round till I found some shirts an' jeans I figured would fit that gent was stayin' with me. After I'd piled it all up on the counter I asked for a couple boxes of .44 ca'tridges that would fit both them pistols an' the Winchester.

The clerk was a bald-headed gent with spectacles an' garters 'round his shirt sleeves. He give me a few curious looks whilst I was gatherin' my supplies. But he didn't say nothin' till I'd had him fetch the ca'tridges an' add 'em to the pile.

"That's a right smart number of shells for most folks 'round these parts. You ain't fixin' to start a war are you?"

"Nope. Just figure if they's anybody come along with that kind of a notion I wouldn't like 'em to be disappointed."

He narrowed his eyes an' looked at me kind of sharp. But then he just licked his pencil an' started totin' up what I owed him on a scrap of brown paper there on the counter.

"Let's see. That comes to three, four, seven . . . nine dollars an' fifty cents." He looked up from the paper an' eyed me over his glasses. "That's a lot of merchandise you've took outen my stock, an' there won't be another boat in here for three, four days. I'll need cash money to fill up my shelves again. So I reckon I can't let you have all of this on credit. Mebbe if you was to come up with half of it . . ."

I grinned an' reached in my shirt pocket for a ten dollar bill I'd got from Cameron. "I 'preciate the offer, but I ain't too much for owin' money." I unfolded the bill an' smoothed it out on the paper he'd used for his figurin'. "I'll just go on ahead an' pay for all the damage today."

That clerk's eyes got kind of big behind his glasses an' he picked up the ten-spot kind of careful to peer at it in the light from the window next to him. They was a few dark blood stains round the edge of it, but after he'd turned it ever which-way, I guess he finally decided it were the genuine article. He shoved it in his pocket an' fished out two quarters to give me for change.

"Don't see that kind of money all of a piece too often," he said whilst I pocketed the coins. "Reckon you maybe had you a job guidin' some Yankee tourists." He bent down to fetch a couple croaker sacks to load up my purchases. "Or somethin'."

I knew what he was thinkin'. Man in the market for a bunch of .44 ca'tridges an' no shotgun shells for huntin' is liable to have other ways of gettin' holt of cash money. 'Specially if it's got them brown stains 'round the edges. But I just looked him in the eye an' smiled.

It give me a idea though. 'Long as he was thinkin' it . . .

When he was done fillin' the croaker sacks I slung 'em over my shoulder an' acted like I was startin' to leave. Then I stopped an' turned back.

"By the way," I said. "I heard tell they's a feller called Gator somewheres hereabouts. Somebody said he might have a job for the right sort of man."

The clerk didn't answer me for the time it might of took to count up to ten. Then he shook his head an' looked down at the floor. "Never heard of nobody like that in this country. Reckon whoever told you that was givin' you wrong information."

"Uh-huh." I shrugged. "Well I guess it don't cost nothin' to ask."

I went outside an' started tyin' them sacks on in back of my saddle. Did a mite of ponderin' whilst I was at it. I'd no doubts that storekeeper knew 'zactly who it was I'd just asked him 'bout. But he weren't of a mind to let on. Acted plumb scared to even have the name Gator brought up.

So like Gator'd suggested, he was a knowed man in these parts. But what was knowed 'bout him didn't 'pear to make him too popular 'mongst the locals. Maybe feared was more like it.

I wondered if that meant they'd be as tight-lipped talkin' *to* him as they was talkin' *'bout* him. All them supplies I'd bought was a right smart amount for only one man. Wouldn't take no great leap of thinkin' to imagine I'd maybe got somebody else stayin' with me. An' that weren't a idea I wanted spread about just at present.

I put my hands on my saddle an' looked up an' down the sandy main street. It was the middle of the mornin' an' that street was 'bout as empty as any street gets to be. Them as had a job was prob'ly doin' it, an' them without one weren't ready to come out in the heat of the sun just at present.

They was houses back in amongst the trees here an' there. But I'd never met nobody that lived in 'em. An' knockin' on some stranger's door to ask 'em questions they didn't want asked an' was prob'ly 'feared to answer didn't seem just the best way to keep from raisin' suspicions an' gettin' myself talked about.

What happened to Cameron had already showed me what that sort of a thing could lead to.

So I climbed up into the leather an' swung my mare's head 'round to the northwest, meanin' to go on back to my cabin an' try to figure out what I'd ought to do next. Maybe that dee-tective I'd got for a house guest would have some suggestions.

I rode mighty slow an' careful, loosenin' my Winchester in its scabbard an' watchin' the trees on both sides for movement 'mongst the shadows. Kept half a eye on my horse's ears whilst I was at it. That animal was frontier-bred, an' what she didn't notice 'bout our surroundin's was prob'ly scarce worth noticin'.

I was well over halfway home when I heard this voice come out from the trees to my left. It was a woman's voice, but I couldn't see right off where she was or what she looked like.

"Heighdy there, neighbor! Been meanin' to pay you a call an' offer a welcome into the country. But I just ain't managed to find no time to do it 'fore today."

She stepped out into the open, a woman my age or a li'l less, kind of handsome but showin' some years of livin. She wore a floppy hat an' a man's shirt an' trousers. Her face was brown from the sun an' it was split wide in a big ole grin.

"Whyn't you come on up to the house an' set for a spell if you got the time? I just made coffee an' they's a pan of gingerbread warmin' in the oven."

Well, I can always do with some coffee. But it was the gingerbread that decided me. I ain't tasted none of that in longer'n I cared to recall.

I drew rein an' swung the mare's head so's I could face her. "Don't mind if I do, ma'am. If it ain't no special trouble."

"No trouble at all. Climb down off your horse an' lead her on up this path. It ain't no more'n a hop an' a skip to my place back in the trees."

Well, it were more like two-three hundred yards. But they was low-hangin' vines an' tree limbs that would of made ridin' in there a caution. That cabin was nigh on to invisible from forty feet away. Woods come almost up to the doorstep an' hung over the place on three sides with just a li'l space for a kitchen garden in back an' what I took to be a stable up under the trees.

Which could explain why I hadn't never seen it before, nor even had a suspicion it was there.

They was a hitchin' post an' a water trough in front, so I tied up the mare whilst that woman went on inside without even a pause or a by-your-leave. Wondered if she was that heedless 'bout all the strangers she met. But when I follered her inside I seen a rifle leanin' next to the door an' a pistol in a holster that was hung from a nail in the wall where it'd be in easy reach. So I reckoned maybe if I'd been somebody like Gator an' them it could of been a different story.

She'd already poured a couple cups of coffee an' set 'em in front of two facin' chairs at this good-sized table she had. Just now she was bendin' over with a cloth in her hands to fetch a pan out from the oven. "Set yourself down an' take a load off your feet," she said. An' I done it, takin' the seat that looked towards the door from out of habit.

If she noticed that she didn't say nothin', just put the pan down on the table with the cloth underneath an' went to fetch a couple plates an' forks from a cupboard next to the stove. Then she plopped down in the chair acrost from me.

I'd took a better look 'round the place in the meantime. They was two openin's, that 'peared to lead to other rooms, both of 'em on my right. Each was hung with strings of shell beads instead of doors, which made a kind of sense considerin' the country we was in. Lots of such cabins didn't have no inside doors, though most folks just covered the space with blankets. It 'curred to me that it'd be mighty hard for anybody to come in or out of these here rooms without makin' a whole heap of racket.

My hostess was busy cuttin' two big slabs of gingerbread to put on our plates, an' afterwards used the knife to take butter from a bowl an' set it to melt on top of 'em. "My name's Marcy," she said whilst she was doin' it. "Marcy McCollum." She finished an' laid the knife down to look up into my eyes. "An' you'd be . . ."

"Barkley," I said. "Tate Barkley's the name."

"Pleased to meet you, Mister Tate. Seen you 'round here an' there, but never knowed what you was called." She picked up her cup an' took a sip of coffee, still eyin' me kind of thoughtful. Then she put the cup down an' shrugged. "I got to ask you to excuse the way I'm dressed. Didn't know I was about to have company." She cut off a bite of gingerbread an' lifted it on her fork. "Women's fixin's ain't so handy for tendin' livestock an' grubbin' round in the garden. An' it ain't like I got that many good dresses to root 'round in an' get all dirty."

She started to eat an' I followed suit, usin' the fork like I'd been taught 'stead of pickin' up the whole slab like I'd usually do to home. Neither of us said much else till they was nothin' left on our plates but some crumbs.

"Want another piece? she asked.

I considered it pretty serious, but then I shook my head. Didn't want it to 'pear like I was greedy or nothin' our first meetin' out of the gate. "No thank you, ma'am. I reckon I'll do for now, though it surely was mighty good. Got to leave some for yourself later on."

"Me an' my son," she said, takin' out the cloth to spread it over the pan. "James Albert would be a tad upset if he learned we'd finished it off without leavin' none for him." She seen my curious look an' went on. "He's 'bout man-growed now an' generally goes out with the oyster boats whenever the weather's fair. Right good provider for his age. Been the only man of the house for upwards of six year now, ever since his pa was brought down by the cholera."

"Well, I'm sorry to hear 'bout your husband," I said. "But havin' a son to carry on must be a considerable comfort."

"It is that. Don't know what I'd of ever done without him." She got up kind of sudden an' went to fetch the coffee pot offen the stove. Kept her back towards me for just a minute like she'd some feelin's she didn't want to show.

When she turned 'round an' come back to refill our cups an' set the pot down on the table she was smilin', an' didn't say no more 'bout her son an' dead husband. 'Stead, after she'd took her seat again she leaned forward acrost the table.

"Now, Mister Tate, tell me all about yourself. An' that other feller you been hidin' out up to your cabin."

Well, I almost spit out the coffee I'd just drunk. Had to grab a napkin right quick to cover my mouth an' the look that was on my face. Whilst I was tryin' to come up with some kind of an answer, I seen that woman was just settin' there grinnin' at me.

"Ain't so awful much happens in this country," she told me, "That I don't know or can find out 'bout. I get around pretty slick in the woods, almost as good as a Injun. An' I been scopin' out your place ever since you went an' moved into there. Curious I guess, or some might call it just plain nosy. But I figure it don't hurt to learn all I can 'bout the folks down here where the law's mostly lackin' an' a passel of miles away."

"I reckon that's true," I said, still not too anxious to tell her nothin' 'bout my house guest that she hadn't already gathered or figured out.

"So I was out there watchin' when you brung the feller in. 'Peared he was either drunk or pretty bad hurt. I reckon it was the last 'cause I ain't seen hide nor hair of him outside your place ever since." She paused an' took a drink of coffee. "An' then I figured out you was hidin' him when I heard what you told that bunch of no-counts come huntin' for him the next day."

"I guess you do get 'round an' see a good bit," I admitted. "If you know that much you prob'ly know I made me some enemies right then. An' why I ain't of much mind to go sharin' my affairs with folks I just now met. Meanin' no disrespect," I added right quick.

"I reckon that's fair," she said. "Whatever you an' that feller are up is your own private business 'long as it don't have to do with me. An' I ain't never been the gossipin' kind. Nobody hears 'bout what-all I learn 'cept sometimes my boy, James Albert. He ain't much of a talker neither, but I don't even let him in on everthing I know."

"I'll take your word on it," I said, thinkin' I didn't have too awful much choice in the matter. "An' I 'preciate you keepin' it all under your hat."

She nodded real serious. "That's a thing neighbors do for each other." Then we were both quiet for a minute or two. Finally she asked, "More coffee?"

"Maybe just one more li'l cup." I was tryin' to figure out how to ask her more 'bout that Gator an' his friends. 'Peared to me if they was anybody in these parts could fill me in on that crowd it'd be Miz Marcy McCollum. But here she'd just now said she didn't go tellin' folks what-all she knew!

I hadn't come up with no good ideas by the time she'd refilled our cups. But then she brought the conversation back 'round to what she'd started askin' me in the first place. Part of it, anyhow.

"What you mean to do now an' in the future ain't none of my business," she said. "But me an' you is neighbors an' likely to be for a spell. I always like to know who it is I'm living next to an' what I might expect from 'em. If it ain't gettin' too personal, you reckon you could tell me a li'l about yourself? Like where you come from an' what you do to make ends meet an' all?"

Well, that didn't cause me no problems. Fair is fair an' she'd already told me 'bout herself an' her son. The more she got to know me the better chanct that she'd maybe let me in on some of her secrets. And o'course whilst I was at it I'd be doin' what I could to cast a favorable light on myself.

I told her 'bout bein' raised up in Taylor an' Lafayette Counties, goin' off to fight in the War of Northern Aggression, an' then travelin' out West till them Yankees got done re-constructin' the hell outen what used to be the Confederacy. Said I'd mostly worked cattle out yonder an' in Florida, with a li'l bit of sheriffin' here an' there.

Didn't bother to bring up none of my shootin' altercations over the years. But I could see her eyin' that tied-down gun at my side an' the Winchester I'd carried into the house with me. Don't reckon she was much fooled in that regard.

In betwixt my talkin' she told me a li'l more 'bout her life, too. Turns out she was a Taylor County gal herself, though she hadn't been back since the war. Her husband was from over Jacksonville way an' they'd started out on a good-sized farm an' cattle operation near the town of Alligator. But that all ended with the Yankee invasion of '64.

They'd burned everthing to the ground an' took all the stock to feed their soldiers. Weren't nothin' much to do then but pull up stakes and start over again somewheres far away. An' this country down here was 'bout as far as they could get an' still be in Florida. Husband made do with fishin' an' huntin', sometimes diggin' coontie root or workin' on the oyster boats if they needed cash money.

After he passed, she an' the boy just stayed on. Didn't have no close relations an' no p'ticular desire to uproot theirselves again. They was doin' all right, with a solid-built cabin an' li'l piece of land, a milk cow an' the kitchen garden, plus the money James Albert brought in together with fishin' an' huntin'. I reckoned if I could be that well off after another couple years I'd be a contented man.

We sat there jawin' at that table for a couple-three hours without no thought for the passin' time. But then I seen it was gettin' on past noon an' I'd ought to get back to my own place an' check up on how that Cameron gent was doin'.

But when I thought 'bout him it reminded me of the job he'd hired me to do. An' like I said, Miz Marcy here were likely the best source of information I'd be able to come up with in a whole month of Sundays. 'Spite of what she'd said 'bout keepin' what she knew to herself, I couldn't let a chanct like this pass me by.

So I just set my coffee down an' took the bull by the horns.

7

"YOU KNOW THEM MEN COME UP TO MY CABIN T'OTHER DAY?" I ASKED. "The ones totin' all that artillery an' led by a feller calls hisself Gator?"

Marcy McCollum's face got kind of grim all of a sudden an' she nodded.

"Well, like I said, I don't believe they took what I told 'em back then too friendly. An' it 'pears you an' me both figured they was huntin' that gent in my cabin. Fact is, somebody put lead into him a day earlier an' I think they was wantin' to finish up what they'd started."

She nodded again, not sayin' nothin' but eyin' me mighty careful.

"What you know 'bout them fellers? Reckon I'm kind of like you in a way. I always want to know who-all's close by, an' what kinds of trouble any of 'em's liable to bring me."

She took in a deep breath an' let it out real slow. "I know 'em," she said. "Knowed 'bout them an' the others for goin' on three years now."

Then she got quiet again an' I had to encourage her a mite. "Others? How many of 'em you reckon they are?"

"'Least a dozen. Prob'ly more."

"I never seen no crowd like that since I been livin' here. They all local fellers?"

"Nope. Got 'em some place they stay 'way back up yonder in the Glades. Generally don't come down into the settlements 'cept when they got goods to sell or a itch to cause trouble."

"What kind of goods is that?' I was thinkin' they weren't a awful lot of value out amongst them swamps an' endless wet prairie. 'Cept fish maybe. Or snakes an' gators. But them was plentiful enough 'most anywheres. Who'd want to pay for what they could get for theirselves without spendin' good money for it?

Marcy McCollum looked at me like I were some kind of a ignoramus. Then I reckon she took pity on me an' figured 'long as she'd gone this far she might's well fill me on the the rest of what she knew.

"They's plumers," she said. An' the way she said it didn't leave much doubt she ranked that some lower'n a skunk or a wood tick. "Kill off all the prettiest birds they can manage to draw a bead on. Thousands an' thousands of 'em—herons an' egrets an' flamingos an' rosy spoonbills. Leave their carcasses to rot an' just pluck out the feathers."

I looked at her mighty strange, not havin' no idea why a body in his right mind would ever go an' do such a thing.

She seen it in my eyes an' went on with a li'l hint of humor in her voice. "You ain't been up north very recent, have you? Or to any big city?"

"Not hardly. Not in a awful long while." Not more'n once or twict in my entire life to tell the truth. Spent a couple nights in Denver onct.

"Well, the fashion amongst all the fine ladies in them parts is great big picture hats mostly covered over with bird plumes. Kind of plumes that can't be had from nowheres else but these southern wetlands." She rose up from the table. "Wait a minute. I think I got a *Godey's Ladies Book* 'round here somewheres."

She fished about in a drawer till she come up with a magazine that were several years old. Come back an' laid it out flat on the table so's I could look at the pictures in it.

Doggone if she weren't right. Them drawin's showed fancy-dressed women all carryin' parasols an' wearin' big wide-brimmed hats that near-bout reached acrost their shoulders. An' ever one of 'em had bird plumes stuck in it, of just the sort she'd been tellin' me 'bout. Must of been a heap of birds had to die to make all them ladies look so smart an' fashionable.

"They's real big money in plumes these days," Marcy said, sittin' down again. "Folks up North'll pay through the nose for good uns. An' Gator an' his bunch is all primed to supply 'em. Pack 'em up for somebody to take to the railroad buildin' just a li'l ways north from here. An' that feller shells out cash money whenever they fetch in a load of 'em."

I looked up from the magazine. "I shot plenty birds an' other game for eatin'. But not no more'n I needed. An' these kinds is fish eaters mostly, not 'zactly the best ones for cookin'." I scowled. "Ought to be a crime to kill so many just only for the feathers."

"But it ain't. 'Least not that I ever heard tell of. They's some folks is agin it. Audubon Society for one. They'd like to have laws made to stop it. But way too much money's bein' had, an' they's too many plumers." She paused, lookin' at me mighty serious.

"I reckon you got some notion now of what you could be up against if you or them plumers choose to make a issue of it. They's a passel of 'em, and the ones that foller that Gator is all meaner'n a rattlesnake in the blind."

Well, I didn't much care for what them fellers out yonder was doin'. But it weren't none of my affair 'less they tried to make it one. I surely didn't want to go off into the Glades to meet 'em. I'd already got plenty to occupy me right here where the ground was dryer.

But then I got to thinkin' 'bout that friend of Cameron's what went missin'. He'd said the feller were a naturalist, an' had what he called a passion for wild birds that lived in the Glades.

Marcy interrupted my speculatin' with what she went on to say next: "I can tell you're a kind of a hard man. An' from what you said to them fellers t'other day there ain't a whole lot of back-up in you. I reckon maybe that's why I went ahead an' talked so free out of school just now. 'Tain't generally my habit. But from the first you've 'peared to be the kind of neighbor I'd like to see stay in these parts."

She smiled, kind of friendly an' grim at the same time. "Wouldn't want nothin' bad to happen that might change that, just 'cause you didn't know all that goes on 'round here."

Well, I 'preciated everthing she'd told me an' I said so. Didn't yet know if I was goin' to have more trouble with them plumers, nor what I'd do if I did. But knowin' who's who an' what's what is always a useful thing.

I took my leave of Miz Marcy not too long afterwards. Went out an' tightened the cinch on my Cracker horse, then led her back out to that trail by the crick 'fore climbin' up into the leather.

I still kept a wary eye out on my surroundin's 'long the way, right up till I drew rein next to my cabin. Hadn't seen nobody nor nothin' I needed to be concerned over durin' my trip, nor not afterwards neither. I led the mare 'round to the stable an' had me a good long look about 'fore walkin' acrost to my door in the back.

When I opened it I found myself starin' smack into the black barrel of a six-shooter. But it was held in the hand of that Cameron gent, him bein' just nearly as cautious as me.

He was settin' at the table with his hurt leg up on a chair an' he grinned as he holstered the pistol. "Coffee's on the stove," he said. "I didn't know how long you'd be gone so I waited to start cooking dinner."

"You'll make some feller a good wife one of these days." I brung in the food an' the other things I'd bought an' set 'em on the bed an' the table.

"I'm already married," he said, still grinnin'. "And besides, you're not my type."

"Just as well. Never had it much in my mind to get hitched up in double harness no way." It was clear this gent were feelin' a heap better'n he did earlier. I figured it wouldn't be a whole lot longer 'fore he was itchin' to be out an' about.

"You were gone long enough." His face got more serious. "Did you find out anything useful?"

"Couple things, I reckon." I poured myself some coffee an' sat down on the bed, there bein' just only the two chairs.

"That Gator'n them is knowed 'round these parts," I said. "though maybe not quite so popular as they'd wanted me to believe." I told him how that storekeeper had acted, tight-lipped as all get-out an' claimin' he'd never heard nothin' 'bout no Gator hereabouts.

Cameron nodded. "That's pretty much the reaction I got from the locals that I talked to."

"Plumb scared, I figure. An' prob'ly with good reason." Then I went on to tell him what Miz Marcy McCollum had said 'bout them all bein' plumers an' livin' away back yonder in the Glades.

Cameron listened with a kind of a scowl on his face but didn't say nothin' till I'd finished. Didn't make no comment a-tall 'bout what them fellers was doin' for money. 'Peared killin' whole flocks of birds for their feathers weren't no special news to him.

"This McCollum woman," he said. "She's been watching this place and she knows I'm here?"

"I reckon. 'Pears to me ain't too much goes on in this country she ain't got her nose into one way or t'other."

"That could be a problem. I'm going to need to stay here for another week or so at least. And when people come together and start talking it's awfully easy to let something slip."

"Well, I think what she said 'bout keepin' it under her hat is pretty much what she'll do. 'Pears like it's a kind of a habit with her. I ain't for sure she's even mentioned you to her son. An' she weren't real anxious there at the first to even tell me nothin' 'bout them plumers."

Cameron studied me thoughtful for a minute, then he shrugged. "Well, I guess there's nothing else we can do for the moment but keep hoping that you're right."

He was quiet for a couple minutes longer, thinkin'. Finally he said, "I expect you're right about people being afraid of Gator and his companions. But there's more to it than that. Every business in this area is making money from pluming. Your storekeeper sells more supplies because there's more money to be spent. Probably the fishermen and oystermen too. And I've no doubt there are saloons and brothels around that welcome the business.

"What this means," he went on, "is that nobody here has much interest in seeing it come to an end. That's reason enough for everyone to avoid giving information to strangers who might be pursuing laws against it. Quite apart from any fears they have."

Well, that made a kind of sense. Not so different from some of the places I'd run acrost 'long the Outlaw Trail out West. Owlhoots a dime a dozen without no law close enough to care. An' nobody wantin' the bad men to leave whilst any of 'em still had money to spend.

Which made me think of somethin' Miz Marcy had said. "I hear tell there ain't no laws agin what-all them plumers is doin'."

"No, and not likely to be any time in the near future. There are a few men in Congress and in the state legislature who are hoping to remedy that. But for now it's just one of many issues they have to deal with. Nor," he said with a shrug, "is it an issue I'm inclined to give my own attention to at present."

I looked him in the eye. "You real certain 'bout that?" I went on an' told him the notion I'd had concernin' that friend of his who'd turned up missin'. "You said he'd got him some kind of a passion towards all the birds in these parts. You reckon maybe he took it into his head to try an' do somethin' on his own to stop the plumin'?"

❧ 8 ❧

"THAT WOULD BE A VERY FOOLISH THING TO DO," CAMERON SAID. "AND almost surely futile as well." Then he got kind of quiet an' thoughtful, goin' on like he was talkin' mostly to hisself. "But it might be just the sort of wild-eyed scheme a man like Richard Summerfield would seize upon!"

He looked over an' met my eyes. "Doctor Summerfield is a renowned and respected scientist with more knowledge and intelligence than I will ever hope to have. But when it comes to practical affairs of the world, he's little more than a child. I'm afraid he's led a very sheltered life. Very different from the two of us."

Well, that last struck me a li'l curious, comin' from a gent who dressed in fancy rich man's duds an' always talked so slick an' educated. But then I'd seen the way he'd handled that six-shooter, an' I'd got a suspicion he weren't no fadin' violet in a fight. Ain't no tellin' what a feller's got in his past that others can't make no guesses about.

"So it is possible," he went on with a frown, "that Doctor Summerfield in his own naive and single-minded way has managed to run afoul of those plumers living in the Everglades. He may have made some rash remark around Lemon City that happened to get back to them. Or worse, he may actually have set out into that watery wilderness with the idea of confronting them on their own ground. He's a tendency to speak with authority, and they'd have no way of knowing how much influence he might have to get laws enacted that could cause them problems."

"Well, from what I seen an' what happened to you," I said, "if he did somethin' like that it don't 'pear too likely he'd live through no meetin' with 'em."

"Possibly, though there's no way to be sure. He may have simply gone into the Glades quietly and peacefully to study the bird life as he'd proposed.

39

There are plenty of dangers he might encounter there without ever coming in contact with Gator or his friends."

After a minute or two Cameron swung his bum leg to the floor an' put both hands on his knees. "Well," he said, "at any rate now I've got more reason than ever to be looking for those men."

I hadn't forgot the way he'd talked 'bout that earlier. He hadn't no intention of lettin' that dry-gulchin' crowd go off without huntin' 'em up an' readin' 'em from the Book. An' I weren't too sure by this time he wouldn't find him a way to do it. But that brought up another question.

"Supposin' they just decide to stay out yonder in the Glades for maybe another month of two? You thinkin' to wait till they show up again here-abouts? Or go on in there huntin' for 'em?"

"If the mountain won't come to Mahomet," he said kind of grim-like, "then Mahomet must go to the mountain."

Well, I reckon that settled it. 'Least after a fashion. How he meant to do what-all he'd said were still a thing needed a mite more considerin'.

We didn't say no more 'bout it right then though. I'd a couple sea bass that needed to be cleaned an' fried up whilst they was still pretty fresh. An' as it turned out that Yankee dude I'd found an' took in proved to be a fair hand at both. We fixed the meal together, with cornbread an' some greens on the side. Onct we'd finished it off we kind of just whiled the afternoon away, talkin' time to time 'bout this an' that.

'Long about evenin' I went outside to throw the slops away from the cabin for the hogs an' then come back 'round to feed the horses. That's when I seen they was three of 'em 'stead of just my two. This big black stallion with a saddle an' bridle on him was standin' up next to the corral stickin' his nose in it an' makin' some kind of horse talk with the others. Ole Roan didn't 'pear real happy with him bein' there an' was kind of snortin' an' pawin' at the ground.

I went inside to kind of settle my animals down an' fork some hay for their supper. Then I come outside again to see what I could do 'bout that black. He wouldn't let me get near 'nough to take holt of the reins, but he didn't show no inclination to leave my place neither. Just blew an' tossed his head a mite whenever I got close an' then sidestepped out of reach without takin' his eyes offen my cabin or Ole Roan.

Well, now this here were a problem. Couple of 'em in fact. I could dab a rope over his neck an' tie him up till his owner come lookin' for him, or I could just leave him out there an' hope he'd finally decide to go off on his own—if he ever did. Second choice might be safer, me bein' new to the country an' all. That were a mighty fine lookin' animal an' I didn't want no touchy folks hereabouts to get the notion I was tryin' to steal him.

Even if I did catch him up they was one thing for certain-sure. Weren't no way I could stable him in together with Ole Roan an' my Cracker mare. Them two stallions would likely kill one another 'fore the night was out.

But what made the situation worse, since that black didn't act like he were goin' noplace if I took him in tow or not, was that anybody that happened to notice I had a extra horse hangin' 'round come daylight was goin' to figure they was somebody stayin' in my cabin with me.

I was thinkin' right hard on all that when I went back inside an' told Cameron what I'd found.

"The General!" he said almost 'fore I'd got done talkin'. "That's my horse that I was riding when I was shot. I was afraid I might never see him again. But it seems he's managed to find me!"

Well, that put a li'l different complexion on the matter. But not a whole lot in light of some of them problems I'd just been frettin' over. I went ahead an' told him so.

"Yes," he said, grabbin' up his crutch to start to hobblin' towards the door. "That's a thing we'll need to consider. But first let's have a look at him. Afterwards we can talk about what might be done to hide him or try and find a place to board him."

It was pretty much dark by now, an' I blew out the lantern on the table so's the light from the open door wouldn't show nothin' to nobody that chanced to be watchin'. Then I follered him outside.

That stallion knowed his master sure enough. He lifted up his head an' started to let out a whinny. Cameron hopped an' scrambled over to him so's he could try an' quiet him down. Then he was huggin' that big animal 'round the neck an' the horse went to nuzzlin' him under the arm.

It was a mighty touchin' reunion. But me, I was thinkin' all the while, big black critter like that wouldn't be too easy to keep folks from noticin'. An' Gator an' his pals had already seen this gent here ridin' him. Where could he be put to that was outen the way an' out of sight so's the word wouldn't get back to 'em?

Livery stable in town was out, 'cause I was pretty sure nobody hereabouts would keep no secrets from that bunch. They was scared of 'em already, an' would be a heap more scared to think what might happen if it was found out somebody'd done deceived 'em. Same was liable to be true 'most any place within a dozen miles of here. I figured Gator an' his crowd was prob'ly knowed all over these parts, leastways good enough to be kind of cautious 'bout.

Might be we could take the stallion up to where the railroad was buildin' an' ship him up to Cameron's home in Georgia. Or maybe put him on a boat an' find a place he could be kept down to Coconut Grove. But I'd a notion this gent weren't goin' to like bein' so far off from a critter he 'peared so attached to an' had thought he'd lost.

Ornery as he was, I reckon I'd of prob'ly felt the same 'bout Ole Roan.

I found myself wishin' I'd been livin' here longer an' got to know more of the folks hereabouts. Friends is a mighty handy thing to have whenever trouble rears its head. An' I'd had me a few of 'em time to time.

Might be, I thought, I'd just come acrost one today. Maybe.

I hadn't no idea what kind of a friend Miz Marcy McCollum would turn out to be in the long run. But she clearly weren't no friend to Gator an' them plumers. An' her place back up in the woods was 'bout as hidden an' private as a feller was liable to find in these parts.

Leastways it was a possibility, an' pretty much the only one I could think of right now tonight. Come tomorrow I wanted that black where it wouldn't be seen 'round my cabin if they was any way a-tall it could be managed.

I reckoned I'd just have to ride over to her place now an' ask if she'd mind puttin' the horse up for a li'l while. Cameron had picketed him under the trees for the time bein', an' was actin' like he meant to take the saddle off when I went over to where they was. I got him to hold up with what he was doin' an' told what I'd been thinkin'.

"You believe that will be a safe place to leave him?"

"I believe if it ain't or if she's afeared to risk it she'll come right out an' tell me. Didn't 'pear to me she's the kind to hem an' haw much when it comes to makin' a decision."

"Well, I agree we can't keep him here very long. So I guess we'd better ride over there and have a talk with the woman."

"We? I was thinkin' I'd just call on her my ownself. It was me she spent time with this mornin', an' you ain't rightly healed up good yet. I'll ride your horse, an' if she's okay with keepin' him I'll make my way back by shank's mare."

The moon weren't up yet an' I couldn't make out his face. But I got a notion that Cameron were grinnin' at me. "You wouldn't get twenty feet. Nobody rides General but me. I've trained him that way and he'd have you off his back and on the ground the minute you hit the saddle."

Well, that were a bit of a insult. An' a challenge along with it. I've broke more'n a few wild mustangs in my day. But then I got to thinkin' that maybe my day were some several years ago. An' I couldn't see gettin' myself all hurt an' stove up just to try an' make a point.

"Your funeral," I said an' went to saddle the mare.

Ole Roan weren't too happy 'bout bein' left behind all alone. But two ornery stallions what already had took a dislike to each other were more'n I wanted to deal with out yonder on the road. 'Specially since I weren't real sure how good Cameron could keep his horse under control in light of his hurts an' all.

By the time we'd got back to where him an' his horse was he was up in the leather an' ready to go. I noticed he was breathin' kind of hard though, an' could guess what it'd prob'ly cost him to climb up there all by hisself. Reckon he'd been too proud an' stubborn to ask for help. 'Peared this feller could be just nearly as bull-headed as me on occasion.

We set out past the cabin at a easy walk an' then 'long that trail by the creek. It were mostly white sand an' no trouble a-tall to see in the light from the stars. Might take a li'l more huntin' to find that path that led up to Miz Marcy's place.

I wondered what Cameron an' her would think of each other after they'd got a chanct to meet. Maybe when the two of 'em had talked a mite he wouldn't be so all-fired suspicious as he'd sounded whilst I'd been tellin' him 'bout her. 'Leastwise I hoped so.

❧ 9 ❧

'Spite of my doubts I didn't have no trouble findin' that path to her cabin. My own tracks was right clear comin' out from the woods, an' 'parently there hadn't been no other riders gone near there in the time since I'd left.

I stopped a li'l way into the trees an' dismounted. We could see they was lights in the cabin, glowin' kind of yellow through all the limbs an' branches. I took a step or two closer an' called out friendly-like, "Hello, the house! Tate Barkley here with another feller, hopin' for a li'l talk an' maybe a spot of coffee!" It was same as I'd told that Gator an' his friends to do, bein' the custom in any civilized country.

After a minute, I saw one of the lights inside move an' start to shine out through the openin' door.

"Heighdy, Tate!" Miz Marcy called. "Didn't 'spect to hear from you again so soon!" She hung the lantern from a rafter over the porch an' kind of stepped back into the shadows. "Who you got for company?"

"Feller we was talkin' bout earlier today. He's wantin' to meet up with you an' maybe ask a favor."

"Well, come on ahead. But do it easy an' careful. We don't generally entertain callers too much after dark."

We went on up to the cabin, mostly guided by that lantern. I led both horses an' Cameron stayed in the saddle, it bein' kind of a long hike for a feller on a crutch. He had to bend over till he was almost huggin' the stallion's neck to keep from runnin' into the branches.

When we got close to where we could tie the horses, Miz Marcy still weren't in sight. But when Cameron got down with a kind of a groan an' she caught sight of his crutch, she come down them steps right quick an' took holt of his arm to lead him up an' inside.

"This here is Major Briand Cameron," I said, followin' behind 'em. "Some time back of the Yankee Army."

"I'm real sorry I didn't greet you out front, Major, as would of been proper." She pulled a chair away from the table an' then scurried 'round to fetch a li'l stool he could rest his hurt leg on. "But things 'round here has got to where we don't let nobody up to the cabin 'less we know who they are an' can see 'em clear." She glanced at me. "Even them we already met an' figure to be friends."

The rifle I'd seen the last time was still leanin' 'gainst the wall, but at a different place from where it was earlier. An' that nailed-up holster didn't have no pistol in it now. I'd a pretty good notion we three wasn't the only ones inside this cabin at the moment.

"That's quite all right, ma'am," Cameron said. Before settin' down at the table he leaned on his crutch an' bowed, takin' holt of her hand an' touchin' her fingers to his lips. Miz Marcy turned beet red when he did it, an' then he went on. "Special circumstances call for special precautions. We're grateful you were kind enough to take the trouble to see us at all tonight."

"Oh, 't ain't no trouble. Not no trouble a-tall." She fluttered around fetchin' an' layin' out cups with saucers an' spoons an' napkins whilst Cameron an' me took our seats. Way she was actin' now give me the idea them two was goin' to hit it off just fine.

Cameron watched her for a minute or two without speakin'. Then he said kind of quiet an' innocent, "Aren't you going to set another place? For the young man who's in the other room?"

Well, she stopped all of a sudden with a pitcher of cream in one hand an' a sugar bowl in the other. "Young man?"

"Your son, I assume. Mister Barkley said you have a son living with you."

Before the lady could say nothin' else they was a rattle of them shell beads from one of the doorways behind us an' everbody turned to look.

He were a right tall youngster, wearin' some kind of a dark shirt, dungarees, an' shoes with rope soles. Hair was a light brown color bleached by the sun an' almost down to his shoulders. Them shoulders was broad an' carried a sizable set of muscles, what I reckoned come from pullin' nets on fishin' boats all day long. Didn't 'pear to be much over sixteen, seventeen year old. But that Navy Colt in his fist was plenty old enough to get my attention.

"You can put the gun away, James Albert," Marcy said. "Mister Cameron an' Mister Barkley here is friends." He give us a long measurin' look, then went an' did like he was told.

He come over to the table an' shook each of our hands 'fore pullin' out a chair to join us. Had a right strong grip for a feller his age, though o' course

I made sure that mine matched it. "My friends mostly call me Jimmy," he said, takin' a seat.

Miz Marcy set him a place, then brung the coffee pot from the stove an' sat down her ownself. "Now," she said, pourin' coffee, "what was that favor you spoke of out yonder?"

Weren't no beatin' 'round the bush with this woman. An' just as well I reckoned. We needed to do somethin' with that stallion of Cameron's right quick. An' if she weren't agreeable to keepin' him, we'd only got till daybreak tomorrow to come up with somethin' different.

I told her what was the problem, an' what it was we was hopin'. She listened, glancin' at her son time to time, an' then nodded.

"I reckon we can do that, for a li'l while at least. They's a kind of a lean-to shed in the back where nobody'd be liable to see him 'less they got up real close. Got a milk cow we keep penned up out yonder an' a mule we use sometimes for ridin'. Plenty of hay at present. You reckon your horse can stand comp'ny?"

"No problem," Cameron said. He looked a me an' smiled. "Just so long there's not another stallion with a mare." Then he went on more serious: "I'm willing and able to pay for his keep. And I'd like to have Tate bring some corn and oats to add to his feed."

"Wouldn't think of takin' money for doin' what's neighborly," Marcy said. "But if you want to contribute to his feedin', it'll be welcome. How long you figure you'll be needin' him to stay?"

"Just a few weeks at most," Cameron told her. "Only until I'm recovered enough to get around without trouble."

"It's settled then. I'll have James Albert take him 'round an' introduce him to the other critters in a li'l bit. In the meantime, we'll just set an' drink our coffee." She paused, lookin' kind of sharp from me to Cameron. "An' talk a mite."

Uh-oh, I thought. This woman ain't goin' to let us get shut of this place till she's dragged ever bit of information she can out of Cameron 'bout what-all he's doin' here an' how he got shot.

She didn't ask him nothin' like that right off though. 'Stead, she wanted to hear 'bout where he come from an' his family an' all like that there. An' he seemed willin' enough tell her. 'Least a part of it, includin' things he hadn't had occasion to tell me.

Seems like he'd spent most the war up 'round St. Augustine, right here in Florida. Afterwards, he'd gone to live out west for a time same as I did. That were a number of years back o' course, for both of us. When he come east again, he got hisself into that dee-tectin' business some way or another. Didn't call it that, though. Said what he did was solve problems for folks who'd got money but didn't have no other way to get help.

'Pears he made him a right sizable stake doin' that, an' finally just decided to ree-tire an' settle down in Savannah with his wife an' a growed-up daughter. I could tell they was plenty more he was keepin' to hisself. But I reckon no man wants everthing in his life to be a open book. What he didn't tell us weren't none of our affair, an' I wouldn't of thought to ask him 'bout it.

Miz Marcy were of a li'l different mind though. "You say you're retired now an' been takin' life easy," she said kind of thoughtful-like whilst pourin' coffee an' not lookin' at him. "But here you are 'way down at the far end of Creation, miles an' miles from that family of yours. You come down here all by your lonesome for just the huntin' an' fishin'? Or maybe for somethin' else?"

Cameron just smiled at her an' took a swallow of coffee. "One of those three," he said. Then it got real quiet whilst they just sat an' looked at each other acrost the table. I glanced over at Jimmy out of the corner of my eye. He was curious too, but I reckon he'd got used to lettin' his ma take the lead when it come to pryin' information out of strangers.

Finally, Cameron 'peared to reach a decision. "Actually," he said, puttin' his cup down, "I came here hoping to find a friend of mine who appears to be missing." He went on to tell 'bout that naturalist gent who'd left out from Coconut Grove. "No one I've talked to seems to know anything about him. It's as if he just disappeared off the face of the earth."

He paused an' looked from one to the other of 'em. "I don't suppose either of you has seen him or heard something about him?"

"Not me." Marcy frowned. "But then I don't make it off this place so very often." She turned to her son. "James Albert?"

He was frownin' too. "I didn't see him, nor no other strangers hereabouts lately. But I recall hearin' one of the boatmen tellin' 'bout some Yankee passenger he'd carried up from the Grove some several weeks ago. Said he was a odd sort of a gent, kind of old an' with a funny way of talkin'. Wore them knickers like some of the northern hunters we see now an' again."

He shrugged an' shook his head. "I was kinda lookin' for him curious-like when I got off the boat that day. But I never did catch sight of him, not then nor later."

Cameron perked up considerable when he heard this. He slapped his hand on the table. "That surely sounds like Doctor Summerfield!" he said. "At least we've now some evidence he made it this far. If only we could find someone who knows what he did after he got here . . ."

None of the rest of us had no suggestions to offer. Me an' Cameron had already learned that if they was any such "someone" they wasn't likely to do no talkin'. An' I reckon Miz Marcy an' her boy knowed the situation 'least as good as us.

After a minute the lady looked acrost at her son. "James Albert, why'n't you go an' see after the gentleman's horse? It's that big black stallion out yonder. Me an' Mister Cameron has a couple more li'l things to discuss. Then we'll let these men go home again an' get some shuteye."

Jimmy McCollum weren't too anxious to leave us just then. He was mighty curious to know what-all was happenin' that nobody'd talk 'bout in front of him. I reckon his ma had been keepin' him in the dark 'bout me an' Cameron's troubles with them plumers.

He was a good hearted young-un though, an' he done what he was told. Dragged his feet a mite as he was walkin' to the door. But he didn't forget to take that Navy Colt along when he opened it an' went outside.

✂ 10 ✄

WHEN HE WAS GONE, MIZ MARCY LOOKED AT CAMERON FIRST, AN' THEN at me. "Like I told you, I don't always let James Albert in on everthing I know, though maybe it's gettin' to be time I did." She spoke kind of soft till we'd heard him go down the steps an' start 'round back with the stallion. "He's a smart young-un an' already has a idea 'bout the trouble them plumers might cause us. An' now he's wonderin' why it is we're hidin' a horse for some gent we only just now met."

"I think you should let him into your confidence," Cameron said. "As you say, he's intelligent and from what I can see he's man enough to look out for himself. Keeping him in ignorance may only endanger him."

She nodded. "I reckon you're prob'ly right. But the trouble of it is . . ." She looked at him real narrow. "I ain't just exactly sure what it is I'd ought to tell him. I know what I seen. But beyond that you ain't neither one give out hardly a clue durin' the entire time that we been settin' here. Somehow or another you got yourself shot up awhile back, an' though I can prob'ly guess who it was that done it I still ain't got no notion of why.

"Maybe you ought to take me into your confidence a li'l bit yourself."

Cameron met her eyes for a minute. An' then he nodded. "I guess that's fair. If there's to be any risk to you and your son on my behalf, though I hope it will be small, I should tell you something of the reasons behind it. At least as much as I know at the moment, which isn't much."

He went on to 'splain 'bout that Doctor Summerfield's feelin's towards what the plumers was doin' an' how he was the kind of feller that wouldn't keep quiet about 'em. When you put that together with the fact they was folks in Tallahassee an' Washington wanted to make laws puttin' a stop to their money-makin' business, it could of 'peared to Gator an' them that they'd all be better off if he just up an' disappeared. An' they'd their own notions 'bout how to make that come about.

As for Cameron, he'd showed up all of a sudden askin' question 'bout the doc, an' if they done somethin' like what we was thinkin' they didn't want none of them questions asked or answered. Looked like maybe it'd be a good idea if he pulled a disappearin' act too. With all the money to be had hereabouts an' him bein' a stranger, they didn't figure nobody'd look too close into the matter.

"That's likely enough," Marcy said. "Them plumers is a mean rough bunch an' the sheriff's all the way up to the county seat at Jupiter. He ain't much inclined to come down here messin' with folks in the Glades—even assumin' none of that money from plumes has managed to reach him."

She thought for a minute. "So all that bein' the case, what is it you got in mind to do now? 'Pears you ain't got no proof 'bout what might of happened to your doctor friend. An' you ain't no actual lawman nohow. You figure to just heal up an' go on home to your wife an' daughter? Forget 'bout what's goin' on in this part of the country?"

They weren't much pleasantness in Cameron's smile when he answered. "A man doesn't forget having two bullets put into him from ambush. I intend to arrange for another meeting with the men who did it and give them a chance to finish what they started. You say your sheriff doesn't show much interest in what happens in this area. Maybe he won't care too much if some others turn up missing in the Everglades."

Well, that laid it out plain an' certain. Miz Marcy looked at him kind of sharp, but she was noddin' whilst she did it. "Ain't the only time such matters been settled in this country without the law takin' a hand. But you'll be facin' a mighty hard crowd. You reckon you're up to it?"

"I guess I'll find out. It won't be the first time, as Tate would say, that I've ever smelled gunsmoke."

"Well, for your sake I'll hope it ain't the last. You 'spect to run acrost 'em 'round here? Or you thinkin' to foller 'em into the Glades?"

"Whichever. If they come here I'll face them here. If they stay away . . ." He shrugged.

We didn't say nothin' else till Jimmy come in the back door. "That's a mighty fine horse you got there, Mister. I could tell he'd been runnin' loose, so after I'd took off the saddle I spent some time curryin' the burrs an' stickers outen his coat. Other'n that he didn't look a bit worse for wear."

"Thank you, Jimmy." Cameron give him a smile. "You know a lot about horses do you?"

"Some. All we got's the mule o'course. But I've cared for other folks' horses now an' again. Never a one like that though. I bet he can go like the wind! Could just picture myself up on that kind of a critter, gallopin' along an' lookin' down on the world!"

"Well, you'd best not try it with the General. He's a one-man horse. But there may be another some time in the future."

"Maybe." Jimmy shrugged. "But I reckon I'll prob'ly stick to boats. I like spendin' time on the water. Rowboats or sailboats, li'l cricks or the big green rollers, I've got to where I like 'em all."

"James Albert's a hand with 'em," Marcy said. "'Most any kind you could name. I been up in the Glades with him in our li'l skiff, fishin' an' huntin' an' such. He knows ever one of them twisty channels yonder just like the back of his hand!"

Cameron glanced at her thoughtful for a second. Then he turned back to Jimmy. "You wouldn't mind owning a horse too, would you? Then you'd have the best of both worlds."

"Oh, sure. If'n I though we could afford it. But I could only have one, a boat would be better. It could bring in money 'stead of just eatin' it up."

Cameron nodded serious-like. Then he lowered his foot to the floor an' took aholt of his crutch. "I think we've taken enough of your time for tonight. I'm more grateful than I can say that you've agreed to look after my horse, General. I hope I won't have to leave him with you for too long."

"However long you need to," Marcy told him. "Come 'round to see him any time you like. 'Course," she pushed back her chair, "I reckon it'll be best you wait till dark to do it."

We got up an' she went to open the door for us. Then she turned 'round with a smile. "Next time you come, I'll try an' have some fresh gingerbread made. 'Tween Tate an' my boy here, none of that I made this mornin' lasted out the day."

Jimmy grinned a mite an' stepped forward to shake our hands. "I'm real pleased to of met you-all," he said. "Don't get so many visitors here, an' none I can recall that ever been out in them western lands. I bet if you had more time you could tell some mighty excitin' stories 'bout outlaws an' gunfights an' what-all."

Marcy looked at him an' shook her head. "James Albert's been readin' them dime novels. Thinks he'd admire to be a western marshal or somethin'."

"Don't be in too big of a hurry to try it," I told him. "It ain't all so simple an' easy like it is in them books. An' far as gunfights goes, you want to remember that folks get hurt an' kilt thataway."

We took our leave, Cameron mounted up on my Cracker horse an' me walkin' 'long beside him. I took my Winchester outen the saddle boot an' carried it in my hands whilst we made that short trip back to my cabin. Didn't see nobody out an' about in the dark, nor nothin' else to concern us. But a feller never can tell.

Neither one of us done much talkin' on the way back. I led the mare 'round to the corral an' Cameron got down an' went inside whilst I unsaddled an' forked out hay for the animals.

Ole Roan was lookin' more'n a little upset when I got there. His ears was up an' he was kind of dancin' 'round an' blowin' through his nose. But I just figured it was 'cause he was mad at bein' left all alone. Or maybe he was still frettin' 'bout that big ole stallion he'd took a dislike to earlier.

When I'd got done with my chores an' headed for the cabin, I seen some shadows movin' past the light in the window. Took me a second or two 'fore I realized they was more'n just one shadow stirrin' 'round inside there.

❧ 11 ❧

I WAS CARRYIN' MY WINCHESTER UNDER MY ARM, BUT IT WEREN'T COCKED right then. An' it surely didn't seem the time to make that kind of a sound out here in the night. I switched it to my left hand an' slipped the thong off the hammer of my six-shooter. Then I snuck up to one side of the window an' took a careful peek inside.

They was two of 'em that I could see. Both was holdin' pistols, them bein' handier weapons for any close quarters work like this. If they'd brung shotguns or rifles along, they must of put 'em down somewheres, an' I was thankful for small favors.

Cameron was backed up 'gainst the unlit stove, his crutch down out of sight an' both hands up over his head. He was listenin' an' them other men was talkin'. 'Peared they was the sort that couldn't just go on an' shoot a man without tellin' him all 'bout it beforehand. Neither one of 'em was that Gator.

"You got yourself into a mess of trouble, Mister Yankee, comin' down here askin' 'bout things that ain't none of your affair." That was the older of the two speakin', all shaggy an' unshaved, though what he'd got on his face weren't 'zactly what I'd call a beard. "Been a heap better for you 'f you'd stayed up north where you come from."

"Nosy," the other one put in. "Just plain nosy." He was a youngster with corn-colored hair an' 'peared to be tryin' to grow a mustache without a awful lot of success. But he'd a real mean cast to his eye that told me he might be even more of worrisome than the feller he was with.

I didn't recognize neither of 'em from that bunch I'd seen earlier. But they was dressed pretty much the same: khaki-colored shirts an' canvas pants that hadn't been acquainted with soap since Methuselah was a pup, together with mud-caked brogans an' floppy sweat-stained hats pulled down over long greasy hair.

What held my attention more at the moment was where an' how they both was standin'. They was keepin' a fair distance between 'em, so I couldn't chance a shot at one without t'other gettin' lead into Cameron. Or into me, since they was eyin' this window kind of frequent. I'd had to take off my hat an' ease up next to the sill real slow an' careful, then drop down underneath an' slip over to the other side so's I could take in the whole room.

They knowed I'd be out here somewheres o'course, an' I'd the notion they was just hopin' I'd come on prancin' through the door all wide-eyed an' innocent. An' I might of too, if I hadn't happened to pick up on them extra shadows movin' past the light.

Right now they wasn't movin' hardly a-tall, each just standin' with his back up against the wall with his eyes shiftin' from Cameron past the window to the door an' then back again. Wondered how long they was willin' to wait for me to come inside there, or make some kind of a noise to tell 'em where I was an' what I was doin'.

Me, I weren't in no hurry to do either one. I didn't much care for the looks of the situation. But 'least so far nobody was doin' any shootin'. An' I was able to keep my eyes on them whilst that lantern on the table meant alls they could see through the window was coal black night.

Meanwhile, that younger feller couldn't keep hisself from talkin'.

"Nosy's what I call him, Jake. Mister all-fired Nosy Yankee." He grinned an' reached down with his left hand to fetch out a fair-sized toad-sticker that flickered a tad in the lantern's light. "You reckon what he'll look like whenever I cut that there nose from off his face?"

He took a step like he meant to do it right there an' then. But the feller he'd called Jake spoke up real quick an' got him to stop. "Hold on there, Willy-Boy. You get up close an' he's liable to try an' fight you. Then we'd have to shoot him an' give a warnin' to that other'n out yonder. Just bide your time a li'l longer an' we'll have the both of 'em under our guns. After that you can do all the carvin' you like."

I could see from Cameron's eyes that he'd been givin' thought to takin' a chanct. An' I'd noticed earlier that his six-shooter was still in its holster with the thong offen the hammer. 'Parently they hadn't tried to take it from him for the same reason Jake had just mentioned.

Willy-Boy didn't 'pear too happy with waitin'. But after a second he give a shrug an' leaned back up against the wall. Kept turnin' the knife to an' fro in his hand kind of nervous-like whilst he did it.

Well, I figured he were the one couldn't stay patient too much longer. What I needed to do was come up with some kind of a plan where he'd get anxious an' do somethin' to change that Mexican stand-off I was seein' through the window. An' hope that Cameron would have sense enough to just keep still until I'd did it.

I looked back over my shoulder an' contemplated them horses I'd got in the corral. Ole Roan was still stampin' an' snortin' time to time, an' the mare 'peared to catchin' some of the excitement from him. Both of 'em was movin' back an' forth real restless inside there an' 't wouldn't take a awful lot to get 'em het up even more.

I slipped on back to where they was an' found a place where I could climb up on the rail an' see through that window good enough to keep watch on Jake an' Willy-Boy. Ole Roan come an' pushed hisself up alongside me like I'd kind of figured he would. An' that's when I took my hat off an' swatted him hard as I could acrost the nose.

Well, he was fit to be tied. He scooted back an' reared up on his hind legs, lettin' out a shrill horse war-cry that were like to make a believer out of Satan. The mare was puttin' her two cents in too, though I reckon maybe it was more from fear than out of anger.

I was busy leanin' over an' dodgin' the hoofs of my stallion. But I managed to get that Winchester cocked as I did it an' in the same instant I give out a yell, "Dad-blasted horses is got loose! Cameron, you hear me? I got to go after 'em right now 'fore they get so far off I can't catch 'em up!"

When I'd managed to set up straight again an' take another look through the window them men inside there was more'n a tad discombobulated. Willy-Boy was startin' towards the door an' Jake was swingin' his head back an' forth lookin' from him to Cameron. If I was goin' off hot-footin' it into the night, they'd small hope of tryin' to find me. An' that left 'em with only the one feller they meant to kill.

But one was better'n none, an' Jake was pretty quick to figure it out. He lifted up his shootin' iron an' leveled it at where I guessed Cameron was still standin'. I couldn't see him now from the place where I was sittin'.

I put a hot piece of .44 lead into the midst of Jake's brisket an' then swung the Winchester 'round to lever two more real quick into that door as it was comin' open.

I heard Jake's shot go off someplace whilst I was jumpin' off the fence an' runnin' over to where the door was. Willy-Boy had made it through by then, but he done it fallin' down. An' from what I could see, that young-un weren't never goin' to be no older.

They was other shots whilst I was pullin' him outen the way. When I'd climbed the steps to look inside, Jake was still on his feet, tryin' his hardest to lift his pistol. But 'fore I could bring the Winchester to bear, he let it drop from his fingers an' slid down the wall to the floor, leavin' a big smear of blood behind him.

I glanced over to my right an' there was Cameron with a smokin' pistol in his fist an' a kind of a grim half-smile on his face. He hadn't moved a inch from where I'd seen him last, an' near as I could tell there weren't no fresh bullet holes in him.

"Sorry about the mess, Tate," he said when he'd reloaded an' holstered his pistol. He was reachin' down to take up his crutch.

Well, I was sorry too. But not near so sorry as I'd been if things hadn't worked out the way they did.

"I reckon you stayin' here ain't the big ole secret we been thinkin' it was," I told him.

"Maybe. I had the impression those two didn't have any definite knowledge of it when they entered the cabin. From what they said, I think they were just suspicious of you, and curious." He made a funny face. "Nosy, you might say."

"Uh-huh. Well, couple dead bodies bein' found on the place is liable to make other folks curious. That Gator an' his friends in particular. I reckon the first thing needs to be done is get these two here under the ground."

"All that shooting may raise a few questions too."

"It could. But prob'ly not so much as a feller might think. Ain't many folks live near this place. An' they's all kinds of shootin' goes on hereabouts time to time. Huntin' deer an' gators an' such."

"At this hour of the night?"

"Best time to do it a good many'd say. Fill up a box with mud an' make a fire in it on a boat. Makes them critters' eyes shine so's you couldn't hardly miss 'em."

Even so, I went back outside an' had me a good long look 'round 'fore gettin' down to that job I'd set for myself. Tried my best to calm them horses some too whilst I was at it. Ole Roan weren't 'bout to forgive me any time soon for what I'd gone an' done to him. But he weren't too concerned over the shootin' that follered after it. Prob'ly just seemed like old times to him.

When I come back, I handed the Winchester to Cameron so's he could keep watch whilst I toted them bodies over close to the woods where the fresh-turned dirt wouldn't be so noticeable. Onct I'd got Willy-Boy situated an' come in to fetch Jake, I finally got a good look at them bullet holes Cameron put into him. You could of laid a silver dollar down an' covered up both of 'em. That there was some kind of shootin'!

After I'd got both bodies laid out an' was headed back from the lean-to with my shovel, I near-bout jumped outen my skin when I heard this loud "Psst!" from the dark woods a couple feet away.

"Mister Tate? You-all gettin' 'long okay?"

Jimmy McCollum stepped out from the trees, holdin' that Navy Colt down by his side. "Ma an' me heard some shootin' a li'l while back. She sent me over here to find out if you was all right."

Well, I 'preciated her concern. But this here was a bit of a embarassin' situation.

They was a tad of light from the cabin's open door an' window, an' a sliver of moon was just risin' up over the trees. Weren't no way the boy couldn't see what it was I was about.

ᵍ 12 ᵍ

ILOOKED OVER TO WHERE CAMERON HAD JUST GOT UP FROM THEM BACK STEPS he'd been settin' on. He was tryin' to make out who it was I was talkin' to, an' he'd cocked that Winchester all ready to shoot. I waved at him an' called out calm as I could manage. "It's all right. Just Jimmy McCollum from over yonder."

I turned back 'round an' started to say somethin', but the boy didn't need no long explanations. He'd heard the shootin' an' he seen the results. He just went ahead an' shoved his pistol in back of his belt an' took the shovel from outen my hand.

He were a worker. With his youth an' them big strong shoulders, an' me takin' a turn my ownself time to time, we had that common grave dug 'fore the moon was midway up the sky. Jimmy weren't stand-offish 'bout handlin' dead bodies neither. Just took holt the shoulders whilst I got the feet an' we rolled them two down inside the hole an' set ourselves to coverin' it over.

I didn't have no spare blankets to wrap 'em in, an' prob'ly wouldn't of wasted 'em on Jake an' Willy-Boy nohow. Onct we'd got done tampin' the earth down good I took some leaves an' pine needles an' spread 'em 'round on top so's the grave couldn't hardly be seen from a li'l distance off.

After I'd went to put the shovel up Jimmy an' me walked back to the cabin together. It were late, but he didn't seem anxious to go home just yet. Cameron had gone inside whilst we was workin', an' when we was washin' up at the pump by the back steps we smelt coffee makin'.

That gent had been busy his ownself. He'd cleaned up some of the worst of the blood with a ole rag mop I'd had an' made a stab at wipin' down the wall a mite too. But I seen it'd take a deal more work to make the place what I'd call livable. Figured I was lookin' at some wearisome hours on hands an' knees with soap an' a holy stone.

But that weren't a thing me nor nobody else wanted to think about right then. We was all of us plumb wore to a frazzle from what-all we'd been through. Jimmy'd already put in a full day's work 'fore he even showed up at my place. An' far as me an' Cameron was concerned, they's just somethin' 'bout fightin' an' killin' an' tryin' not to get kilt that purely takes it out of a man.

We just sat 'round drinkin' coffee an' nobody had a awful lot to say for several long minutes. Jimmy an' Cameron was acrost from each other at the table, an' I sat hunched over on the bed, mostly starin' at the floor.

Finally Cameron spoke up, kind of quiet an' thoughtful-like: "Jimmy, your mother mentioned you've spent some time in the Everglades. She seemed to think you could find your way through the area pretty well with a boat."

"I reckon. Been goin' out yonder by myself ever since I was knee-high to a tall grasshopper. Knowed my way through them sawgrass creeks an' hammocks long 'fore I ever set foot on no sailin' ship."

"Have you ever acted as a guide for hunters or fishermen?"

"Done it a time or two. But the work ain't steady like fishin' an' oysterin'. An' a lot of them Yankees what call theirselves sportsmen ain't got the good sense to take shelter from the rain. They shoot off their guns at everthing that moves an' then ain't got no earthly idea what to do if they manage to hit somethin'." He frowned an' shook his head. "Some of 'em's right uppity towards local folks too. An' ever one I ever met drinks whiskey. Ma an' me just finally decided they wasn't fit comp'ny for a God-fearin' young-un."

I was lookin' over at him whilst he spoke an' had to cover up a grin with my hand. He weren't tellin' nothin' I hadn't seen for myself.

"But recently," Cameron went on serious-like, "I guess it's pretty dangerous to spend time out there alone with all those plumers in the area."

"Well," Jimmy said, "it's always been some dangerous with the snakes an' gators an' poison plants like that manchineel tree. I reckon them plumers makes it a li'l more so. But what a feller wants to do is keep hisself from bein' spotted by 'em. An' that ain't so hard as you'd think considerin' all them miles an' miles of swamp an' hammock 'tween here an' the Gulf. I been payin' attention to the routes them fellers usually take, an' I got a idea or two where they got their stands an' camps out yonder. 'Long as I stay shut of them places they don't never guess I'm around."

"So you've been out there lately and kept an eye on them."

"Near-bout ever day that I ain't gone to work on the fishin' boats." He looked 'round from Cameron to me. "Ma don't know that's what I been doin' an' I'd be grateful if you-all didn't tell her. She'd be apt to worry. Alls I ever say is I'm goin' out after mullet or crawdads or such. Usually come back with enough to keep from rousin' her suspicions."

Well, I had my own ideas 'bout that. From what I'd seen of Marcy McCollum, I weren't convinced that Jimmy nor nobody else was goin' to keep her in the dark for long. But I just nodded, an' Cameron give him a smile.

"Your secret is safe with us," he said. "And it's good to know someone who can provide information about the plumers. Neither Tate nor I have been able to learn much." He paused a minute, frownin'. "But you still haven't seen any sign of that older gentleman who went missing? My friend Doctor Summerfield?"

"Nope. Ain't seen nobody a-tall like you described. You reckon them plumers kilt him?"

"It's possible," Cameron admitted with a scowl. "But I'll keep hoping for the best."

"You want I should ask around a bit? Might be folks'll talk more free with me."

"No. I'm afraid that could prove even more dangerous than your forays into the Everglades. Let's keep my search for him to ourselves for now, along with my living in Tate's cabin."

After Jimmy'd finished his coffee an' left for home, I looked over at the gent at my table. "You reckon you bein' here is still that much of a secret? Maybe we'd best be huntin' some other place you can hole up."

"And where would that be? Neither one of us knows anyone we can trust in the area besides the McCollums. And even if they were willing, I wouldn't ask them to take the risk."

He'd got a point. Only other possibility was to hide out in the woods somewheres. An' that weren't no real safe bet neither. Some hunter or fisherman was sure to come acrost his sign soon or late.

"No," Cameron said, "the best thing for me to do is stay right where I am for the present. Those two who were here when we came back from our visit seemed genuinely surprised when I walked in the door, though it's clear they'd seen or heard of me someplace. They took me by surprise too, of course. Though if it hadn't been for this crutch . . ."

Well, I'd a idea what he meant. This gent was right quick on the draw from what li'l I'd seen. An' I knew for a fact he could shoot mighty straight.

"But," he went on kind of slow an' careful, "I'm assuming you're still willing to have me here. Maybe you'd rather I took my problems elsewhere."

"Never crossed my mind," I said, an' I pretty much meant it. Jake an' Willy-Boy had been layin' for me too, which didn't make me feel no fondness for 'em. An' I'd already figured me an' that Gator feller was goin' to have to have it out betwixt us sometime.

What's more, I'd took on the job of helpin' an' lookin' after him. An' Tate Barkley ain't never been no quitter. Not to mention all the cash money I'd been promised.

I fetched the coffeepot an' refilled our cups. Then I sat down an' changed the subject. "You asked Jimmy McCollum a heap of questions just now. He seems a knowin' lad, an' I reckon you're right that he could tell us plenty 'bout them plumers an' where they hang out an' all. But I got a feelin' you was fishin' for somethin' a li'l more." I looked him in the eye. "You're thinkin' to take him 'long for a guide if it turns out we got to go up in the Glades huntin' 'em."

He didn't say nothin' for a minute an' then he shrugged. "I'm afraid neither one of us would have much luck running those men to ground in all that watery wilderness—even if someone like Jimmy were to give us directions. And it would be much safer if we could avoid being seen by them until we could come upon their camp."

All that were true o' course. Me an' Ole Roan had found our way 'round pretty good in that high dry country out west, an' in the swamps an' piney woods of Florida too. But them Everglades was another matter. Weren't nothin' but sawgrass an' water out yonder, with dry land near scarce as hen's teeth. No trails an' no tracks a-tall that a feller might foller. Without some kind of a knowin' guide we was liable to wander about for weeks an' finally just wind up food for the gators an' buzzards.

But whilst Cameron an' me might be fool enough to risk our hides thataway, there weren't no call for Jimmy to do it with us. Whatever troubles we might have with them plumers, none of 'em was his. An' anyways, I reckoned if he didn't have the good sense to tell us no, his ma would get up on her high horse right quick to lay down the law.

I said somethin' of that sort to Cameron an' he just shrugged again. "If the time comes," he said, "all we can do is ask."

❧ 13 ☙

THE SUBJECT DIDN'T COME UP FOR THE NEXT COUPLE WEEKS, DURIN' WHICH me an' Cameron kept a even closer watch over my place than we'd been in the habit of earlier. Didn't see no sign of them plumers the while, an' it was startin' to 'pear my guest had been right when he suggested them two that got in there was just snoopin' 'round without no good reason to believe he was there.

All that watchin' an' worryin' kept me to home more'n I'd of liked. But we had food enough, what with that I'd bought an' the chickens an' all. An' I couldn't think of nobody in close ridin' distance that would of answered the kinds of questions we wanted to ask anyway. 'Least it give us plenty of time to clean up that mess ole Jake had made of my cabin.

Jimmy come 'round to see us time to time, usually after sundown when he'd got done with his day's work. An' some nights he took Cameron over to see his black stallion whilst I stayed home to make sure there weren't no more surprises waitin' for him when he got back.

'Peared the boy was still keepin' a eye on them plumers durin' his days off. But he said they hadn't showed theirselves near the settlements for a spell. Too busy shootin' an' pluckin' birds, I reckon, though maybe they was a mite cautious too since a couple the fellers they'd been hangin' out with had gone missin' without no clear reason for it.

I'd got the idea him an' Cameron had been talkin' more 'bout such things whenever I wasn't with 'em. Maybe Miz Marcy heard some of it too, but I weren't so sure 'bout that.

As the days passed, that gent livin' with me 'peared to be mendin' up just fine. He'd got rid of his crutch an' was able to walk without hardly a limp. An' his shoulder didn't seem to bother him no more neither. He even told me he'd took to ridin' his horse now an' then of a evenin' so's it could get some exercise. Didn't go far, just up an' down that sand road by the creek whenever it looked to be empty of travelers.

An' whilst we was coolin' our heels there at my place, he spent hours practicin' with that six-shooter, drawin' it an' pointin' it an' whippin' 'round like he'd heard somebody behind him. Didn't risk shootin' it off most times, though onct in a while he'd bust up some bottles after dark.

From all I could tell he didn't much need all that practice. He was smooth an' fast an' when he shot at somethin' he hit it. I figured he was near-'bout good as me, maybe even just a mite better.

One thing Jimmy did talk 'bout when we was all three together was how after them plumers had a bait of feathers gathered up they took 'em to somebody that paid cash money for 'em. Then they'd all of 'em go on a spree. Said they'd spend a week or so hoorawin' 'round the country gettin' drunk an' bustin' things up an' partakin' in the pleasures of the flesh. 'Pears they was places all 'long the edges of the Glades that was ready to cater to such doin's.

Whenever an' wherever they set out to do that 'most anything could happen, none of it good. Folks livin' close by just had to hunker down an' wait it out till they finally run out of steam an' money an' went back into the Glades. Way it sounded to me, 't weren't so awful different from when a hurricane hit these shores.

An' that could be the time to go to out lookin' for 'em.

'Least that's what Cameron an' me figured. Wouldn't be no need to go chasin' off into that mis'able wet wilderness after 'em 'cause they'd be right where everbody knowed they was. An' at a time when they wasn't 'zactly sober 'nough to be too careful 'bout watchin' their back trail.

Trouble of it was, we hadn't no idea when they'd decide they'd got enough plumes to want to sell 'em. Nor where they'd go to do it or who they'd sell 'em to, much less where they'd choose to do their celebratin' afterwards. Somehow or another, we'd got that to find out.

Cameron, he said he didn't have no wish to go after that entire crowd. He just wanted to find the ones that put lead into him, an' maybe some others he could ask 'bout that Doctor Summerfield that was still missin'. If it turned out he'd been kilt like we more'n half feared, then they'd be some other choices to make.

So what we needed to do next was try an' find out where they meant to sell their plumes. Most likely spot would be further up the coast where they was a railroad could take 'em to the big cities in the North. Near as we could learn that'd be somewhere south of Palm Beach at the present time. That Mister Flagler'd built him a big ho-tel on the island there, an' now he was layin' tracks on south like there wouldn't be no tomorrow.

'Course it was possible they'd send their plumes off by boat instead. But Jimmy said he hadn't heard of no boatmen takin' part in such traffic, an' it'd be hard to keep that kind of thing a secret even if somebody thought there'd be a reason for it.

So soon as Cameron was feelin' up to it he went an' got his stallion from the McCollums, I saddled up Ole Roan an' we started off up the coast to where that new railroad was buildin'. Might of been wiser to take the younger horse for such a distance, but that ole partner of mine weren't in no mood to be left behind again. He were still a animal that liked to see fresh country, an' anyway we didn't plan to do no hard ridin' on this trip.

Him an' that horse of Cameron's 'peared to of reached a agreement to get along without causin' us no trouble. Prob'ly had to do with the fact they weren't no mare along for them to be jealous over. They both just pointed their noses to the north an' went along real steady an' peaceful.

Jimmy an' his ma would be keepin' the Cracker horse whilst we was gone, an' they'd have a watchful eye out for my cabin an' property. We hadn't seen no plumers nor no other strangers about for quite a spell an' hadn't no reason to expect they'd be trouble. But still we warned 'em not to come up to my place without first lookin' her over mighty careful.

Best we could figure it'd be somethin' over thirty miles to where we was headed an' we wasn't in no hurry. We walked the horses most the way, just raisin' 'em up to a trot now an' then where the country was open enough. It was generally all sandy an' flat, but with scrub oaks an' palmettos an' sometimes a stand of big ole palm trees. They was creeks that had to be crossed too, but we kept inland a bit an' never met with no real deep water. What with that an' them barrier islands off the coast, we never hardly got a peek at the ocean.

We camped in a stand of hardwoods with a li'l grass an' low-growin' bushes an' plenty of Spanish moss hangin' about for the horses to feed on. Made a li'l fire an' cooked up some bacon an' pan bread an' coffee 'fore spreadin' our blankets for the night.

We'd seen a few folks round an' about durin' the day, but not too many an' none that 'peared anxious to talk to us. Which suited us fine, 'cause we'd a mind to keep what we was doin' up here to ourselves till we'd figured out how to learn who might be buyin' plumes for shipment to the North.

They was a few ramshackle cabins we passed here an' there, even a couple made all outen the fans of palmettos. Feller that lived in one of them would keep outen the rain sure enough. But he'd prob'ly have to share his lodgin's with a whole passel of bugs.

Next afternoon we come up on the end of the tracks an' found a heap more folks 'round that place than they was in Lemon City an' all the country 'tween there an' here. Most all of 'em was men, gandy dancers an' saloon keepers an' supply sellers an' such. I reckoned they was women somewheres too. But they wasn't showin' theirselves in the daytime. Likely slept late an' mostly plied their trade at night.

Cameron an' me'd talked it over an' decided we'd make ourselves out to be would-be plumers, new to the area an' huntin' a market for all the goods we was hopin' to get. I'd brung along a ole shotgun I'd had, givin' it to Cameron to carry in the boot of his saddle. It had a pitted barrel an' weren't of much account. But I figured nobody with any sense would go to birdin' with a rifle.

It kind of helped us to look the part, though I'd done loaded it up with double-ought buck. It weren't birds we was so much concerned about when you come right down to it.

Cameron was still wearin' the duds I'd got him at the general store, an' them Boston boots of his hadn't been polished up for a week. So I reckoned he could pass for some no-count travelin' feller huntin' a easy dollar. 'Cept maybe when he talked. We agreed I'd do most of that.

We tied our horses at the rail next to a hollowed-out log that served as a waterin' trough, then stood for a bit just kind of lookin' things over. They was one long wide bare patch that some might call a street, follerin' along next to the tracks an' 'bout ankle deep in sand. Weren't no proper buildin's in sight, just tents put up ever which-way with a few of 'em havin' short boardwalks in front. Railroad office 'peared to be a ole boxcar pulled off onto a new-laid sidin'.

I made out what I calculated to be maybe a dozen or more saloons with hand-lettered signs like "RORY'S RETREET" an' "BUCKET O' BLUD" an' such-like. Generally these was where you'd go to find out whatever there was to know in some new place you hadn't been to before. But 'fore I could pick out one to start our in-vestigation, Cameron nudged my arm.

He pointed to a sign on another tent a dozen yards away that said "EATƧ" in great big letters. "First things first," he said. "No offense, but I've gotten a little tired of our own cooking. Maybe this won't be any better, but at least it'll be different."

I didn't have no objection. We hadn't put nothin' in our bellies since sun-up, an' then it was only a couple strips of bacon with some cold corn pone an' coffee.

❦ 14 ❧

WE WENT IN THE PLACE, WHICH 'LEAST HAD A PLANK FLOOR AN' SOME skeeter nettin' hung up to catch the spiders an' bugs from over our heads. They was a couple long tables with benches down each side an' a feller was settin' at the end of one of 'em. It was some past the noon hour, an' I reckoned 'most everbody else was already back at work.

This gent didn't 'pear like he too often worked up a sweat. He was wearin' a kind of a white suit with a shiny vest, but no necktie an' no collar on his shirt. Right then he was smokin' a cigar an' drinkin' coffee whilst lookin' over the grease-stained newspaper he'd got laid flat in front of him.

We took seats at t' other end of the same table he was at. When a man in a dirty apron showed up with cups an' a coffee pot, we ordered from the cardboard menu nailed up on a rafter. It give us the choice of fried mullet or fried mullet, together with some cooked swamp cabbage an' whatever was left over from that mornin's biscuits.

Anyhow, it was different.

Whilst we was waitin' for the food to be brought, I looked over at that feller at the end of the table an' tried to start up a conversation.

"'Nother right warm day," I said. He glanced up from his paper an' nodded, then went on back to his readin'.

"Lots of work to be had hereabouts I reckon, layin' out ties an' rails, then swingin' a double-jack to drive in the spikes." The gent didn't even look up this time. I took a swaller of coffee an' shrugged. "Liable to get a man all sweaty an' wore to a frazzle. Me an' my partner here figure they's better ways to make a dollar." He turned a page of his paper, still without lookin' at me.

"We hear tell they's mighty good money in shootin' birds an' takin' the plumes to sell. Wondered how a feller'd go about gettin' into that business."

The gent had took up his cup to take a sip of coffee. Now he put it down real slow an' stared down the table at me. He took a long drag on his cigar an' flicked the ash on the floor 'fore he spoke.

"My advice would be to do a little traveling. Maybe to Louisiana or some place like that. The market for plumes here in south Florida is all sewed up."

Well now, this here were a thing worth pursuin'. How'd that feller know 'bout the market for plumes hereabouts, an' why'd he say it was all sewed up? 'Less'n maybe he had a hand in it hisself?

"You real sure 'bout that?" I said. "'Pears to me there ain't no shortage of birds an' feathers everwhere. Ought to be room for a couple more fellers to have a piece of it."

The gent put his cigar on the edge of the table an' studied me an' Cameron for what felt like a long time. Then he folded up his paper an' stuck the cigar back in his mouth.

"There's no room here for any hunters to be working on their own. The men involved in the trade don't like competition."

He got up from the table an' started to go outside. Then he stopped in the entrance an' turned. "If you think you'd be able to take orders and a smaller share of the profits," he said kind of careful, "you might ask around for a man they call Gator. He may take you on with him, and then again he may not. If he doesn't," the gent shrugged an' turned his back, "you probably won't be seen again."

That give us a li'l somethin' to think about when we started in on our mullets.

"Well," I said after I'd took a couple bites, "what you figure we'd ought to do next? It's a brass-bound cinch neither one of us is goin' to ask after that Gator. He knows us already, an' we ain't goin' to get nothin' but grief if he learns we're about."

"Yes." Cameron put down his fork an' took a minute to finish his chewin'. "I've an idea from the way that man spoke he isn't here at present. But we need to keep an eye out for him just in case. And for anyone we see that seems curious and is likely to report to him."

He took another bite of fish, frownin' a mite. "Still, I think we ought to stay here for another day or two and see what we can find out. That man we just talked to clearly knows something about the pluming business. It could be he's the very agent who pays Gator and ships the feathers up north."

"Might be," I said. "But if he is, how do we go about learnin' it? An' then what do we do if it turns out he's the one?"

"First we'll ask a few questions here and there. Very discreetly. Buying and selling plumes is not against the law, and there's no reason it should be cloaked in secrecy. But how Gator deals with competition may be another matter." He shrugged. "I don't think it would be a good idea to let him know there's anyone looking into it."

We finished eatin' an' left the place, splittin' up to go callin' on some of the stores an' saloons in the area. Me, I figured I'd seek out the saloons an' just idle 'round inside 'em, keepin' my ears open an' my mouth shut. Cameron, he had his own ideas.

In Florida like in the West, saloons was where men generally met an' talked 'bout whatever was happenin' locally or was fresh on their minds. Often as not deals for cattle an' other goods was made there too. Feller could learn a good deal just standin' at the bar an' listenin' to what was said.

It were the middle of the afternoon an' not close to quittin' time for railroad men, which generally didn't come till the sun was goin' down. So none of them drinkin' establishments was what you'd call crowded, nor even much busy. Some didn't have a soul in 'em 'cept the owner or barkeep, who didn't have nothin' better to do but hope some idler'd come in that had money an' no job.

I didn't spare more'n a glance into them places, just long enough to see they was empty. Feller tendin' bar was sure to know a few things. But to find 'em out, I'd need to do a deal of talkin' my ownself. An' I weren't of a mind to bring so much attention to myself.

Finally I come to this mildew-streaked tent kind of off the beaten track an' backed up under some trees. It didn't look too promisin' on the face of it. But they was a couple horses tied to some bushes close by, an' I figured I might's well give it a shot.

The bar was a couple planks laid over two barrels an' the only whiskey in sight was in a dusty gallon jug that weren't near so easy to see through as the liquor inside it. Two rough-dressed fellers was bellied up there with a couple fruit jars in front of 'em.

I nodded a greetin' an' walked over to where the big beefy bartender stood restin' his bare arms on the planks.

"You got any beer?" I asked, hopin' I wouldn't have to sample none of that white lightnin' just so's I'd appear to be sociable.

"I reckon." He turned an' reached down into a box behind him, takin' out a brown bottle that he opened by knockin' the cap off on the edge of the bar. It foamed up a mite when he set it down, but I was just thankful it were somethin' looked reasonable safe to drink an' not of his own private makin'.

I laid my nickel on the bar an' took a couple steps back. Didn't say nothin' else right then, just lookin' them other three over whilst they was studyin' me.

"Ain't seen you 'round here before," the bartender said after a minute. "You come huntin' a job with the railroad?"

"Not so's you could notice" I shrugged. "Lately I just been travelin' a mite. Got a li'l left from the last job I had an' thought I'd take a look at the country hereabouts."

"Ain't much to look at," one of the two at the bar said. He were a older feller, 'round my age but less'n half my size. All tapered down to rawhide an' bone with a face that might of wore out two bodies. "Just sand an' scrub an' wet prairie 'most everwhere a body can see."

"But we like it," the younger one said. "We like it just fine. You wouldn't go noplace else, Judd, an' you might's well admit it." He were some inches taller'n his companion with broad shoulders an' the slim hips that told me he were a rider.

"I reckon maybe," the other agreed. Then he shook his head an' scowled. "If'n all these new folks 'round here would just go on back to where they come from an' leave all of it be. Gettin' so you can't hardly toss a pine cone 'thout hittin' some Yankee pilgrim with plans to muck out a swamp an' start a town."

"There's that." His partner nodded. "Railroads an' ho-tels an' rich tour-ists an' what-all. Started up in Saint Augustine a couple years ago, an' now I hear tell they don't mean to quit till they reach Miami an' Coconut Grove. Some say that Flagler feller's thinkin' to build bridges an' such all the way down to Key West."

"Don't reckon they's too much chance of that," the bartender said. "First hurricane comes along an' them bridges an' trains'll all be under water or back up in the Glades."

The older feller shrugged an' took a drink of his 'shine. "Well, that all ain't the worst of it. I reckon I could stand to let 'em spread out along them useless beaches an' islands next the ocean. Trouble of it is, they's plenty comin' inland too, diggin' after phosphate or plantin' orange trees on ever piece of ground they can latch onto. 'Fore you know it, they won't be free range enough left to feed a dozen cows."

"Well, I don't know 'bout that," the younger one told him. "They's still lots of country ain't been settled on yet. An' them couple freezes lately has sort of put a crimp in the orange business. Still, it's a kind of a worrisome thing."

He paused an' glanced over at me. "Us two are cow hunters. Just got done with the mammyin' up and havin' ourselves a li'l break 'fore headin' on back to the home place."

"Been at it a passel of years," the man next to him said, "our families has. An' I seen more changes in the last dozen years than our paps an' grandpaps ever knew in their entire lifes."

Well, that answered the question I'd been mullin' over a mite. Had a feelin' these two wasn't plumers, but I couldn't be real sure. An' it wouldn't of been too smart or safe to bring the matter up if it chanced that my hunch about 'em was wrong.

I still didn't plan to ask no questions straight out on the subject. They was that man standin' back of the bar, an' I didn't know nothin' 'bout him. 'Cept fellers in that line of work just naturally got a tendency to talk.

Way it turned out they weren't no need for me to bring up nothin'. That older cow puncher had sampled enough 'shine to go right on ahead with his talkin'.

❧ 15 ❧

"'N OTHER THING THAT GETS IN MY CRAW," HE SAID, "IS HOW ALL THEM folks that come down here want to shoot up the place an' kill ever livin' critter they can draw a bead on. I seen bear an' deer an' gators just layin' out in the sun with maybe a head or a piece of hide cut off an' the rest of it left to rot!"

He spit tobacco juice into a sand box at his feet. "An' birds? Hundreds of 'em, maybe even thousands. More in a day than any ho-tel full of tourists could ever eat in a year!"

He drained his fruit jar, an' the bartender uncapped the jug to pour him a li'l bit more. "An' you know what for? 'Sides makin' pictures of 'em to show their friends up North? Feathers! They pull the feathers off 'em an' send 'em up to Noo Yawk an' Boston to be put on their womenfolks' hats!"

He shook his head in disgust an' finally 'peared to of run out of things to say. After a minute his partner took it up.

"I reckon you're right 'bout all that, Judd. But the last you can't just lay on the Yankees. They's local boys does a heap of that killin' for plumes. Best part of it from what I hear. They fetch 'em in an' sell 'em to some feller that sends 'em off up yonder to the cities."

"What I heard too," the older man said mighty grim. "An' maybe somebody ought to take a gun an' see how they like bein' filled up with shot an' have all the hair pulled offen their scalps!"

He got quiet of a sudden an' looked about him, realizin' maybe he'd been talkin' too free. "Well anyhow," he finished up some milder, "if'n the Yankees didn't pay so much for them feathers, wouldn't nobody be workin' so long an' so hard at it."

I'd been standin' a li'l apart from them fellers, just drinkin' my beer an' keepin' my thoughts to myself. But I figured they'd ought to know that

"

whatever they might have to worry 'bout from them plumers it wouldn't be 'cause of me.

"First time I ever heard tell of such a thing," I lied, shakin' my head. "Mostly I've lived up in the north an' west parts of the state. Never guessed nobody'd pay cash money for feathers."

"Oh, they do it," the bartender said with a knowin' nod. "An' you'd be surprised how much money they is in it. Makes them plumers more'n willin' to take whatever steps is needed to be sure nobody ever tries to stop it."

The two cow hunters glanced at each other an' then finished their 'shine pretty quick "I reckon we'll be ridin'," the younger one said. "Like to put some miles behind us 'fore the sun gets too far down the sky." He follered his partner outside an ' a couple minutes later we heard the jingle of spurs an' the sound of horses trottin' away through the trees.

I finished my beer an' was fixin' to leave out from there my ownself. But when I come to set my empty bottle down the bartender give me a sly grin. "Good thing them two is leavin' now an' not a day or two later. Word is all the plumers will be comin' here 'bout sundown tomorrow. An' when they do they'll have feathers to sell an' a mighty big hankerin' for whiskey an' women. I seen 'em other places, tearin' 'round the country an' needin' the best part of a week to get shut of all the cash money they'll have."

He looked at me an' one eye closed in a slow wink. "Word to the wise, stranger."

Onct Cameron an' me had met up again it was comin' on to supper time an' we got us a meal in a diff'rent eatin' place. 'T'weren't a whole lot better'n the first, but anyhow, the food was different. This time we had a kind of a stew made out of what I figured was beef an' venison, with a li'l taste of bear meat throwed in.

We didn't get no chance to talk right then 'bout what-all we each had found out. Them tables was so crowded we was elbow to elbow with a whole passel of hungry railroad men an' others that we didn't know an' who might be inclined to repeat what they'd heard.

After we left there an' got our horses we found us a place back up in the woods a li'l ways off from all the activity. It weren't lookin' much like rain an' we didn't want to sleep in that big tent they called a ho-tel. It were just a couple long rows of bunks kept separate here an' there by sheets. Not even close to what a body'd call private, an' neither one of us thought much of bein' shut in with strangers on ever side. We'd slept in the open the night before an' was just as pleased to do it again.

We picketed the horses on a li'l patch of grass in a grove of live oaks where they could give warnin' in case we had visitors. It was warm enough that we didn't need no fire to let everbody see where we was. So we just spread our bedrolls out an' sat down on top of 'em in the dark to talk things over.

Cameron had spoke to some folks in that railroad office an' found out they did ship plumes up to the North time to time. An' sure 'nough, the gent we'd met in that first eatin' place was one of them that paid for the shippin'. Nobody had said he were the only one, but it 'peared likely from what he'd told us 'bout how Gator an' them all felt towards competition.

The man's name was John Patrick McCarty, an' he'd come down to these parts from Boston some five or six months earlier. Nobody knowed too much 'bout him, 'cept that he always had money an' he'd hired him a house someplace over near Jupiter where he stayed a part of the time. Rest of it he spent travelin' here an' there, sometimes hirin' a carriage to drive off in towards the South, an' sometimes takin' a train up to the North.

Cameron seemed to think they were somethin' 'bout that gent might be worth a closer look, though he admitted he didn't know of nothin' he'd done hereabouts that were agin the law. Me, I'd leave that kind of in-vestigatin' to him. Didn't 'pear to me he were the one we'd most cause to be concerned about.

Them plumers on the other hand, was liable to be a caution. Onct they'd got paid for their plumes they'd be raisin' holy hell for what could be miles around. Cameron said he'd got the idea they'd be some more money changin' hands, put up by Flagler an' his railroad comp'ny to get them fellers to take their drinkin' an' hoorawin' off someplace else where it wouldn't cause no delays in the layin' of tracks.

If so, it meant that barkeep I'd talked to had maybe got his information wrong an' where they meant to come an' sell their plumes weren't here at the end of the tracks a-tall. In which case we'd have to find out where that was if we'd any mind to run acrost 'em. An' Cameron had him a powerful wish to do that, both for meetin' up with them as ambushed him an' tryin' to find out what ever happened to that doctor friend of his.

For a couple minutes there he got quiet an' thoughtful. Then he said, "How many do you think there are in that gang of plumers all told?"

"Bartender didn't say. Miz Marcy allowed it were a dozen or more."

"Hm. Too many to face all at one time, even if they've been drinking."

Well, I reckon he'd got that right. Onliest times I'd had me any kind of a difficulty with a crowd that size I'd had some powerful help. Or else I'd been runnin'.

I pondered on it for a couple minutes. "Maybe," I said, "they'll split up some after they been paid off. If we could come up on 'em in twos an' threes it might give us a chanct to whittle 'em down a li'l."

"You mean ambush them? Or catch a few apart from the others and force a shoot-out?"

I could tell from the way he said it the idea didn't set too good with him. We still didn't know for sure who in that bunch might of put lead into him. Nor if they was any others of 'em that needed killin'.

I shook my head. "Neither one if we can help it. What I was considerin' was that if we talked real firm to some of them boys we might bring 'em 'round to see the error of their ways. It could be they's a number of 'em ain't had no hand in shootin' at nothin' but birds. You an' me got no partic'lar quarrel with them. But they's still liable to back Gator if it comes to a show-down.

"Now, s'posin' . . ." I was thinkin' ahead whilst I was talkin', "we was to give 'em to understand we'd got in mind to declare out-an'-out war on plumin' in these parts? Shoot up an' burn down their camps, hole their boats, steal or trash any plumes they've gathered. Might be they'd figure it's a sight healthier to go somewheres else to do their bird-huntin'.'"

"Do you think we could follow through on such a threat? Only the two of us?"

"Maybe. An' maybe not. But I reckon we could do enough damage to make 'em wonder. They ain't for sure we'd be all alone in what we're plannin'. There's others don't look real kindly on what they been doin'. Like them cow hunters I talked to."

"So your idea is we might scare some of them off?"

"Wouldn't say they was the kind to be scared too awful easy. But could be they'd be a li'l smarter in the way they looked at the situation. Shootin' down helpless birds is one thing. Gettin' shot at yourself whilst you're at it is somethin' else again. No matter how much money a feller makes, he ain't goin' to spend none of it from underneath the ground."

"And what if none of those we talk to are persuaded?"

"Then I reckon we'll just have to try a li'l harder to persuade 'em." I looked over to where I could make out his dark shape settin' acrost from me. "You figure you'd be up for that kind of a game?"

"I took cards when I first came down here, though at the time I'd no idea of the stakes. Now that I know them I think I'll play out my hand and see what turns up at the showdown."

"Good 'nough for me. 'Pears like we got us all day tomorrow to do some figurin' an' find out a couple things. Right now I've a mind to get some shut-eye."

❧ 16 ❧

WE ROLLED OUT AT FIRST LIGHT AN' SADDLED UP THE HORSES. THEN WE rode into the work camp an' got ourselves some breakfast. I picked the second place we'd ate at. Didn't figure nobody could mess up eggs an' bacon an' hotcakes too bad. But still I weren't anxious to risk that one was fryin' fish the day before.

It was full up to overflowin' same as it had been at dinner, an' neither one of us did much talkin' whilst we filled our bellies an' drank three-four cups of coffee. Afterwards, Cameron had a notion to go an' send a telegram, so I just waited for him with the horses at the hitch rail an' watched the all locals go about their business.

Hadn't been there too long when that McCarty gent come struttin' up the street. He were lookin' mighty pleased with hisself, an' I figured it was 'cause he was expectin' to get another batch of plumes right soon an' was already countin' up the money he'd have after he'd sent 'em on up North. Didn't take no dee-tective like Cameron to tell me that whatever he give to them plumers wouldn't be a patch on all the dollars he'd make out of that deal his ownself.

He seen where I was an' come over next to me. "Good morning!" he said real cheerful-like. "Still here, I see. Have you found someone to ask about seeing Gator over that matter we were discussing?"

"Not yet," I said. "Been considerin' on it some, but weren't too sure how we'd go 'bout meetin' up with him."

"Well, you're in luck. He and his men will be coming in from the Glades this very evening. We've some business to transact, and then they may be in the area for several days longer." He give me a sly look. "But if I were you, I'd not waste any time finding him. They all like to celebrate a little after being paid for their goods, and then nobody will be much in the mood to talk business."

"That so? Well, we'll surely have it in mind. Only we ain't quite made a decision yet 'bout whether we want to hitch ourselves to another feller's wagon."

The gent's smile disappeared. "There are only two choices you have to decide between. Either you join his group, or you leave this country entirely. And if you choose the second, I'd advise you to do it before nightfall. Things may not be so safe after that."

"I reckon you could be right," I told him. "'Course it ain't never too safe for them as goes 'round packin' guns." I grinned. "Not nobody a-tall."

He didn't have nothin' to say to that. Just looked at me kind of sharp for a second, then turned his back an' walked off down the street.

I noticed 'fore he done it though, that he'd give a li'l glance at that tied-down six-shooter on my hip.

When Cameron had got back, we agreed to kind of stay in the background whilst keepin' our eyes an' ears open for anything more we could learn 'bout Gator an' his plume-huntin' associates. What we wanted to know most of all was where they'd be gatherin' that evenin' to turn over their plumes an' get the money for 'em.

Didn't 'pear to be much doubt that this McCarty gent was the one who'd be doin' the gettin' an' the givin'. So it looked like a good idea to watch over him on the sly in hopes he'd do or say somethin' that would give us a clue as to how he'd go about it. But as it turned out that weren't so easy as it might of seemed at first glance.

He spent most the mornin' over coffee an' his newspaper in that same eatin' place where we'd first met him. We managed to keep a eye on the entrance to it by kind of idlin' 'round a couple stores an' saloons acrost the way. But by noontime we was gettin' some sharp looks from the owners an' managers of them places, 'cause we hadn't hardly bought nothin' 'cept a couple small beers an' some triflin' odds an' ends.

Two fellers with no partic'lar place to go nor nothin' special to do was bound to make folks curious, an' were liable to cause talk. Which was 'zactly what we was tryin' not to have happen.

An' yet ole McCarty didn't 'pear in no hurry a-tall to leave where he was at an' go on 'bout his business. We caught glimpses of him inside there time to time, just smokin' his cigar an' lookin' like he'd be happy to spend the entire day just settin' at that table an' not doin' another thing.

We'd 'bout decided we was goin' to have to move on an' come up with some other way to find out what we wanted when the noon whistle blew, an' right then a man wearin' a floppy hat an' work clothes went inside the eatin' place. He weren't in there a dozen minutes 'fore he come out again in what 'peared to be a all-fired hurry. We watched him stride 'long real lively till he turned an' made his way back in amongst some tents so's we couldn't see him no more nor guess where he was headed.

Had to of been McCarty. Who'd gone inside to see 'cause there weren't nobody else in the place just then 'sides the cook. Me an' Cameron glanced at each other an' then I lit out after the man in the floppy hat whilst he headed over to the tent that had the "EATş" sign on it.

Trouble of it was, that whistle had done turned loose a whole army of hungry railroad men an' we near-bout had to run a bunch of 'em over to make it to where we was goin'. Some of them boys was right sturdy built an' not much in the mood to have theirselves get run over. Could of turned into a reg'lar Saturday night shindig if the two of us hadn't had sense enough to stop an' let the crowd thin out a mite 'fore makin' our way on past 'em.

Upshot of it was that I never got another peek at that feller I was tryin' to foller. An' when I come back 'round to the front of the eatin' place Cameron was frownin' an' shakin' his head.

"McCarty slipped out back through the kitchen," he said. "Probably while we were still watching that man he met walk away."

Well, it didn't make neither of us real happy, since we'd just gone an' wasted the entire mornin' standin' 'round without learnin' a doggone thing. What's worse, it 'peared we hadn't been near so sly an' stealthy as we'd wanted to believe we was. That McCarty must of seen us or been told 'bout us watchin' him, then come up with a plan to leave us there twiddlin' our thumbs whilst he went on an' did what he was meanin' to do all along.

"It happens." Cameron said after I'd cussed an' told him what I thought of the situation. "The question is, what do we do now?"

"Well, if he's leavin' out to meet them plumers sometime soon, an' not just foolin' 'round with us like he's done so far, he's got to have him a way to travel to wherever its is they're plannin' to meet. An' that means he'll need a horse or a rig of some kind to take him there."

"Of course! And no one I've talked to ever mentioned him having a horse of his own. In fact, I remember someone said he was in the habit of renting some type of horse-drawn vehicle every time he made his periodic trips into the country."

"So what we got to do now is try an' find out where he might get aholt of one. An' if he's done hired somethin', it could be that whoever he got it from has a notion of where he'll be headed."

We split up again an' made the rounds, lookin' for corrals an' stables that had animals to rent. There weren't that many of 'em, 'specially with rigs to let out an' teams to pull 'em. After li'l bit I come acrost one, kind of back up in the woods with some rope corrals an' a shelter for the horses made outen palmetto fans an' canvas.

☙ 17 ❧

Feller that run the place was friendly enough but kind of close-mouthed 'bout who his customers was an' if he'd done any business with 'em in the last hour or so. I didn't bring up the subject right off o'course. Didn't want him to get the notion I might be huntin' somebody, nor that I was in a special hurry to ask questions. Which o' course, I was. But I did my best to pretend like I wasn't.

I'd done left Ole Roan back at the hitchin' rail so's I could show up afoot an' make out like I was wantin' some transportation for myself. I spent a couple minutes lookin' over the horses an' mules he'd got there for sale an' rent, but didn't show a whole lot of interest in none of 'em.

Which didn't take no special play-actin' on my part. They was as sorry a collection of critters as I'd seen to one place in a month of Sundays. Sway-backed an' old, most of 'em, with a few youngsters that was likely not half broke. An' one ornery ole mule that tried to take a bite out of me when I started to get too close.

I backed off an' shook my head. "Don't reckon none of these here would much suit me. You got anything else? Maybe a couple you're holdin' out back?" They was a split log fence I could see past the trees, which might or might not of been a part of his outfit.

"'Fraid not," the hostler said. "Horses ain't so plentiful hereabouts as they might be other places. An' the Yankees tend to favor them older gentle ones. 'Specially their womenfolks."

"Well . . ." I said like I was considerin', "I was huntin' a good ridin' horse. But if you got some kind of a rig you could hitch a couple of these here to, just for a li'l spell till I can find me somethin' better . . ."

The feller spit a stream of tobacco juice an' shrugged. "Like to. But I won't get my surrey an' trotters back till tomorrow or the next day. Just now rented it out to this Yankee from up North."

"One of them bosses with the railroad?" I asked casual-like as if I didn't much care.

"Never got 'round to askin' him what his business might be. But I'm pretty sure it ain't the railroad. He comes here ever now an' again, always takes the same surrey an' team an' pays for 'em in advance." He spit again. "Pays mighty good too, so I try an' hold that there rig for him special."

"Meanin' you prob'ly wouldn't let it out even after he's got back?"

"Maybe. An' then again I might. Depends on what he tells me 'bout when he wants to use it again." He squinted at me kind of suspicious from under his hat brim. "An' whether a feller's got cash money enough to meet my price."

"Well, I got a friend who'll put up the money if it comes to that. When you say you expect that gent back?"

"Tomorrow evenin' at the earliest. Maybe the day after."

"Wonder where he'd be goin' to durin' all that time. Couldn't be a place too terrible far away I imagine . . ." I kind of let my voice trail off in hopes the hostler would offer a li'l hint.

"He didn't say an' I didn't ask." He looked at me kind of sharp. "Why'd you want to know?"

"Just curious." I shrugged. "You reckon he's sparkin' some li'l gal he knows in the vicinity?"

"If he is it ain't no least part of my business. Nor yours."

I agreed an' left out from there pretty quick, figurin' I'd just nearly pushed my luck a tad too far. I did take the time to suggest I might come back with that well-off friend of mine. Maybe if this feller thought they was good money in the offin' he wouldn't be so anxious to repeat any suspicions he might of had.

'Peared like I'd done found the place where Mister McCarty rented that rig he traveled in. But 's far as where he meant to go with it this time I'd no more idea than a mule has of five card poker. Less, prob'ly.

Turned out, though, that whilst I was solvin' that first part of the puzzle, Cameron had come up with a clue to the second.

"There's a small river some four or five miles south of here," he said after we'd managed to get back together again, "which flows out from the Everglades. You may recall we crossed it on our way here."

"Uh-huh." They was a number of them creeks we'd crossed. Couldn't be too sure which one he was talkin' 'bout now.

"Well, it seems that's the one the plumers intend to use to come in and meet with their agent. They'll be in boats of course. After they've been paid, they could just turn around and go back into the Glades." He give me a kind of a lopsided smile. "But I've strong reason to doubt it."

Well, I doubted it too from what I'd heard 'bout how they generally acted after they'd got holt of some cash money. An' Cameron 'peared to know more 'bout it than he'd told me so far.

"You got a look on your face like a big ole tomcat settin' outside a li'l mouse's hidey-hole. What else you found out 'bout them plumers an' their doin's?"

He let his grin fade a mite when I said that. But I could see he was still mighty proud of his dee-tectin' skills.

"As I was making the rounds of the camp in search of corrals or stables that might have horses to rent, I noticed something else that caught my interest. Some men were busy loading casks and barrels onto a heavy mule-drawn wagon partly hidden in the trees behind one of the saloon tents. From the looks of those barrels it was pretty clear they contained liquor. Since it will be some time yet before the rails have advanced far enough to relocate the saloons, I wondered why anyone would be taking whiskey away from here rather than bringing it in.

"To make a long story short, I was curious enough to slip back through the trees and do a little eavesdropping. It seems that whiskey is being taken to where Gator and his men are expected to make their appearance. This way those bringing it will get first crack at their money before they can go anywhere else."

"An' you heard 'em say where they was goin'? Described it good enough so's we could find the place our ownselves?"

"Not exactly. But that's a heavy wagon and it can't move very fast on what pass for roads in this country. All we have to do is follow its tracks while keeping out of sight of the teamsters and those they're expecting to meet."

Meanin' that McCarty gent an' the plumers o'course. I reckoned we could prob'ly do it. An' it were the best chance we was likely to have to come acrost them at their meetin' place.

"Let's go fetch the horses," I said.

Onct we was in the saddle, Cameron took me to where he'd watched 'em loadin' up the wagon so's we could pick up their trail without needin' to ask nobody 'bout whether they'd seen it nor which way it was headed. No sense gettin' folks to wonderin' why we was askin' or what it was we was up to.

'Peared them fellers on the wagon had kind of the same idea. Them deep ruts they'd left weren't no trouble a-tall to spot. But they'd circled 'round through the trees so's not to pass through the settlement an' be noticed by somebody that might get curious the way Cameron had done. They didn't mean to share their profits with no others that had whiskey for sale.

After they'd gone a li'l ways west an' was out of sight of all the tents, they turned south onto this sand road that had grass an' weeds growin' up betwixt the ruts. There'd been a mite of travel on it time to time, but not so much that we couldn't make out their tracks mighty plain. An' if they ever went to turn off somewheres, the tore-up dirt would be somethin' even a blind man would notice.

But they held to the road an' so did we, walkin' our horses so's not to come up on 'em unexpected. I figured there weren't no reason to hurry. The sun hadn't even started to brush the tree-tops yet.

After we'd made it a couple-three miles Cameron drew up all of a sudden an' got down off his horse. He squatted on his heels in the road an' pointed to a narrower track that were mostly covered over by the wider wheels of the wagon an' the bigger hoofs of the mules.

I leaned over in the saddle to see what he was lookin' at. "Smaller rig come 'long here earlier today," I said. "You reckon it's that McCarty in his surrey?"

"I'd be willing to bet on it. The tracks were made after the sun dried the ground, which indicates late morning or afternoon. And . . ." He'd been lookin' all 'round the place where he'd squatted. Now he got up an' stepped over to the side of the road. "There's a discarded cigar butt." He bent down an' touched it. "Still warm at the end. He must have passed this way not very many minutes earlier."

"An' the liquor toters is right behind him. So they's both pretty close up ahead now. Could be a good time for us to give the horses a li'l rest an' take stock."

Cameron nodded an' went to take up the reins of his black. He led him off the road into a stand of trees a few yards to our right. I got down from the leather an' follered him with Ole Roan. We kept our voices just barely over a whisper whilst we stood there an' talked things over.

❧ 18 ❧

"From what we've heard," Cameron said, "the meeting with Gator and his men is supposed to take place shortly before dark. It could happen sooner, but let's suppose for now that this is the plan. Then it will be several hours more until they make their appearance."

"Uh-huh, likely enough. This is a far piece from their usual stompin' grounds west of Lemon City. An' nobody moves real fast whilst polin' a boat."

"So even at their present pace, McCarty and the men on the wagon must be expecting to reach their rendezvous early and wait there for the plumers. I think for his part he just saw an opportunity to give us the slip and took it, setting out quickly to minimize the chance of being followed. Once he left the encampment behind, he'd no particular need to hurry."

"Assumin' where he's goin' ain't so awful far from where he started. How much further you reckon that place is from where we are right here?"

"Five or six miles I'd guess, following the road. Maybe as little as half that."

"What 'bout them fellers with the liquor wagon? 'Pears they left out kind of early too."

"Probably for the same reason. To avoid calling attention to themselves."

"You reckon McCarty knew they was comin'? Or did their showin' up behind him come as a surprise?"

"Well, somebody must have told them where the meeting place was. He may have intended to keep the plumers there until he could hurry back to the railroad and arrange a shipment north."

"'Fore them boys got to thinkin' they might just take his money an' sell their plumes elsewhere?"

"It's possible, though I doubt if Gator would take a chance on killing the goose that laid the golden egg. And if my suspicions about Mister McCarty are correct, he has associates who could make things very dangerous for anyone who crossed him."

Well, that were somethin' I might want to ponder on sometime—if this gent here ever give me more'n just a hint as to what he might be talkin' 'bout. But instead he turned back to the subject at hand.

"I'd like for us to arrive early at that meeting place too, since it seems we have the time. If we can find a hidden place to watch whatever goes on there, we may get a chance to single out some of the plumers and speak to them privately."

"Meanin' tell 'em what we'd a mind to do from here on out, an' offer 'em a opportunity to mend their ways." It was what we'd talked 'bout the night before, an' this here looked like as good a place as any to make a start.

"Exactly." He nodded. "There are too many on the road ahead to make any secret approach that way. But since we don't know exactly where the meeting is to be, it seems we can't afford to lose track of it either. It presents a problem."

Well, I'd a idea or two 'bout that. But I weren't real sure how good a Injun Cameron would be if it come to skulkin' through the woods.

"Mebbe," I said, "we could try an' come at it a different way." He looked at me kind of curious an' I went on to explain. "Them fellers'll be comin' down outen the Glades in boats, follerin' the creek you heard tell of. Now, they's a passel of creeks they might of chose for the purpose, but it stands to reason they'll use the one that's closest to this road, or 'least meets up with it. So if we was to find us that creek an' foller it upstream a ways . . ."

"Of course! It should lead us right to the meeting place!"

"Uh-huh. 'Course it may not be so easy as all that. They's swamps an' thickets right next to 'most them creeks hereabouts. Might not be too easy to foller even after we'd managed to find it."

"It's worth a try at least. And now that I think of it, since they're all in boats and have no other way to travel except to walk, it's likely they'll use them to go farther downstream after they've been paid, in search of brothels or other entertainment. Even if we don't reach the place where they're to meet McCarty, we still might come across some of them afterward."

"Maybe. But that's a bridge we'll cross when an' if we come to it. First we got to find us that creek."

"You have any idea how to locate it?"

"Just the one. Since we ain't yet come to no water on the way here, I reckon it's got to be somewheres to the south. Can't say how far, but from how them folks on the road don't 'pear to be in much hurry I figure there ain't a whole heap of ground to cover. An' since 'most all them creeks run out from the Glades to the sea, we're just naturally bound to come acrost it sooner or later."

"Then what are we waiting for? Lead on, MacDuff!"

I hadn't got no idea what he meant by callin' me that. But I didn't take no time nor trouble to ask him. I just took the reins of Ole Roan, an' after a careful look up an' down the road, I led him acrost it an' in amongst the thick woods on the other side.

'T'weren't no sense in us gettin' mounted up again. They was low-growin' limbs an' vines near everwhere you looked. It was trouble enough just to find us openin's where the horses could follow. Figured we'd have to leave 'em behind 'fore too very long. But I surely didn't want to leave 'em near that road where somebody was liable to find 'em.

Turned out that creek we was huntin' weren't more'n a quarter mile away. An' a right good thing too, 'cause we was all havin' our difficulties makin' our way amongst them trees an' vines an' devil's walkin' sticks an' what-all.

When we got close to the water we held up for a bit an' took ourselves a breather. The sun was down behind the trees now, but I figured we'd still got another good hour or more of daylight 'fore it come on to full dark. An' I knowed from earlier that they'd be a three-quarter moon risin' not too long after.

I handed the reins to Cameron an' stepped out onto a cypress knee, wrappin' one arm about the tree for balance. That way I could kind of lean over an' have me a gander both upstream an' down.

Weren't a awful lot to see. That li'l stream curved an' twisted so much that only a hundred yards or so was in sight in each direction. Weren't no boats anywheres about, which was good if a feller was worried 'bout them plumers gettin' past us somehow. But at the same time I'd been thinkin' how much easier it'd been if they was some kind of a boat we could latch onto our ownselves to use just now.

'Fore I stepped back onto solid ground I glanced downstream one more time, an' thought I seen a li'l feather of smoke risin' up from behind some trees a good ways off yonder. Could be somebody had 'em a cabin or a fishin' camp alongside the creek thataways. I wondered if they knew 'bout Gator an' his friends. An' what they'd do onct that bunch got all liquored up an' started in to travel.

Well, whatever they did or didn't know was their own lookout just now. We'd got us other places to go an' other fish to fry.

We come to a li'l grassy clearin' not too much further upstream, with tall pines an' cypress to hide it from the creek an' the woods all 'round. Looked like a good place to picket the horses after we'd give 'em a chance to drink. I made sure they was room to get in betwixt the trees on the north side towards the road. Then I spent a couple minutes studyin' on how the tops of 'em all looked 'gainst the sky in that direction.

Could be we'd be in a bit of a hurry when we went to leave out of that place. An' I didn't mean get all turned 'round an' start goin' the wrong direction.

I happened to notice that Cameron tied his black to the picket rope usin' a slip knot same as I was doin'. That feller'd had occasion to make him a sudden departure or two his ownself somewhere along the line.

It were some easier makin' our way beside that creek without two big ole stallions in tow. An' when it come to Injunin' through the woods Cameron 'peared to be just nearly as good as me. He surely weren't the tenderfoot I'd half suspected he was. He stepped mighty careful an' took his time, watchin' the ground ahead an' pushin' aside them vines an' branches so's they scarcely made a whisper.

It didn't take us long to get close enough to spot where that meetin' was to be. It were just a li'l clearin' amongst the trees, with the road runnin' down to a flat grassy patch alongside the creek an' some low sandy islands off in the water that made what looked to be a ford.

Them fellers with the whiskey was busy standin' one of the barrels up on the tail of the wagon an' drivin' a tap into it near the bottom. Whilst they was doin' that an' settin' out some tin cups an' a cigar box where they planned to keep their money, that McCarty gent was just settin' in his surrey alongside 'em smokin' one of his cigars. He'd gone an' turned his rig 'round so it pointed back up the road, makin' it clear he didn't mean to waste 'round none gettin' shut of the place just quick as his business was over.

I seen he was wearin' a pistol in a holster now, an' he'd got another one layin' next to him on the seat. 'Spite of what Cameron had said 'bout his dangerous associates, this gent weren't plannin' to take him no chances.

After a bit we heard Gator an' his crowd hootin' an' hollerin' a good ways off, long 'fore they got to where we could see 'em. They sounded in a rowdy mood already, lookin' forward to gettin' started on their drinkin' spree just quick as they got hands on the money to do it.

19

Cameron an' me hunkered down a li'l lower in the bushes whilst they poled their boats in an' jumped out to drag 'em partways up from the water. Miz Marcy had said she thought they was a dozen of 'em or maybe more. She'd been right 'bout that last part anyway. I counted eighteen as they come up onto the bank, with eight or ten flat-bottomed boats an' canoes that was lined up by the creek.

We'd found us a pretty good hidin' place, not so close to that wide open clearin' as to run much risk of bein' noticed back under the trees, but where we could still keep a eye on the greatest part of it an' see what-all was happenin'.

We'd figured we was goin' to have to set there for a spell without movin', till that whiskey got to flowin' an' the plumers was feelin' it enough to spread theirselves out a mite an' not pay too close attention to what was around 'em. Most of 'em was totin' shotguns, an' some had pistols shoved down in their belts too. I seen Gator stridin' acrost to the surrey with that rifle he'd had when him an' his friends come up to my cabin.

It was gettin' dark now an' the fellers from the wagon had lit a couple torches atop some poles they'd stuck into the ground. They had 'em a coal-oil lantern too, settin' on the tailgate right next to their cash box. Where we was hidin' the shadows was too deep for anybody to spot us 'long as we stayed away from that light from the torches.

When Gator got next to McCarty, they had a few words, then Gator turned an' waved for his men to come on over to where they was. They'd been busy fetchin' things out from the boats in the meantime. Some of 'em 'peared to be folders they'd made out of leather an' cloth, but there was also a bunch of cushions an' pillows. What surprised me a mite was that a few of them fellers was totin' good-sized books. I could of swore one was a big ole family Bible.

"They press the feathers between the pages," Cameron whispered in my ear. "It preserves and protects the best and most valuable."

We watched 'em load all their bundles into the back of the surrey an' then walk away from it whilst McCarty kept his eyes on 'em with his hand on the seat a couple inches from his pistol. When Gator was the only one still close by, McCarty reached in his coat an' fetched out a big roll of greenbacks. He held it out in his left hand whilst pickin' up the reins with his right.

Gator took the money an' stepped away to start dealin' it out to his men. Soon as he done that, McCarty slapped the reins to his horses an' lit out up that sand road like Ole Scratch an' all his devils was a-standin' right behind him.

Which maybe weren't so far from the truth.

Them fellers sellin' the whiskey was right wary their ownselves. I'd seen a sawed-off shotgun an' a couple ax handles layin' in easy reach near that barrel on the wagon. I reckon nobody 'round here trusted nobody else too much, what with all the cash money that was bein' spread about.

We watched them fellers get their pay an' start congregatin' 'round the wagon like a pack of hungry hound dogs. They took to that whiskey like it was cold spring water an' all their innards was ablaze. After li'l while an' a heap more hootin' an' hollerin', they started spreadin' out 'round the clearin', a mite unsteady on their feet an' callin' out to each other 'bout gettin' shut of this place an' findin' some different entertainment.

We seen two of 'em go down to where the boats was beached an' start pushin' one out into the water. We give some thought to sneakin' over there to meet 'em, but 'fore we could make up our minds to do it a couple others wandered off into the woods not a dozen yards from where we was. We follered them instead, an' onct they'd got back into the darker shadows they went to answerin' nature's call.

They'd leaned their shotguns against a tree trunk to do it, an' they was a mite surprised when Cameron an' me come alongside 'em whilst they was busy buttonin' up. We'd slipped the thongs off the hammers of our six-shooters earlier, but didn't feel no need to fetch 'em out just yet. Had in mind to do a li'l talkin' first.

"Evenin', gents," I said. "How 'bout we step over a li'l deeper into the woods so's we can have a quiet conversation?"

Feller I was standin' next to jerked his head 'round an' seen my hands was empty, which caused him to make a wrong decision. 'Stead of answerin' he just kind of grunted an' swung his big hairy fist up all of a sudden, thinkin' to fetch it 'longside my jaw.

Only my jaw weren't where he expected it to be. I'd pulled my head to the side an' brung my arm back for a blow of my own. His fist went over my shoulder an' I hit him hard as I could right underneath the breastbone. He were a good-sized feller, some heavier'n me an' maybe a inch or two taller. But ain't nobody goin' to stand up to gettin' hit where I hit him when he ain't set for it. He bent over gaspin' an' chokin' whilst I took holt of his collar an' the seat of his pants to hustle him off amongst the trees away from the clearin'.

Didn't have no chance to watch what Cameron was doin' till I'd banged that feller's head up against the trunk of a good-sized hickory. But when he moaned an' went down on his knees I looked 'round an' seen my partner had fetched the other'n along with us. Had his arm shoved up betwixt his shoulder blades so hard that his only choices was to have it broke or go to the ground alongside his compadre.

Cameron stepped back an' shucked his six-gun. "Now we'll have that talk," he said, "without interruptions."

We was far 'nough off by now that I reckoned he was right. 'Specially since all the others was makin' so much hooraw they prob'ly wouldn't hear us.

But that feller he'd just let go of reared up like he meant to give out a holler. So Cameron clicked back the hammer of his six-shooter. "All you have to do," he said, "is sit there quietly and listen while we do the talking. Afterward we might turn you loose."

He glanced at me. "Were either of these among the men who came to your cabin asking questions?"

"Nope. I got a pretty good recollection for faces an' I never set eyes on them two 'fore tonight."

"All right. Then what we have," he said as he looked back at the fellers on the ground, "is a proposition for you to consider. You've just completed what I'm sure were a number of uncomfortable months in the Everglades. You've been well paid for your time there, and now you've the chance to reconsider your choice of vocation. Or at least where to practice it. I'd suggest some place far off from here, where the climate would be more conducive to your health and well-being."

Them two just stared at him. I'd a notion the big words he'd been usin' were a tad more confusin' to 'em than convincin'.

"What my partner means," I said, "is that you-all had best leave out from here an' go do your bird-killin' elsewhere. We got us a mind to declare war on the plumin' business hereabouts—burnin' up camps, holin' boats, an' just generally makin' it too much trouble for the gatherin' of feathers. Prob'ly involve a mite of shootin' too, here an' there. So you'd likely find if safer if you was somewheres else onct we got started."

"You're crazy in the head!" the smaller one squawked. "We ain't breakin' no laws, an' you-all ain't got no right to set yourselves agin us thataway!"

"What we got a right to do," I told him, "an' what we're liable to do is two separate things. 'F I was you, I'd be havin' a peek at my hole card an' decidin' if what's in the pot is worth takin' the chanct."

That feller I'd knocked in the head was comin' 'round by now, an' he got real red in the face. "I'll be damned if I'll let no pair of tinhorns tell me what to do or how!" He hunched his back like he meant to get up an' have another go at me. I was ready, but he happened to spot Cameron's cocked pistol 'bout then an' it settled him down a mite.

"More'n likely be damned if you don't," I said. "But you-all can do whatever you're a mind to. Anyway you've been told."

The other'n weren't ready to let go of it just yet. "You try somethin' like you said an' we'll have the law down on you both!"

"From what we've heard," Cameron said, "the law doesn't have much interest in what happens in the Glades. But if they do, there are some shootings and a possible murder they might look into while they're at it."

"Murder? We ain't had a part in no murders! Nor no shootin' neither, 'ceptin' at birds."

"So you say." I give him a hard look. "But they's sure 'nough somebody in that crowd of yours that has. You reckon you could 'splain to the hangman it weren't you?"

Sounded like Cameron's mention of shootin's an' murder were news to these two. But maybe not a total surprise. From the way they'd glanced at each other right then I figured they'd a notion of who could of done it.

"Anyhow," I said, "If the question come up an' you-all wasn't here, I 'spect we might forget that we seen you."

Whilst they was mullin' that over, 'peared like a good time to bring this meetin' to a end. We backed off an' left 'em settin' there, Cameron still keepin' 'em covered with his pistol. When we got to where they'd left their shotguns we took 'em up an' shucked out the shells, then went over by the creek an' slung 'em off in the middle of it.

Afterward, we kind of circled 'round, watchin' out for others of that bunch an' tryin' to figure who else we might put a li'l bug in the ear of.

They'd been several more left out in their boats by then, an' we heard some talk that give us to believe that maybe there was some kind of a hog ranch a li'l farther downstream. I figured it could of been that place I'd seen the smoke risin' from earlier, though 'course we couldn't know for sure.

It were worth givin' a bit of thought to. Might be where we'd catch a couple plumers with their pants down, in a manner of speakin'.

Trouble of it was, we hadn't no idea which side that twisty creek it'd be on if we found it. An' if it turned out it were the far one then we'd either have to swim our horses over or use that ford right here in front of the rest of 'em.

So we decided to save that idea for later an' try makin' our case to a few others 'fore they all got gone from this place.

✆ 20 ✇

I'D BEEN KEEPIN' MY EYES ON OLE GATOR PRETTY CONSTANT, AN' HE DIDN'T look near ready to leave just yet. He'd been doin' his part with the drinkin', but it didn't 'pear to of had much effect on him. His swaggerin' walk was just as steady as a feller leavin' church. Carried that rifle under his arm the entire time, with his right hand on the action all ready for use. Done his drinkin' from a tin cup in his left.

They was four, five other hard cases that never got too far from him, ever one of 'em armed to the teeth too. An' the way their eyes kept turnin' towards the dark edges of the woods time to time made Cameron an' me right cautious 'bout gettin' too near to that clearin'. We just kept ourselves back in the shadows so's we could study on the situation.

'Fore very long we spotted them men we'd done our talkin' to kind of sneakin' 'round through the trees towards where all the boats was beached. I'd been more'n half expectin' 'em to stride right up to Gator an' tell him 'bout us an' what-all we'd said. If they done that, it wouldn't of left us much choice but to fade back into the dark real quick an' go fetch the horses. But 'least they'd of been spreadin' the word 'round so's the rest of that bunch would know that life in the Glades was 'bout to get some less agreeable an' prob'ly more risky.

The way them two was actin' though, they wasn't real anxious to even be noticed by Gator. Nor by nobody else in that crowd neither. They was doin' their level best to get theirselves away from this place without bein' seen.

Could be they was a mite embarrassed 'bout losin' their guns back yonder. Or maybe what we'd been sayin' 'bout murder an' hangin' had started 'em to thinkin'. Not everbody's willin' to risk a noose for money, no matter how much money it is. I reckoned maybe these two wasn't the stone cold killers I suspicioned Gator an' some others to be. 'Least not killers of men. Birds was another matter.

I watched 'em go down to their boat, an' whilst they was pushin' it off an' gettin' situated inside I seen somethin' else. I give Cameron a li'l nudge with my elbow.

"'Nother boat back yonder," I whispered. "A li'l apart from the others an' nearly hid from sight amongst some bushes an' reeds."

"Any idea which of these men arrived in it?"

"Nope. But it surely weren't Gator. I seen him climb out of that cypress skiff right there in the middle."

"It could be another one or two we might talk to about leaving."

"Maybe. If we was to 'splain things to 'em kind of quiet-like."

He eased a couple branches apart an' studied the place I'd pointed to. "Do you think there's a way we can get over there without being seen?"

"I reckon. If we kind of circle 'round an' take it slow an' careful."

"Let's go then. We're wasting our time staying here."

We backed off, keepin' some trees an' bushes betwixt us an' the light from the torches. 'Most all of them that was still in the clearin' weren't strayin' too far from that wagon with the whiskey. An' the fellers that brung it was still doin' business, though not quite so fast as they had at the first.

It took us a good half-hour to make our way 'round to where we could hunker down in the dark a few yards from where I'd noticed that boat. They was a mess of twisted-up roots an' reeds 'twixt where we was an' it was, which meant we'd got to get down on or hands an' knees an' crawl through 'em 'fore we was could get up by it. An' that took more time, what with tryin' not to make no noise nor signs of movement we didn't purely have to.

After all that it was kind of a relief see that whoever'd left that boat hadn't decided to come get it an' take off in the meantime. Made up just a li'l bit for the scratches I'd got on my face an' hands, an' the mud all over my knees an' boots.

I reckoned Cameron hadn't come out of it a whole lot better. But I'd already learned he weren't the kind to complain.

Onct we was there we backed up under some branches where we wouldn't be noticed right off if a feller come along by the shore. 'Specially not if he'd been swallerin' much of that rotgut whiskey.

An' then we waited.

Some of the others come an' got their boats to go off down the creek. But it were dark as a black cat at midnight just where we was, an' none of 'em seen us. Didn't even glance in our direction.

Seemed like we crouched there a right long time 'fore we heard some-body comin' near us. I was startin' to get concerned 'bout whoever it was belonged to this boat here. Wondered if they'd just passed out on the ground somewheres an' wouldn't stir till mornin'.

Finally we heard footsteps stumblin' over some loose rocks by the water, an' a couple low cusses along with 'em. Then we spied two dark forms 'gainst the lighter color of the sky. Neither one was too steady on his feet, but they didn't leave no doubt that this was where they was headed.

We perked up an' got set to make our move. I had my feet under me an' was just on the verge of jumpin' on the one leadin' the way when I heard a loud thump! an' he all of sudden disappeared. Next thing I heard was loud bangin' an' cussin' in the bottom of the skiff.

"Damnation, Luke! Why in hell did you pick such a infernal out-of-the-way spot to put us ashore? I near-bout killed myself 'fore I could figure where to put my feet!"

"'T'weren't dark when we got here," the other'n said. "An' all the other landin' places was took." He come up an' tried to peer down into the boat. "Mebbe 'f you was a mite soberer you'd have some better idea of where you was goin'!"

First feller cussed at him an' tried to set up. That was 'bout all the conversation they had time for, 'cause then I was over the side an' in there with him. Cameron got a arm 'round Luke's neck an' pushed him down to join us.

Both was surprised an' discombobulated, so it didn't take more'n a couple raps on the skull to quiet 'em down. I got holt of a oar and pushed us off into the water whilst Cameron sat on one an' took the other's shirt in his fist so's he could twist it up against his neck.

I let us drift with the current a ways till I figured we was far enough off from everbody else that our talkin' wouldn't cause much notice. Then I steered us over to the bank an' fetched up amongst a bunch of cypress knees under the trees.

Weren't no rope to tie the boat with that I could find, but we didn't actual need one. We couldn't drift far without bumpin' into some of them knees an' we'd likely just keep goin' back an' forth betwixt 'em till we got ready to leave.

It was pretty dark where we was, but they was enough light from the moon that could make out faces pretty good. I put down the oar an' reached over the side to splash some water over them fellers an' wake 'em up a mite. They sputtered an' complained some 'fore they come to theirselves. But then their eyes popped open an' they started to get a notion of where they was an' the kind of a fix they was in.

Cameron was settin' on a thwart lookin' down at 'em with his six-shooter held sort of casual acrost his knees. It weren't 'zactly pointed at 'em, but it weren't 'zactly pointed no other place neither. Their own guns was on the bottom of the boat in back of him an' weren't no way either was goin' to lay a hand on 'em.

I'd made my mind up I'd do most the talkin' this time 'round, an' after I'd started Cameron held his peace. He just sat quiet, smilin' down at 'em. It weren't what a feller would call a friendly smile.

"How you boys doin'?" I said. "Have yourselves a good li'l nap?"

'Peared neither of 'em felt much like answerin'. They just stared at me kind of bleary-eyed, tryin' to shake the cobwebs outen their heads an' guess what was goin' to happen next.

"Reason we brung y'all out here in this boat was so's we could 'splain a few things 'thout bein' interrupted by Gator or none of his close friends." I paused an' looked at 'em kind of sharp. "You ain't by any chance countin' yourselves amongst that number of close friends are you?"

"He's the chief," the one I'd heard called Luke grumbled. "We do like he says, an' he fixes it so's we get paid cash money for the plumes we take. Friendship ain't much a part of it."

"Still an' all," the other'n piped up, "we ain't got no complaints to make. He's done right good by us so far. That's more money'n either of us ever seen in a life of hard livin'!"

"Likely more'n he's seen too," I said. "You figure he's sharin' it equal?"

They didn't voice no opinions 'bout that. The one who'd been talkin' just shrugged.

I looked at Luke. "Now, you said you do like Gator tells you. He ever tell you to hunt down an' kill somebody?"

"Nope. An' I don't figure he's liable to. 'F a feller needs killin' it's some-thin' a man's got to decide for hisself. Ain't sayin' I mightn't do it. But not on Gator's say-so. Nor on nobody else's."

"Way I kind of look at the matter my ownself," I said. "But we ain't so sure everbody in that crowd you been hangin' 'round with sees it the same way. We got reason to believe they's some killin' been done. An' my partner here's had a touch of lead poisonin' his ownself. Just pure-dee luck he ain't under the ground right now." They looked over at Cameron an' could see he'd stopped smilin'. "Near as we can figure, ever bit of what's happened is on that chief of yours' say-so."

Well, that give 'em a bit of a pause. I seen the wheels turnin' inside them two uncurried heads. They didn't look awful quick on the uptake, even when more sober than they was just now. But they both knew Gator, an' whether or not they believed what I'd told 'em was true they knowed that it could be. It just weren't a thing they'd considered 'fore now, nor much wanted to.

"There will be consequences," Cameron said, speakin' for the first time. "Either from the legal authorities," he paused, narrowin' his eyes, "or without their involvement. I don't like being shot. And when the shots come from ambush I like it even less. What my friend and I have in mind will involve not just Gator, but everyone who's associated with him. Before we begin we're offering you the chance to take what remains of your earnings and find a healthier climate."

"What he means" I said, "is they ain't goin' to be no more warnin's. You got you one chanct to get shut of this country 'fore we start in to readin' to your crowd from the Book."

They didn't like it, not even a li'l bit. No man likes to be handed his walkin' papers by a couple fellers he don't know from Adam's off ox. But they was somethin' 'bout the way Cameron's voice got real cold when he talked, an' maybe somethin' 'bout how I looked too, that told 'em whatever we'd in mind weren't goin' to be no Sunday school picnic.

We didn't give 'em no other hints, nor no chance to argue neither. When that feller next to Luke opened his mouth to speak, I just slapped him hard acrost the face, forward an' back, then took holt of his collar an' belt an' heaved him in the water. Luke made it over the side under his own steam, encouraged a mite by the eared back hammer of Cameron's pistol.

I took up the oar an' poled us out of there whilst they splashed an' spluttered towards what I hoped for their sake was dry land. Anyhow, it was a nice moonlit night for a li'l swim. An' it'd prob'ly sober 'em up a tad too.

We got back out into the current an' since we had us a boat now, I figured we'd at least ought to see if we could locate that hog ranch we heard was downstream. Might be too far to off fool with tonight. But weren't no way to know without we looked. What we'd do when we found it—if we did—we could make up our minds 'bout afterwards.

As for Luke an' his crony back yonder, I didn't waste a heap more thought on 'em. Maybe they'd take what we told 'em to heart, an' maybe they'd just cuss us an' keep on with what they'd been doin'. Might talk it over with Gator or some of the others 'fore decidin', though it's a thing I'd want to consider kind of serious first. If they'd been killin's done that they hadn't known 'bout, bringin' up the subject could bring on a embarrassin' situation. Not to mention maybe a unhealthy one.

That creek widened out some as we kept on downstream, an' the moon was bright enough that it showed ever shoal an' sawyer on the way. Would of made that boat we was in mighty easy to see too if we'd stayed in the middle of it. But we held in close to the bank as much as possible, where they was cypress an' bays to offer a li'l cover.

Cameron had found him a paddle somewheres, an' he were doin' a right fair job of helpin' us along, me polin' with the oar whenever I could touch bottom an' him mostly doin' the steerin'. We kept at it for what I guessed was three, four miles, with so many twists an' turns that I figured we weren't more'n half that from where we'd left the horses.

Finally, we rounded another bend an' come out into this wide open stretch of water where it 'peared they might be some springs off to one side that made a kind of a lake in the midst of the creek 'fore it flowed on past an' took another turn on its way to the sea.

At the far side of that lake were one of the doggonedest sights I'd ever seen.

❧ 21 ❧

THEY WAS THIS BIG OLE TWO-STORY FRAME HOUSE THAT HAD PILIN'S AN' A dock stretched out in front of it 'longside the water. Dock had posts ever five-six feet with coal oil lanterns hung, all burnin' a bright yellow. In back of these ever single window of the house was lit up too. An' 'round the outside, in amongst the trees an' Spanish moss, was dozens of them li'l colored paper lanterns like I seen one time in Denver when I went to a Chinese eatin' place.

I mean it couldn't of been much brighter if it had been downtown Jacksonville at noon—though just now I figured it were comin' on to midnight. I could hear the sound of a pi-anna inside there too, playin' a lively tune of the kind I'd heard somebody call ragtime.

We'd come up on that big stretch of water unawares, an' Cameron started backin' up from it right quick. Soon as I could get myself over my gawkin' I pitched in to help him. Out in the open with all that light from the house an' the moon we was feelin' like a li'l fly settin' down on a white sheet under a window.

We got ourselves back into the shadows of the trees an' set ourselves to thinkin' an' talkin' 'bout what we'd found.

"Not exactly what I'd have expected to see," Cameron said' "out here miles from the closest city or town."

I nodded, agreein' with him but not havin' nothin' to say. 'T'weren't what I'd of expected to see 'most any place a feller could name.

"I've an idea that's the bawdy house we heard those men back there talking about. I can't imagine what else it would be, so far from civilization and doing business at this hour."

"I reckon maybe. But if it is they sure ain't hidin' none of their lights underneath a bushel."

101

"It pays to advertise. I don't imagine it's any secret in this area. The sheriff probably knows all about it. He either doesn't care what happens away from the homes of respectable citizens, or he may be getting paid to look the other way. He could even be a customer!"

"Makes sense I guess, when you 'splain it that way." I was quiet for a few seconds, bendin' over to peer past the trees at all the lights of that li'l backwoods Babylon. "What you figure to do? If they's any plumers inside there we might's well just leave 'em to their pleasures an' go on back to the horses. We sure ain't goin' to sneak up on nobody in such a place."

"No . . ."

There was somethin' 'bout the way he said that caused me to glance back over my shoulder. Doggone if the gent weren't grinnin'!

"We'll just go over there to the landing, climb out of this boat, and walk right in the front door!"

Well, we done it. Paddled acrost that stretch of water bold as you please an' found us a rope hangin' from a pilin' at the far end of the dock. Where we tied up there it was mostly out of the light an' not too likely to be noticed 'less'n a body got up close. I put a slip knot in the rope just in case we wanted to leave out kind of quick-like.

Then we took few minutes to try an' spruce up a mite, reachin' into the water to wash our hands an' faces an' get the worst of the mud off our pants. Cleaned our boots off best as we could with the paddle an' the side of the boat.

It seemed like the proper thing to do, though I was pretty sure nobody here was goin' to turn away two visitors of the male persuasion what 'peared to have cash money in their pockets.

Now I got to confess it weren't the first time I ever been in that kind of a establishment. They was places 'most everwhere you went that offered up liquor an' female comp'ny, together with more private kinds of hospitality. But when we come up to that fancy front door with the cut glass panels an' it swung open to let us in, I couldn't find nothin' in all my earlier experience that even held a candle to what were on the other side.

I mean, if we'd just stepped into the parlor of Mister Henry Flagler hisself, I didn't figure they'd of been more silk an' velvet fixin's everwhere you looked. There was plush settees an' wing chairs scattered about a big ole room that had walls covered in red an' gold with what 'peared to be velvet too. Overhead was this big collection of hangin' pieces of glass with lighted candles in amongst 'em. An' soon as we got our feet inside they sunk down into this thick carpet of a darker red with some kind of gold pattern all over it.

Place weren't too crowded at this hour of the night, but it weren't 'zactly empty neither. They was folks settin' about here an' there, women in fancy dresses holdin' onto the arms of gents in collars an' ties. Didn't 'pear to be nobody what looked like a plumer anywheres. After all them months out in the Glades, I reckoned any of 'em that come into this place wouldn't be a mind to waste 'round just passin' the time of day.

An' Cameron told me later that he figured them that run the establishment would of hustled 'em back out of view of the regular customers as soon as they showed up.

All down the far wall was this long mahogany bar with a brass rail an' a big ole mirror hung behind it. Weren't nobody standin' in front of it just now, but behind it a wide-shouldered bartender with a bald head was restin' his arms on the top, keepin' a close eye on everbody in the place.

Off to one side of the bar were this funny-lookin' pi-anna like nothin' I'd ever seen before—low an' kind of round in shape, with what 'peared to be a lid propped up by a li'l stick at one side. It was painted all over in white enamel, an' behind it sat a colored feller wearin' a white shirt with a bow tie an' garters on his sleeves. Right now he were doin' his level best to make them ivories jump.

'Fore I'd even half got done takin' all this in, there was a lady in a long blue dress standin' right beside us. She looked like a lady anyhow, tall an' elegant an' right handsome into the bargain. Couldn't make a guess at her age, what with all the paint she was wearin'. An' maybe they was a tad more white skin showin' over the top of that dress than you'd see at a revival meetin'.

"Welcome, gentlemen. What might be your pleasure?"

Cameron give her one of his winnin' smiles. "I think we'll start with a few drinks first. Then we'll see what develops."

"In that case you can just step over to the bar and two of our young ladies will join you. They'll be pleased to answer any questions you have, or simply keep you company and engage in light conversation."

We was startin' to turn away when she held out a arm to stop us. "But first I must ask you to check your weapons over there." She pointed to a li'l closet a couple feet away with a half-door an' a counter on top of it. "That's a policy of our establishment, and I'm sure you'll understand. We like each of our guests to enjoy his stay with no concerns for his safety."

Well, that there policy didn't please me a whole lot. But I reckoned it made sense when you thought about it. We went over an' shucked our gun belts together with our hats, an' a smilin' young gal in back of the counter handed each of us a numbered ticket so's to keep track of who belonged to what.

Then we ambled over to the bar an' ordered a couple beers. Cameron told me he recognized most the bottles on the shelves behind it an' weren't much need to worry 'bout the whiskey here. But without no idea of who or what we might run into in the next li'l while we'd a mind to keep our wits about us.

The bartender drew the beer an' set it out in heavy glasses with stems on the bottom. Almost 'fore we'd got our hands on 'em good, a couple young women had eased in next to us. Both was smilin' like we was two long-lost cousins they hadn't seen in a month of Sundays.

They was dressed near as elegant as that lady who'd first greeted us, an' the one by me put a hand on my arm right off, not 'zactly takin' holt of it but just kind of friendly.

"Evenin', gentlemen," the blond-headed gal next to Cameron said. "Buy a lady a drink?"

"Of course." He smiled at her an' turned to the bartender. "Bring these ladies whatever they'd like."

Neither one of 'em said nothin' to that feller 'bout what kind of a drink she wanted. He just set about pourin' some kind of a colored concoction into a couple long-stemmed glasses an' put 'em down in front of 'em. Cameron laid a gold half-eagle on the bar an' 'fore a feller could blink it disappeared. Looked like these folks here was right proud of their whiskey—or whatever it was them gals was drinkin'.

The one by me took a li'l bitty sip an' then squeezed on my arm a tad. "My goodness," she said. "What big strong muscles you have. I'll bet you could bend an iron horseshoe if you put your mind to it."

"Done it," I said, kind of quiet an' embarrassed, "a time or two." I never been comfortable braggin' to women over what-all I'd done. An' this one was right pretty underneath all that paint, with lots of flamin' red hair piled up on the top of her head. Prob'ly young enough to be my daughter too.

'Fore she could make any other suggestions 'bout what she thought I were strong enough to do, Cameron started in talkin' an' lookin' from one to the other of 'em.

"We saw some men earlier this evening who spoke about coming here, but I don't see any of them around. I thought we could have a word with them if we happened to meet." He shrugged. "Just a small private matter between us."

Them two might be young, but neither was slow on the uptake.

The gal with the blond hair frowned. "You mean you've had trouble with them. Well, whatever it was you leave it outside. We don't allow that sort of thing here."

"This is a real friendly place," the one with me agreed, an' she squeezed my arm a li'l tighter. "Everyone here wants to keep it that way, and they'll do whatever is needed to make sure of it."

Both of 'em was glancin' over towards the bartender, who was down at the far end an' prob'ly didn't hear what was said. Prob'ly. But he'd been keepin' a close eye on us just the same.

I hadn't seen no other men that 'peared to work here 'sides the pi-anna player. But it stood to reason they was others in hailin' distance. An' if they was anywheres near as big an' mean-lookin' as that bartender I reckoned they was able an' ready to keep the peace.

An' none of them would of been told to check their weapons at the door.

Cameron, he just smiled an' lifted up his beer. "No trouble," he said. "I only asked out of curiosity. We're in a friendly mood ourselves tonight." He took a swallow an' put down his glass. "Would either of you ladies care to dance?"

Well, I looked at him. An' then I looked past him. They was a place without no carpet back there that I hadn't paid no mind to earlier. An' sure enough, that blond gal grinned an' took holt of his arm to lead him out into the middle of it. He spoke to the colored pi-anna player as they went by an' put a coin down where he'd see it. Without even a pause that feller changed in mid-tune to some kind of a waltz an' them two commenced to dance.

I mean this gent I'd been travelin' with knowed how it was done. He swung an' twirled that li'l gal 'round the floor till she was breathin' hard an' near-'bout lost her footin'. But she kept up with him pretty good, an' was laughin' an' gigglin' the entire time.

Finally he led her back to the bar an' ordered another drink for her. Then that redhead by me stepped up an' demanded to have her turn. He took her in tow without hardly missin' a beat, an' the two of 'em pretty much done the same.

Me, I was happy to just stand by an' watch. 'T'weren't no kind of dancin' I'd ever thought to try my ownself, an' I'd only seen the like a time or two. Truth of it is, I ain't had much experience with dancin' of any kind. Back when I was a young-un goin' to frolics an' such, I was one of them fellers outside under the trees that only showed up for the fightin'.

When Cameron an' his newest partner made it back to the bar, both them gals was some wore out an' frazzled. Weren't too long 'fore they asked if we'd excuse 'em for a bit whilst they went in the back to powder their noses.

"Take all the time you need, ladies," he said with a smile an' a bow. "We've no other pressing plans for the evening."

Then soon as their backs was turned he glanced at the bartender a good ways off an' leaned over to speak in my ear. "This will give us the chance to look around a little. Maybe we can learn if anyone else we know is here."

☙ 22 ❧

We finished our beers an' Cameron ordered a couple more. Then we left 'em settin' there on the bar whilst we ambled kind of casual-like acrost that big room, actin' for all the world like we was comin' right back for 'em soon as we'd took a look 'round an' maybe found a place to powder our own noses.

We passed two double glass doors in the wall on our right, leadin' out to where we could see all them colored lanterns flickerin' amongst the trees. That weren't much interest to us at the moment, 'cept as a possible way to leave in a hurry if the need arose. What we was huntin' was stairs that would take us up to the second floor where we figured the more private doin's took place.

It didn't take no real lengthy search to find 'em. Just past that wall with the li'l closet where we'd left our six-shooters was a long hall with the stairs risin' up alongside it. They was carpeted over 'same as in the big room, which were a comfort since we wouldn't make much sound when we started up 'em.

We took a glance back 'fore we rounded the corner, an' it didn't 'pear none of the folks behind us was payin' the least mind to what we was doin'. The bartender had his back turned, polishin' some glasses on the shelf behind him. The pi-anna player had gone off somewheres, prob'ly takin' a li'l break from all his poundin' on the keys. An' the few gents an' ladies that was still settin' 'round looked way too caught up in what they was doin' to even think 'bout turnin' away from it.

The second-floor hall was lit by candles in li'l glass chimneys that was 'tached to the wall. It had carpet down the middle of it too, with a row of doors on each side that was so close together I didn't reckon the rooms behind 'em could of held no more'n a bed of some sort an' maybe a chair.

Ever one of them doors was closed when we come out at the top of the stairs, an' weren't no way to guess if they was folks inside or not. I glanced

at Cameron an' he kind of shrugged, knowin' good as I did that one thing
we didn't want to do was pull any of 'em open to have us a look-see. Kind
of commotion that would bring on would make us no friends an' a passel of
enemies, includin' some of the men I suspected was employed here. They'd
of had clubs or guns an' no regard for our safety.

So we just light-footed our way down that hall, pausin' ever now an'
then to listen at a door. What we heard ain't worth repeatin' an' it didn't offer
no clues to whether any plumers was still up there or had gone off by this time
for someplace else.

When we got to the far end they was another set of stairs leadin' down,
some narrower this time an' without no carpet to cover up the bare wood.

Well, that meant we'd got us a decision to make. We could go on back
the way we come, havin' found out nothin' a-tall we didn't already know.
Or we could go a li'l' further with our explorin' an' see what they was at the
bottom of these stairs.

A sensible feller would of took the first choice. We'd no reason to think
they'd be anything down there 'cept maybe a kitchen an' some storerooms or
a few private quarters. An' if we was gone much longer that bartender an' the
gals we'd been with would be wonderin' where it was we had got to.

But me, I'd always had this hankerin' to see what was 'round the next bend
or over the next hill. An' it 'peared like Cameron had him the same weakness.

"In for a penny, in for a pound," he whispered an' started off down the
stairs.

They weren't no light inside that stairwell an' we took it careful, puttin'
our feet down at the side of each step so's to try an' keep that ole wood underneath us from creakin'. I figured we wasn't makin' hardly no sound a-tall. But
when we'd turned at the landin' an' gone three-four steps further, this bright
lantern with a reflector lit up all of a sudden an' a man with a shotgun was
standin' right there in front of us.

In back of him, shakin' out the match in her fingers, was that tall elegant-
dressed lady that had welcomed us into the place.

"I'm afraid we don't allow guests into this part of our establishment," she
said, givin' us a kind of half-smile that weren't no wise friendly. "Nor do we per-
mit them upstairs unless accompanied by one of our ladies." She turned an' took
our hats from where they'd been hung over the posts of a chair alongside her.

"Since it appears that you . . . gentlemen . . . have no regard for our
rules nor for the privacy of others, we'll ask you to leave. And you won't be
welcome here in the future."

After he took his hat Cameron give her with a li'l bow. "We apologize
sincerely," he said, soundin' almost like he meant it. "Our only excuse is a
natural restlessness and ill-advised curiosity."

The lady nodded without speakin' an' I didn't imagine for a second she believed him. The feller with the shotgun just gestured with it towards a door at one side of us.

"I have your weapons here." She took our gun belts from the same chair where she'd got our hats. "We've taken the precaution of removing the cartridges and replacing them in their loops. Please wait until you're off the premises before reloading them."

The feller with the shotgun backed up an' eyed us mighty careful whilst we belted 'em on. Then the lady stepped up an' held her hand out to Cameron.

"There's still the matter of our fee. You have enjoyed the company of two of our most accomplished young hostesses. How you've chosen to spend the time is of course no concern of ours." She named a price an' Cameron paid it, smilin' an' not even blinkin'. I kept my thoughts to myself 'bout how many women a feller could of had a dance with up in Jacksonville or even Denver for that amount of money.

She went to the door an' opened it, usherin' both of us out into the night. I seen we was on the far end of that landin' that run in front of the house next to the water.

We started off down it to where we'd left our boat an' I had a thought to load up my six-shooter right then 'spite or what the lady'd done told us. But when I looked back over my shoulder that feller with the shotgun was standin' in the open door a-watchin' us all the way.

"This is quite a place," Cameron was sayin'. "It compares favorably with some of the houses I've known in Newport and Saratoga. All-in-all, I wouldn't have missed the experience for the world!"

"'Pears to me it were a complete an' total waste of our time," I grumbled. "Not to mention the money it cost you. We never even set eyes on no more of them plumers. Could of spent the hours we took comin' here an' cuttin' a dido with them gals rolled up in our blankets an' snoozin' what's left of the night away."

"For a man who's traveled as much as you've said you have, you don't seem to possess much curiosity or spirit of adventure."

"Heard a feller say onct that what some folks call adventure is mostly just the outcome of bad plannin'."

Cameron turned to look at me an' prob'ly make some smart reply. But he didn't get the chance, 'cause right then he just nearly run smack into a couple fellers that was climbin' up on the dock from out of their boat.

They cussed him an' stumbled backwards, almost fallin' over the side an' into the water. Took 'em a minute to get their feet situated again, an' durin' that minute I got a good look at who they was. Doggone if it weren't that

Gator an' one of them men he'd been hangin' out with back yonder where they sold their plumes.

Gator still had that rifle of his, right under his arm like it were some kind of a part of him. His friend had a pistol shoved down in his belt, an' unlike ours I hadn't no doubts it were loaded. That rifle prob'ly didn't have no empty places in it neither.

Cameron had stepped to one side an' muttered a apology, then started on past without takin' no time to look at their faces. Me, I just stood there eyin' them two, wonderin' what my chances was of bull-rushin 'em both off into the water.

An' not gettin' myself kilt in the process.

Gator had looked at Cameron right sharp as he went by, so it seemed clear that he'd recognized him. An' when he turned his eyes on me I could tell he knowed me too. I was that feller with the Winchester what had invited him an' his companions to leave my cabin an' not come 'round askin' questions no more.

Might be he also had him a notion or two 'bout what happened to cause ole Jake an' Willy-Boy to go missin'. But since we'd buried 'em fast an' hadn't said nothin' to nobody 'cept Jimmy McCollum an' his ma, I figured he couldn't of had nothin' to go on but guesses.

They was a long minute whilst the three of us just stood right still an' looked into each other's eyes. Then Gator said somethin' to his companion kind of under his breath, an' both of 'em turned an' went up the steps to the front door of the house. Time it opened to let 'em in I'd got nearly down to that place where we'd tied up our boat.

When I climbed into it, Cameron had got it loose from the rope, an' 'fore I could get myself settled good he was usin' his paddle to back us off into the shadows of some trees alongside the creek bank. Soon as I'd filled up my six-shooter I took the oar I'd been usin' earlier an' helped him.

We got ourselves turned 'round an' headed back upstream the way we'd come. Then after a couple minutes when I figured our voices wouldn't carry too far I reported on what happened back yonder at the landin'.

Way he'd kept on walkin' after almost runnin' into Gator, I'd figured he didn't even realize who them two was an' the kind of a fix we'd almost been in. But when I mentioned it he just smiled an' kept up with his paddlin'.

"I saw them," he said. "But I also saw that man with the shotgun take a few steps out from the door. He had his eyes on the three of you while Gator and his companion were watching him. We were told that private quarrels aren't permitted at that establishment, and I'm sure Gator was well aware of it. If any of you had thoughts of causing trouble the shotgun presented a strong argument against it."

❦ 23 ❧

IT WAS A MITE MORE WORK GOIN' UPSTREAM THAN IT'D BEEN COMIN' DOWN. But the current weren't so strong as to slow us down a whole lot, 'specially not in close to the bank where we stayed till we was well out of sight from that house with all its lights. After that we crossed over to the far side of the creek an' started lookin' for a place where we could get ourselves ashore an' be in walkin' distance from our horses.

'Long the way we talked some, 'spite of the fact we was both dead tired an' felt a powerful need for shut-eye. My thinkin' was that we'd ought to just camp somewheres close by, maybe even at that spot we'd left the horses, an' then head on back to Lemon City without even goin' near that end-of-the-tracks place again.

I figured we'd done all we could for now, warnin' a few of them plumers 'bout the difficulties they was liable to face if they just went on back to their killin' of birds in the Glades. Maybe they'd take what we'd told 'em serious or maybe they wouldn't. But 'least we'd got 'em to thinkin'.

I hadn't no doubt the word would spread, 'specially after everbody was a mite more sober. The ones we'd seen had 'em some cuts an' bruises that could bear a tad of explainin', plus they'd all of 'em lost their shotguns an' would need to replace 'em if they wanted to go to shootin' birds again.

Cameron hadn't no objection to spreadin' our blankets hereabouts for the rest of the night. We both figured none of that bunch would still be in the neighborhood now, havin' left out to seek more excitin' kinds of entertainment. Far as we knew Gator hadn't no reason to guess we'd been watchin' 'em earlier, nor how we'd happened to show up where we did. Anyhow he was liable to have other things to keep him busy for the next several hours.

Only thing that gent was dead set against was leavin' to go back to Lemon City without him havin' a chance to see if he'd got any answers to them telegrams he'd sent off. An' maybe to send a couple others.

I'd no idea what he thought was so important 'bout them wires, an' he didn't 'pear inclined to explain it. But I reckoned I could possess my soul in patience till he got all done with what he planned to do. 'Nother day away from my home place weren't likely to make much difference, what with Jimmy an' Miz Marcy to keep a eye on it in the meantime.

We found a place 'long the creek that I thought I recognized from when I'd stepped out on the cypress knees to have a look about—where I'd seen the smoke risin' from what I now figured was that house we'd visited. "Hog ranch" didn't seem like quite the right words after we'd been inside it. Cameron had called it a a "bawdy house" an' I reckon that was close enough.

I couldn't be sure where we'd come to were the exact same spot we'd been at earlier, it bein' night an' comin' at it from a different direction an' all. But the distance felt 'bout right an' they was a way we could ease past them trees stickin' up from the water an' get to a piece of dry land. By this time we was both more'n ready to climb outen this cramped li'l boat an' stretch our legs, so we decided to give it a try.

I sunk the boat in the water close to where we landed, partly out of meanness so's them plumers couldn't use it, an' partly 'cause you never could tell when a feller might come this way again an' want a boat. It was made from cypress, so weren't no worries 'bout it rottin' any time soon.

We set off away from the creek, me lookin' all 'round above us tryin' to recognize somethin' in the way the tops of the trees 'peared 'gainst that pale moonlit sky. I'd a fair recollection of what I'd studied earlier, but nothin' looks quite the same at different times an' places.

It was plumb dark down on the ground where we was an' we had to make our way mostly by feel an' guesswork. But after a half hour or so I reckoned I hadn't done too bad a job of gettin' my bearin's. 'Cause right then I heard a familiar snort an' a nicker that I knowed were a greetin' from Ole Roan.

Cameron's stallion spoke up alongside him, an' in another couple minutes we'd found our way into that li'l clearin' where the branches let through enough light so's we could see what was what. Everthing 'peared just like we'd left it, the saddles an' bedrolls off to one side with my Winchester an' that ole shotgun I'd lent Cameron still in their scabbards. All the same, I knelt down to check 'em both out mighty careful. Weren't no call to take nothin' for granted when they was fellers like Gator somewheres about.

The horses acted glad to see us, though 'course Ole Roan tried his hardest not to show it. We led 'em down to the creek to water 'em, then brung 'em back an' moved 'em over to where they could get at some fresh grass. Then we spread out our bedrolls an' rolled ourselves in the blankets. Weren't near cold enough to need 'em for warmth tonight. But 'long 'bout daybreak all the skeeters in the country would be out huntin' their breakfasts.

Didn't give no thought to buildin' a fire neither. We'd get coffee an' somethin' to eat when we got back to where they was people. In the meantime we was just as pleased to keep our whereabouts hid an' let them horses stand watch over us.

The sun was in my eyes time I finally got 'em open. With them trees all 'round, that meant I'd done slept a good part of the mornin' away. I looked over towards Cameron an' he was still abed too. His eyes was open though, an' he'd propped hisself up on one elbow watchin' me.

"It's about time. Did you have a pleasant night's rest?"

"Good 'nough I reckon, though I got to admit I miss my ole cabin with its shingle roof an' the soft bed I been lettin' you appropriate."

"We'll work something out about that after we get back. I'm grateful for your hospitality, but I'm almost completely recovered from my wounds now and I may have taken advantage of it longer than I needed to." He threw off his blankets an' reached for his boots. "Speaking of getting back, are you ready to do some riding?"

"More'n ready. Let's get shut of this place an' go find some coffee an' vittles."

I got my hat an' boots on whilst Cameron left to take the horses to water. Time he come back I'd got our beds all rolled an' ready to tie on in back of our saddles. We throwed them saddles over the animals an' led 'em out to that sand road we'd been on earlier. Then we climbed into the leather an headed back up to the end of the tracks.

We didn't see nobody on the way, an' from the heavy dew layin' over the ruts of that whiskey wagon I figured the fellers ridin' it hadn't waited 'round for daylight to go on home their ownselves.

We found us some eggs an' bacon in a different eatin' place from the two we'd ate at earlier. All the railroad men was hard at work by then, an' it 'peared that McCarty gent had gone off somewheres after he'd got them plumes he'd bought ready to send up North. Anyway, he weren't in sight, an' none of the plumers was neither. 'Prob'ly paid like Cameron heard to keep their celebratin' away from this place.

Still an' all, we wasn't much mind to call attention to ourselves this time 'round. We found a out-of-the-way spot amongst some trees an' I waited with the horses whilst Cameron went to the railroad office to see after his wires.

He was gone some longer'n I expected, an' I was startin' to get a tad worried. But finally he come stridin' 'long just casual as you please. Weren't 'zactly smilin' when he got close. But I could tell he'd a feelin' of satisfaction from the way he was actin'.

"It turns out our Mister McCarty is fairly well known in Boston and its environs," he said as we tightened our cinches an' got set to mount up. "At least among the less reputable elements in the city. And as I suspected, he has a number of associates who are of more than passing interest to the authorities. I've reported his activities here in Florida to them, and while they find those of little interest they do plan to look into how the plumes he provides are distributed."

Well, that was more'n Cameron had let on to me so far 'bout his thinkin' on McCarty. But it still weren't 'zactly what I'd call crystal clear an' obvious. I'd a couple questions I'd a mind to ask. But 'fore I could do it he'd stepped up into the saddle an' started his horse away from me.

I followed as best I could, an' we made our way 'round that tent settlement kind of quiet an' careful 'fore headin' off down the coast towards Lemon City.

It was late afternoon by then, but we figured we'd get us a start an' then find a place to camp without no other folks around. They was a need to be cautious an' watchful on the way, lest we come up with any of them plumers that might of got theirselves in front of us.

'Course it was them creeks we had to cross that we needed to be most careful 'bout. Far as we knew them fellers was still travelin' in boats. But we didn't take nothin' for granted on dry land neither. Though it meant travelin' kind of slow, we still made six or eight miles 'fore it come on to dark.

With a early start an' no trouble ahead we'd ought to make it to my home place by close of the followin' day.

❦ 24 ❧

THEM STORES AN' HOUSES IN LEMON CITY 'PEARED TO ALL BE SHUT UP TIGHT when we rode down the street betwixt 'em. 'Course it was kind of late in the evenin' by then, an' folks hereabouts wasn't much for stayin' up an' socializin' after it got dark. Candles an' coal oil cost money, which weren't in too great supply for most of 'em.

But this had a kind of a different feelin' 'bout it. It was awful quiet for one thing. All the birds an' crickets 'peared to of took the night off. An' here an' there I seen a curtain in a window pulled aside just a tad so's whoever was behind it could peek out without bein' seen. They was watchin' for somebody or somethin', but bein' mighty cautious 'bout it.

Cameron could see what I seen, an' we both had us a notion that maybe some of them plumers was somewheres about. Or else somebody'd come an' spread the word that they was on their way.

I shucked my Winchester an' laid it acrost my saddle bow, an' Cameron reached a hand back to slip the loop off the hammer of his six-shooter. We kept on ridin' kind of slow an' easy, till them houses was behind us an' the dark trees rose up on either side. That li'l crick 'longside the road was lookin' like a silver ribbon in the moonlight.

We didn't see nothin' much till we'd got up next to that path amongst the trees leadin' to where Miz Marcy an' her boy had their cabin. Then we seen a kind of a yellowish glow comin' from somewheres back off there. 'Peared a mite too big to be just a lantern at the cabin.

An' 'long 'bout the same time we caught a real strong smell of woodsmoke.

I looked at Cameron an' he looked at me. "What do you think?" he said quiet-like. "Do you suppose there's been trouble there?"

"Maybe," I said. "But let's go on up to my place first. Afterwards we might ride over an' look in on them folks."

When we come up to where my cabin had been it weren't there no longer. They was just a big pile of tumbled-down logs, lookin' like some giant's one-time campfire. It was still smokin' an' glowin' in places, an' the moon was shinin' down on that cast-iron cook stove of mine settin' up real lonely in the midst of it. I could see behind the place that all the corral bars had been pulled down, an' the palmetto-thatched shed where I'd kept my hay were burnt to cinders too.

'Case I had any doubts about how it happened or who might be behind it, they was a dozen or so dead herons an' egrets strung up by their feet from the scorched branches of a ole willow that used to shade my front stoop. Their white bodies looked kind of spooky an' ghost-like there in the moonlight.

I rode 'round back an' took a look 'round. Weren't no sign of my Cracker horse anywheres. Could be she'd been stole or run off, but 'least she hadn't been kilt. I'd a notion the men that done this was the kind would of shot her down right where she stood if she'd given 'em the chanct. So I guessed she'd been smart enough to high-tail it soon's them bars was down an' she could see her way clear.

To say I was mad right then would of been to put a heap more rosy complexion on the way that I was feelin'. I was fit to chew up nails an' spit 'em out, or to take that ole Winchester of mine an' shoot it plumb empty on the first livin' thing that moved.

Might of done somethin' nearly crazy as that a few years back when I was younger. But right then I just choked down my anger an' kept it inside, kind of simmerin' an' seethin' like them burnt logs that had used to be my home: the only home I'd ever had since back when I was a young-un.

'Course weren't nothin' much that couldn't be rebuilt over time. An' I reckoned I'd have it to do. But not now. Nor tomorrow nor for some days to come. First they was a bunch of men I'd a mind to seek an' to read to 'em from the Book.

I looked back an' seen Cameron still settin' his stallion right where we'd first come up to the place. He hadn't spoke nor hardly moved ever since, just watchin' me an' keepin' his thoughts to hisself. Weren't much that he nor nobody else could of said just then. I reckon he could guess how I felt an' were wonderin' what I'd do.

I walked Ole Roan back beside him an' spoke without meetin' his eyes. "Might's well ride on over an' see how Jimmy an' Miz Marcy is farin'. Ain't nothin' can be done here with it dark an' all. 'Least maybe they could fill us in a bit on what's gone on since we left."

He nodded without answerin' an' swung his horse's head 'round. We went back onto the road an' down to where we could turn in towards that other cabin back in the trees. Then we dismounted an' led the animals a li'l further to a spot where we could tie 'em out of sight from anybody travelin' on the road. Didn't want to get too close to the cabin just yet, not without lookin' things over first an' callin' out to tell Miz Marcy an' Jimmy who we was.

We Injuned through the trees to where we could have a good long look over the place. The cabin was still standin' anyways, though weren't no lights inside it nor no sign of nobody movin' 'round, neither inside nor out. It all 'peared quiet an' still as a graveyard at midnight.

I thought I smelt a li'l smoke comin' from somewheres, though I couldn't see none risin' up into the sky from that stick an' wattle chimney. Could of just been what were still in my memory from bein' at my own place.

We both kept our guns ready for the least li'l hint of trouble, me with my Winchester an' Cameron with his pistol. Them plumers had surely been in the neighborhood earlier, an' for all we could know they still might be around. We took our time, lookin' an' listenin' mighty careful whilst we eased our way a couple dozen yards to the left an' then back to our right.

Weren't nothin' we could see nor hear to suggest they was anybody in them woods. Nor nobody inside that dark an' silent cabin neither when you come right down to it. I was wonderin' if Miz Marcy an' her boy might of lit out onct they heard the plumers was comin'. Tried not to think what could of happened if they'd been caught unawares by that murderin' crowd.

Finally we decided they were nothin' else to do but call out an' see if they was anybody in there that was still alive to answer. I situated myself in back of a scrub oak to be safe, an' Cameron found him another one a couple feet away.

"Hello the house!" I called. "Miz Marcy?! Jimmy?! This here's Tate Barkley an' that Mister Cameron that you–all met! We'd like to come in an' see you if you're able an' of a mind to!"

There weren't no answer for what felt like a right long spell. I was 'bout to call out a second time when I heard Miz Marcy's voice cut through the stillness of the night. It sounded sharp an' maybe a li'l afeared, but loud an' firm enough.

"Come on in, Tate! You an' your friend! But step out real slow an' easy into the moonlight first, so's we can see you ain't got comp'ny!"

We done like she said, keepin' our shootin' irons to hand but with their muzzles towards the ground. I finally made out a couple dark shapes behind the windows. But the door between 'em stayed shut. Then after a minute one of the shapes moved an' I heard the bar bein' pulled up.

"Step up on the porch an' come inside," Miz Marcy said from back of the other window. They was a faint gleam of moonlight on the barrel of her rifle as she moved a li'l to one side. "You'll have to pardon us if we don't light no lamp in here. They was a passel of drunk hooligans shoutin' an' threatenin' all kinds of mischief awhile back. An' doin' a mite of it too. We sent the ones we could spot packin', but didn't go outside to find out if any's still left. Ain't no sense lettin' nobody see who or what's inside here, 'case they's some with further plans."

We went in the door an' Jimmy dropped the bar down behind us. "They's coffee on the stove," Marcy said. "He'p yourselves an' then you can help us keep watch whilst we talk."

The only light in the room was the faint glow of the fire in back of the grate on the stove. We found a couple cups in the cupboard an' filled 'em, then took places where we could set an' look out the windows in the back whilst Jimmy an' Marcy was watchin' the front.

Marcy glanced over at us whilst we done it, then went back to peerin' out into the night. "Now tell us where you-all been gone this past week," she said without lookin' at us. "An' what you managed to find out if anything."

Me, I weren't in much mood for talk right then. Cameron just kind of shrugged.

"We confirmed some things we'd guessed and learned a few others," he said kind of quiet-like. "We can give you a full accounting later, if you don't mind a couple of house guests. As it turns out, we've nowhere else to go now."

"I was 'fraid of somethin' like that," Marcy said. "We seen what looked like a mighty big fire off there beyond the trees."

"They burned Tate's cabin and property," Cameron told her. "And right now what we'd like to hear from you and your son is all that's happened here since we left."

"Won't take a long time to tell it," she said, "'cause nothin' much went on 'fore today." She turned toward us. "But first tell me if you got your horses with you. I didn't see 'em in front of the house."

We told her we did, but left 'em in the woods till we'd had a chanct to scope out the place.

"Well, you'd best go an' fetch 'em first thing, lest some of them plumers is around an' wants to steal 'em. James Albert'll put 'em in the back. Ain't much hay left after them men got done puttin' a torch to it. But we dusted 'em a mite whilst they was at it, an' I reckon they decided it weren't worth gettin' filled full of holes to try an' do no more damage."

"'Cept Ole Bess the milk cow got a knife cut on the shoulder," Jimmy said with a scowl. "An' I'd sure like to meet the man that done it."

We left our coffee settin' an' went back out in the dark after the animals. Kept our eyes out mighty careful for trouble whilst we was doin' it. But we still didn't see hide nor hair of no plumers nor nobody else in the vicinity. Figured maybe Gator an' them had went on back into the Glades now, havin' used up their money an' got their fill of fun from scarin' townsfolks an' burnin' down cabins an' such.

Me, I was a tad disappointed none of 'em had hung 'round long enough to meet up with an' discuss their handiwork with 'em.

$\mathfrak{F}$ 25 $\mathfrak{L}$

W E LED THE ANIMALS 'ROUND BACK AN' UNSADDLED 'EM, CALLIN' OUT
quiet-like to Jimmy that he might's well just stay in the cabin an' keep
watch. That manger where they'd kept most the hay had been burnt up, but
we found enough layin' 'round here an' there to make 'em a scant supper. An'
we took the time to give both critters a rub-down with some ole sackin' we
come acrost. They'd had 'em a long trip same as us, an' 't weren't their faults
if things wasn't as settled an' comfortable as we'd all been hopin'.

Whilst we was doin' that we could make out bullet scars on the rails of
the corral, showin' up white in the light from the moon. An' on our way
back into the cabin we seen others 'round about the door an' the window on
that side. 'Peared like Miz Marcy an' Jimmy'd had 'em a reg'lar set-to here
for a spell.

When we come inside they was fresh heated-up coffee waitin' for us, an'
we took up places by the windows again so's we could look out time to time
whilst we talked matters over.

Them plumers had showed up not too long after noon the day before,
drunk as lords whilst laughin' an' hollerin' out to let the whole world know
what-all they planned to do to that feller they'd had words with awhile back.
An' to the "Yankee meddler" they figured I'd been hidin' out.

Must have been some put out when they seen we wasn't neither of us
to home right then. They spent a hour or two thrashin' through the woods
here an' there, huntin' after us or some signs to show 'em where we'd gone.
Didn't find nothin' o'course. But along in the process they'd come up on Miz
Marcy's cabin a li'l ways off.

'Peared like they hadn't knowed it was there when they'd first started
out, an' didn't have no reason to guess whoever lived there had been helpin'
us the way they had. But the place was close by, an' they'd already made

up their minds to turn my own cabin into kindlin'. So one more li'l con-flagration wouldn't of seemed too much trouble. An' they was drunk enough an' mad enough to do it just from pure meanness.

Only they hadn't figured on Miz Marcy's rifle an' Jimmy's Navy Colt bein' inside them thick walls all ready for 'em. Thing like that can kind of sober up a feller pretty quick. It weren't too long afterwards that they got tired of dodgin' bullets an' figured to let these folks be whilst they turned their attention to that job they'd planned to do earlier.

Which were to wipe out my place an' fix it so's I'd have to pull out an' head off to somewheres that I wouldn't no longer be a bother to 'em.

I reckon them stories that been floatin' 'round 'bout Tate Barkley hadn't made it this far south. Or they didn't put no stock in 'em. I'd a mind to learn 'em different 'fore too much time was past. If they'd thought I were a bother to 'em earlier, it weren't a patch on what they'd got in store for 'em now.

Whilst I was thinkin' such thoughts Cameron were givin' a account of what-all we'd done an' found out durin' our travels up the country. Seemed like he sort of forgot to mention that fancy house we'd paid a visit to. But he told the rest of it plain enough. We'd found out who was buyin' up plumes hereabouts an' we'd done what we could to try an' discourage some of them others from keepin' the company they'd been keepin'.

Didn't sound like a awful lot when you come right down to it. But he said he'd some hopes he might find a way to upset the trade with that Mister McCarty. Surely wouldn't stop the traffic in plumes over the long haul, 'cause they was too much money to be got. Might slow it down a mite though, if the plumers needed to find theirselves another buyer.

How he meant to do it he still didn't say, an' right then none of the rest of us was too concerned with Mister McCarty. It were Gator an' his crowd that was uppermost in our minds.

It got quiet after he finished talkin' an Miz Marcy refilled our cups. Then she sat down again an' looked from one to the other of us. "Well," she said, "what you-all got in mind to do now? Myself, I believe I've had just 'bout enough of drunk hooligans a-roisterin' through the country. Weren't they was some mention of takin' trouble to 'em at their hang-outs out yonder in the Glades?"

"If that's where they've went back to it's where I'll be goin'," I said. "An' the sooner I do it the better I'll like it." Them was the first words I'd spoke in more than a hour, an' the way they come out didn't leave much doubt 'bout the kind of trouble I was meanin' to take 'em. "I sure ain't goin' to wait for 'em to make up their minds to come 'round to the settlements again."

"I've a score of my own to settle with some of those men," Cameron said mighty grim-like. "So I think I'll just come along for the party."

"Well an' good," Marcy said. "Far as it goes. But how you reckon you'll manage to find 'em? Or see 'em first, 'fore one or more of 'em gets you two under their guns?"

Well, that were a question I hadn't been givin' as much thought to as I should whilst I was busy bein' mad, so I closed my mouth an' set myself to considerin' on it. But 'fore I could get started good Miz Marcy popped right up with her answer.

"What you got to have is a guide. Somebody knows them Glades 'bout as good or maybe better than Gator an' them he's been runnin' with." She looked over to where Jimmy was settin' up a li'l straighter 'gainst the wall watchin' her. "An' I reckon my boy here is the one that can fill the bill."

It were a idea Cameron had mentioned to me once upon a time. But I hadn't been much mind to rope the boy into nothin' like that, where he might catch a bullet just 'cause of a private affair he didn't have no stake in. An' we'd both of us figured even if he'd been willin' Miz Marcy wouldn't no ways let him do it.

Cameron said somethin' like that to her now. "Those are dangerous men, Mrs. McCollum. And going after them into the Everglades where they live will almost surely be at the risk of our lives. There's no reason James Albert should take such a chance with us. After all, it's our fight and not his."

"You reckon?" She looked at him real hard for a second. "They done shot into our home an' burnt up our hay out yonder. Had it in mind to burn this cabin down 'round our ears along with it. We was both of us at considerable risk of our lives right then. So I got me a li'l different notion 'bout whose fight this is. 'Pears to me it's everbody's fight that wants to live peaceful an' safe in this country."

She shook her head. "Folks hereabouts been puttin' up with such goin's on for way too long already. Just for a couple extra dollars now an' then, whenever them plumers has enough left over from their drinkin' an' whorin' to buy some more shotgun shells an' food!"

She sat quiet for a second, then spoke more calm: "James Albert an' me done talked it over whilst you two was out back with the horses. We kind of figured you wasn't neither of you the sort to just set back an' let bygones be bygones. An' if what you'd in mind were to go up into the Glades after them men, then we meant to do all we could to help you to do it."

Jimmy bobbed his head real serious to show he agreed. "Like Ma says, it's everbody here's fight. I still owe somebody for what he done to Ole Bess. She wouldn't hardly hurt a fly an' weren't able to defend herself."

All of a sudden Marcy hauled off an' slapped the butt of her rifle. "Doggone it! If I didn't have the livestock an' this place to look after I'd be itchin' to come with you my ownself!"

26

I WAS WISHFUL WE COULD OF SET OFF INTO THE GLADES THAT VERY NEXT mornin'. But they was things had to be took care of first. For one, we'd got to lay in some supplies an' ammunition, 'cause weren't no food nor nothin' else we could use where my cabin used to be. 'T'weren't right we should ask Miz Marcy for nothin' like that. She'd little enough for herself an' Jimmy. An' Cameron still had that money belt he was wearin'.

So after breakfast the two of us took a ride into Lemon City. The general store was open an ready for business. Fear of whatever mischief the plumers might do weren't near so great as the fear of missin' out on any dollars they'd bring in there to spend.

But weren't ary sign of Gator nor any of his crowd in the vicinity. Nor much of anybody else out an' about neither. Most folks was keepin' kind of a low profile till they was pretty sure things had settled down an' was gettin' back to normal.

They was one ole white-bearded feller a-jawin' with the storekeeper when we tied up our horses an' went inside. 'Peared like he'd plumb run out of tobacco sometime durin' the night, an' weren't no kind of a danger powerful enough to keep him from seein' after that need. He'd come 'long totin' a shotgun under his arm, not trustin' to luck nor nobody's good intentions to keep his trip peaceful.

He left right soon after we got inside, givin' us a sideways glance an' a quick nod as he went past. Didn't say nothin' by way of a greetin', an' both them fellers had fell quiet pretty sudden onct they seen us. But we'd caught us a couple words of the conversation whilst we was still out on the boardwalk.

Seemed the older gent were talkin' up the notion of formin' a posse to go after the plumers an' invite 'em all to leave the country, or else hang 'em if they wouldn't do it. He didn't give a hoot 'bout the birds they'd been killin',

125

but said folks an' property was a different matter. He was mighty tired of havin' to hide out an' worry 'bout what they was liable to do ever time they come into the settlements all liquored up an' on a tear.

The storekeeper weren't havin' none of it. Said 'far as he knowed they hadn't kilt nobody yet, an' whatever damage they done weren't so great that it couldn't be fixed with all the cash money they'd been spendin' hereabouts.

I'd got my own notion 'bout that. But I kept it to myself an' just bellied on up to that rough wood counter an' looked him in the eye.

"What's for you, gents?" he said, smilin' in such a way that I figured butter wouldn't melt in his mouth. I looked over the shelves behind him an' picked out some canned goods I reckoned would keep an' not need no fire to fix 'em, since we'd be tryin' to keep ourselves from bein' noticed out in the Glades. Had some beef jerky in a jar on the counter an' I ordered a bait of that too, along with some hard crackers from a pine box that was settin' close by.

"Headin' out on some kind of a long trip?" the storekeeper asked as he stacked the things on the counter an' I told him to put everthing in croker sacks 'stead of that brown paper he'd started reachin' for.

"Somethin' like that," I said without offerin' no explanation. He looked at me kind of curious but I just let him keep right on with his wonderin'. What he didn't know he couldn't repeat to nobody he happened to meet up with later on.

Cameron had come 'long next to me an' was lookin' past my shoulder. "Isn't that a Winchester rifle you have hanging there behind you?"

"Yessir. Finest firearm ever made. That one's new an' .44 caliber, 'stead of the .38's folks hereabouts tend to favor. Shells cost a li'l more, but to my mind the results are worth it. Want to have a look?"

Cameron said he did an' took it from the feller like it weren't the first time he'd ever put his hands on one. He looked it all over mighty careful, workin' the action a couple times an' then checkin' the barrel out for straightness an' any signs of pittin'. "It isn't really new," he said, "but it appears to have been well taken care of."

The storekeeper was drawin' hisself up like he wanted to argue, since he'd been passin' it off as comin' straight from the factory. But that gent I was with were one you kind of thought twict 'bout 'fore callin' him a liar. An' when he said, "I'll take it," the storekeeper just settled down an' smiled.

They spent a couple minutes hagglin' over the price. Cameron weren't much worried 'bout the money, just 'bout makin' his point that a used rifle oughtn't to cost so much as a brand spankin' new one.

We added a couple good-sized canteens to the lot, not wantin' to trust that black swamp water out in the Glades no more'n we absolute had to, an' a few other things includin' a coffee pot 'case we did get a chanct to make a fire. After that we ordered a couple hundred rounds of .44 ammunition, which would fit our two pistols an' the rifles.

That got more'n just a curious look from the storekeeper, anxious though he was to sell us everthing he could whilst we was there an' in a mood for spendin'. "You fellers must be plannin' to do a heap of shootin'," he said, kind of lookin' from one to the other underneath his eyebrows. "You ain't thinkin' 'bout startin' no war?"

"Nothing you need to be concerned about," Cameron told him with a smile. "Just a little shooting at targets we might find out in the wilds away from houses and people."

Can't say that were a lot of satisfaction to the feller's curiosity. But he didn't ask no more questions, an' he helped us to truck everthing we'd bought outside so's we could hitch it in back of our saddles. Then we went back inside an' Cameron paid him off, takin' gold an' greenbacks from out of his money belt an' layin' it all out real careful an' deliberate on the top of the counter.

That storekeeper was all smiles an' wavin' at us onct we was mounted an' started our horses out of town. I done a li'l calc'latin' an' figured them plumers prob'ly wouldn't of meant so much profit to him in the course of a month as he'd just got from us in a single mornin'.

I mean we'd just near-bout emptied the place of a good part of his stock, 'specially them canned goods an' the .44 shells.

We took it easy on the way back to Miz Marcy's, loaded down like we was with all them heavy cans an' such. Wouldn't be so much trouble after we started off into the Glades, 'cause then we'd be ridin' a boat instead of horses.

Jimmy told us he'd went to check on that boat of his whilst we was gone, an' found it in fine shape. He'd had it hid amongst some reeds a good ways from the cabin, an' nobody in that crowd of Gator's 'peared to of come acrost it or even guessed it was there. Drunk as they all was, I figured it'd be a wonder if they'd found anything smaller'n a house durin' the time they'd been roisterin' about in the area.

My li'l Cracker horse had showed up too in the meantime, some frazzled an' skittish after her night in the woods. But she settled down pretty good after Miz Marcy had took her in an' talked to her a mite.

Cameron an' Jimmy an' me spent the rest of the day gettin' our gear ready an' talkin' things over 'twixt the three of us, makin' what few plans we was able to. Jimmy said they was some good-sized tree islands rose up from that big stretch of sawgrass an' water off to the west of us, maybe fifteen, twenty miles from the place we'd be startin' out. They was all growed up with pines an' bays an' hardwoods, cut through by dark twistin' channels that 'peared like they led somewhere but often as not went noplace a-tall.

He said they was land on them islands that were solid enough so's a feller could walk a fair piece without hardly gettin' his feet wet. But they was other places that just looked that way, all covered over with leaves an' such that had deep holes or quicksand underneath. A feller had to watch an' step mighty careful any time he got hisself out of a boat.

An' o' course they was a passel of snakes an' gators an' wildcats an' bears to look out for whilst he was at it. Not to mention a occasional painter or what Jimmy said was a actual crocodile like them they had in Egypt.

I was startin' to think the plumers with their shotguns was liable to be the least part of our worries.

Jimmy had explored a good piece of that country now an' again, though lately he'd had to take to doin' it on the sly whenever Gator an' them was around. He told us he'd spotted some of the stands they used to shoot birds from, an' places where they'd camped for a couple weeks or so. But onct they'd cleaned out a partic'lar roostin' place they just moved on an' went to huntin' another place. If they had 'em any kind of what might be a permanent camp or settlement he hadn't never found out where it was.

They was miles an' miles of Glades t'other side of them islands he told us 'bout that he'd never even been out into.

That night Miz Marcy fixed a bait of grub, fried chicken an' biscuits an' greens cooked with fatback, an' fresh-churned butter an' syrup to go with the biscuits. She'd even made another batch of gingerbread, thinkin' special of Jimmy an' me.

It felt almost like a big Sunday dinner, or maybe some kind of a celebration. Only none of us was in that much mood to celebrate. We'd pretty much talked ourselves out in the course of the afternoon, an' durin' the meal we mostly kept whatever other thoughts we had to ourselves.

Everbody turned in early. Me an' Cameron rolled up in our blankets on the floor of the main room like we'd done the night before, made a mite more comfortable by a couple pillows Miz Marcy had found for us. 'Fore daybreak we was all up drinkin' strong hot coffee the lady had fixed to see us on our way.

They was a low heavy fog layin' across that big open stretch of grass an' water when we loaded up the boat an' pushed out into a li'l stream that led through the midst of it. Leastways weren't nobody liable to see us comin' for a while, assumin' they was any watchers off to where we was headed.

❧ 27 ❧

WE ALL TOOK TURNS POLIN' AN' PADDLIN', AN' IT SEEMED LIKE WE WAS makin' pretty good progress. By the time that fog had started to lift I looked back an' couldn't make out the place we'd started from. They was sawgrass an' reeds all 'round us, near-'bout high enough to swaller up that li'l flat-bottomed boat an' anybody weren't standin' in it upright.

'Course it ain't 'zactly easy polin' a boat whilst settin' down, so whoever done that had to be on his feet. Jimmy took that job hisself mostly, so's he could watch where we was goin' an' look out for sandy shoals an' bends in the channel. The water weren't more'n a few feet deep even where it weren't filled up with reeds an' hyacinths. Seemed to have a mite of current to it though, which was prob'ly why it weren't plugged up entire.

'Li'l after midday we seen off in the distance the first of them tree islands Jimmy'd told us 'bout, just a long dark green shape risin' up from that wide open stretch of sawgrass an' water that was everwhere else in sight. Couldn't make out much more from where we was, but Jimmy said it were a right big place—some five-six miles long an' maybe half that wide.

We kept watchin' it mighty careful as we come closer an' closer, listenin' all the while for any sounds of shootin' or voices that might carry 'crost that open space betwixt us. Weren't nothin' much we could hear though, 'cept the calls of birds that had so far managed to keep from gettin' kilt. An' ever onct in a while the splash of a mullet jumpin' out from the water.

We eased up with our paddlin' when we was some fifty yards off, makin' no more noise than we could help an' listenin' some more. Jimmy had sat down in the boat by then, an' after a couple minutes he leaned over to whisper to Cameron an' me, "They's a landin' place an' a spot they used to camp at 'round to our right. Last time I seen it, it 'peared to be abandoned. But ain't no way to know if somebody might of come back."

Cameron nodded an' whispered back, "There's only one way to find out."

We held our Winchesters ready whilst Jimmy took a paddle an' sculled us next to that island real slow an' careful, not makin' scarcely a sound. They was dark water an' cypress knees 'long the bank, an' it was shaded from the sun by overhangin' trees. Mighty still an' quiet too, 'cept when a eight foot gator slipped off into the water from a log where he'd been restin'.

Weren't nothin' else we could see, so we kept on 'round huggin' the bank till we spied that landin' place that Jimmy'd done told us 'bout. It looked empty sure enough, no boats anywheres in sight an' no tracks we could make out in that soft ground next to the water.

We pulled in a li'l distance off an' beached our boat where it wouldn't be too noticeable from out in the Glades. Then we got out an' eased our way through the trees so's to have a good look at that camp.

They was a raised walkway made out of ole weathered planks that led up from the water to what looked like some kind of a lean-to shanty, with palm trunks at the corners an' some more of them rough boards along the sides. It was roofed over with palmetto fans an' didn't 'pear like nobody'd spent a awful lot of care an' effort in its makin'. But I reckoned it'd prob'ly keep the rain out, or most of it anyhow.

They was four, five other lean-tos an' shanties in amongst the trees, lookin' even more sorry an' run down than that first one we seen.

Jimmy kept watch outside with his Navy Colt whilst me an' Cameron went on to take a better look 'round an' inside them places. What we found give us the idea them plumers hadn't gone off an' left this spot here permanent-like. We found canned goods stacked up on some cobbled-together shelves, 'long with boxes of shotgun an' rifle shells. They was a number of clay jugs here an' there too, an' I reckoned I could guess what was inside 'em. But I pulled the cork on one just to be sure, an' that whiff of white lightnin' near-'bout took my breath away.

It looked pretty clear this were a camp ole Gator an' them had stocked up with a mind to use it as some kind of a home base in betwixt shootin' expeditions or maybe 'fore they took their plumes off into the settlements. So they'd be comin' back to it soon or late, an' the only questions was how soon or how late. An' just 'zactly where they was now.

I went back to where Jimmy was standin' at the rail of that walkway lookin' out acrost the Glades. "Seen any sign of boats or men anywheres about?" He shook his head an' I asked the question that come to my mind almost soon's I'd figured out what this place prob'ly meant to the plumers.

"How fast you reckon we could get away from here if we was a mind to, an' find us some spot where we could hide from anybody come huntin' us?"

He looked at me kind of curious an' thought for a second. "They's 'nother good-sized island not too far off," he said. "An' a channel through the sawgrass that leads to it. We could make it over there in maybe a half or three quarters of a hour with all of us pitchin' in. An' it's got a kind of a twisty creek runs through it that ain't too easy to find or foller." He looked at me an' shrugged. "That's assumin' nobody ain't there afore us, or in betwixt that place an' this. Which is somethin' I wouldn't guess or guarantee."

I nodded an' thought about it for a minute. "Be takin' that kind of a risk 'most anywhere we go from here on out. You willin' to chance it?"

"Why not?" He shrugged again. "Didn't figure on this bein' be no pink tea party when we started out."

"I been a mind to make right sure of that after I found what they done to my cabin. Just wanted to see if you was thinkin' the same way."

He give me a kind of a lopsided grin. "In for a penny," he said, "an' in for a pound."

"Good man." I give him a slap on the shoulder an' sent him off to fetch the boat an' bring it 'round to the landin' where me an' Cameron could get ourselves aboard without losin' no time. Then I went back an' helped my partner do the thing we'd talked 'bout earlier.

First off we piled up all the blankets an' beddin' that was in them shacks on their floors in the middle. Then we took that white lightnin' together with some coal oil an' turpentine we found an' soaked them piles all over real good. Lastly we shucked all them shotgun an' rifle shells outen their boxes an' spread 'em 'round on the tops. That part was to give them plumers somethin' extry to worry 'bout 'case they showed up real soon with a notion to try puttin' out the fires.

Tryin' it prob'ly wouldn't of done 'em no good nohow. Them dry palmetto fans that was used to thatch the roof would of lit up like torches with the first flames that reached 'em. An' them ole weathered boards of the walls wouldn't need much help neither.

Cameron an' me scurried 'round droppin' lighted matches here an' there, then hot-footed it down to the landin' an' jumped in the boat.

Jimmy was ready for us an' had us poled out into clear water 'fore we'd even got a chance to reach for the paddles. With all three of us all slavin' away like the devil were behind us we was out amongst the sawgrass 'fore you could say Jack Robinson. Kept glancin' over our shoulders whilst we was at it, an' pretty soon black smoke started risin' through the trees. Time that smoke got higher an' thicker we heard a whole bunch of shoutin' an' cussin' from somewheres t'other side of it.

'Peared like them plumers had been a heap closer than any of us guessed. But lucky for us they was on the far side of that camp where they likely couldn't see us. We kept right on paddlin' an' polin', an' after another couple minutes we heard the first of them shotgun an' rifle shells goin' off.

'Fore long it were soundin' like the Fourth of July over yonder, an' I figured them boys was prob'ly too busy to spend time lookin' for whoever or whatever had caused the con-flagration. Sounded like maybe some of 'em was doin' a mite of shootin their ownselves. Likely thought they was bein' attacked what with all them shots goin' off all 'round 'em.

When we got close to that next island Jimmy held up with his polin' long 'nough to explain that onct the shootin' was over them fellers would all be in a sweat to keep the flames from reachin' the dried-out tops of the sawgrass that lay everwhere about. Wildfire in these Glades was a mighty fearful thing, spreadin' out with the wind to burn acres an' acres without hardly nothin' to stop it. Kind of like a couple grass fires I'd seen in Kansas an' Nebraska a while back.

It were a thing I hadn't give no thought to when I figured to burn down them plumers' homes like they'd gone an' done to mine. An' I reckoned neither had Cameron. Jimmy 'course weren't consulted 'bout our plans.

It all turned out good enough in the end though. When we come to that li'l creek Jimmy had spoke of there weren't no flames showin' in the Glades, an' the smoke had already started to grow less over towards where that camp had been.

'Sides riskin' a wildfire out of ignorance, I weren't feelin' no regrets a-tall 'bout the destruction we'd caused. 'Cept maybe just a tad that I weren't there to see it with my own eyes. Would of made the memory of my own place a li'l easier in my mind.

'Far as Gator an' his bunch was concerned, it weren't like nobody'd give 'em no warnin'.

❧ 28 ❧

It was gettin' late in the day when we follered that narrow twistin' creek into the midst of the second island. When Jimmy finally brought us to a stop there weren't nothin' but trees an' Spanish moss an' black water everwhere 'round us. Couldn't even get a glimpse of the sun, nor that big sawgrass prairie we knew to be all about.

We dug into our supplies for a bite to eat an' then decided we'd spend the night right there in the boat. Jimmy said he'd been on this creek a time or two, but hadn't never stepped more'n a dozen feet away from it. Without knowin' what we might find out there an' it comin' on dark, seemed like it made more sense not to take no chances on gators or quicksand till we was able to see things more clear.

Not that sleepin' in a boat with two other men was what a feller could call comfortable. Each of us took a turn keepin' watch whilst the others tried to find a place they could halfway stretch out usin' lumpy sacks of supplies as cushions.

Time daylight come an' we was able to climb out on a li'l piece of land I was so stove up that it took a couple minutes 'fore I could get myself to standin' up straight. Felt an' prob'ly looked like some feller a hundred year old. An' the two that was with me weren't actin' a whole lot younger.

We all managed to get the kinks out finally, an' I fetched out the pair of moccasins I was in the habit of carryin' in my saddlebags. Left my boots in the boat whilst I slipped 'em on. They wouldn't be much good 'gainst snakes or prickly pear, but they made walkin' in the woods a heap easier an' quieter. More comfortable too.

When we'd got us some jerky to chew on, I asked Jimmy if he thought it'd be safe to build a li'l fire an' make us some coffee. He 'lowed it were prob'ly 'bout as safe as us bein' here in the first place, 'long as I picked a spot where the smoke would be spread out through the branches. They was already a smell of smoke in the air, left over from that fire on the neighborin' island. A li'l more shouldn't call no special attention to itself.

I rustled 'round an' found some reasonable dry wood an' bark here an' there, 'long with some suckers I pulled off the trees. We'd brought a mite of dry tinder an' fat pine shavin's with us in the boat, so 'fore long I had us a hatful of fire goin' an' a pot of water set by it to boil.

Meantime, Jimmy shinnied up to the top of a big ole cypress so's he could take a good careful look 'round where we was. Cameron was occupyin' hisself with wipin' the dew off our weapons an' checkin' the loads. We wasn't near outen the woods yet, like a feller might say, an' we figured to have use for them rifles an' pistols more sooner than late.

Time the coffee was ready Cameron had finished with what he was doin' an' brought my Winchester over to me from outen the boat, along with some cups he'd got from our packs. Jimmy made it back down to earth a couple minutes later, an' whilst we stood 'round tastin' our coffee he told us what he'd seen.

"Right now them fellers is mostly just millin' 'round what's left of that camp they had an' kind of siftin' through the ashes. Some of 'em has brought boats 'round from t'other side the island where I reckon they'd been when you-all started the fires."

"How many you figure is there?" I was hopin' Cameron an' me had managed to discourage 'least a few of 'em from stickin' with Gator after we'd told 'em what-all we was plannin' to do. I'd counted eighteen at that place where they'd sold their plumes, an' that were a sight more'n I wanted to deal with if it come to some shootin'.

'Peared from Jimmy's answer that the odds had improved a li'l, though not so much as to make me real happy with 'em.

"They was eight or ten that I could see. Maybe a couple others back off in the woods."

"Did you see any sign they intend to make a search of the area?" Cameron asked, knowin' the way we'd went about settin' the fires wouldn't give nobody to think they was accidental.

"Not right away, though they was some acted mad enough to do it. But that Gator was goin' 'round talkin' to 'em like he meant to hold 'em off till he'd a chance to consider on it a mite. He'd prob'ly guessed from what you-all said to some of 'em earlier that you was the ones behind it. But he'd no way of knowin' how many others might be in it with you. An' even if it turned out to be just you two, it didn't make no sense to go pilin' into boats an' headin' out in the open where they'd all be like ducks in a pond for somebody up in the trees with a rifle."

We could understand his thinkin', an' it prob'ly give us some time to talk over what we'd ought to be doin' our ownselves. Whilst tryin' to guess what Gator an' them's next move might be.

Jimmy said they was a third tree island a li'l ways north of where we was now, near-'bout big as these first two. When that creek we was on let out into the Glades a li'l further on you could see it, an' they was a channel through the sawgrass to get there. That made three islands in a couple miles of each other that give us some choices 'bout where we might go an' keep from sight whilst watchin' for another chanct to bring trouble to them plumers.

Or keep shut of trouble our ownselves, dependin' on what Gator an' his crowd decided to do 'bout us.

We put out the fire an' got back in the boat, then made it down to the other end of that creek. They was a patch of higher ground at one side of it that looked big enough to lay out our bedrolls an' get a decent night's sleep for a change. But only if we happened to stay the night there, which weren't too certain an' a good many hours in the future in any case. Right then the sun weren't even high enough to get itself over the tops of them cypress trees.

There was some willows an' bays growin' next to the Glades, which made a good place to stay out of sight an' keep watch over towards that other island we could see in the distance. Trouble of it was, we couldn't see nothin' behind us where Gator an' the rest of them plumers was. So Jimmy found him another good-sized tree an' shinnied up to the top to look off that way an' find out if we'd somethin' to worry about.

He was up there a right long spell, an' I was startin' to wonder if maybe he'd fell asleep, curled up in a notch betwixt two branches. Or worse, got hisself snake-bit by one of them moccasins that dearly loved to climb in them cypresses, an' weren't able to call out that it happened.

But finally they was a li'l rustle an' stirrin' of the leaves an' he slipped on back to the ground. I could see from the look on his face that whatever news he'd got for us weren't goin' to be good.

"They's headed this way," he said when I handed him a cup of fresh coffee I'd made. "Six or eight in boats an' canoes, all of 'em armed to the teeth. Don't reckon they're for sure that we're here. But they spent most the mornin' searchin' all 'round that place that was burnt an' didn't find nobody there. So it was natural to think of the next closest place."

"Six or eight?" Cameron asked. "Didn't you say there were more of them earlier?"

"Uh-huh. They was 'least a couple stayed behind, together with one of their boats. Those I seen didn't 'pear real anxious to risk crossin' them open Glades out in view of God an' everbody. I reckon if they'd been a bunch of us with rifles on t'other side of this island they'd of had 'em a mighty good reason."

"But it's too far now to go back that way before some of them can get into the cover of the trees. And we've just two rifles."

"Pretty much what I thought," Jimmy said. "Looks like we got to make us another run for it. That stretch of sawgrass 'tween us an' the far island is out of sight from where them fellers is now. An' from anyplace they're liable to land. Ought to give us time to make it over yonder an' find a place to hole up."

"Mebbe." I'd been doin' some thinkin' my ownself. An' getting' madder an' madder 'bout the notion of us runnin' an' hidin' ever time we seen that bunch make a move in our direction. "Or mebbe we'd just ought to wait an' dust 'em a mite 'fore settin' out to that place. Let 'em know this here ain't the same as treein' no coon. Nor shootin' down helpless birds whilst hidin' in the bushes. None of them critters is able to shoot back."

Cameron looked at me for a second an' then nodded. "You're right. If nothing else it ought to slow them down and make them more cautious." He took a minute to study what he could see of the ground 'longside the creek an' then he turned to Jimmy.

"It looks pretty solid for a hundred yards or more through there. What do you think?"

"I seen a couple outcroppin's of limestone on the way here. An' they's pine trees in there that need soil to sink their roots. Ground's prob'ly a li'l higher than most other places hereabouts. But still you got to step careful an' look out for leaf covered holes or quicksand, test things with your foot 'fore puttin' your weight down. Reckon I'd ought to lead the way since I been in this country all my life."

"That would be a good idea," Cameron said, "except we'll need you to be ready with the boat. If things go the way I expect, we'll be coming fast when we come back here. And we'll need you to push off for that neighboring island the instant we make our appearance."

Jimmy agreed that made sense, an' he went to puttin' the fire out an' gatherin' up our things whilst Cameron an' me took our Winchesters an' set out along that creek. We was real careful an' cautious 'bout it the way he'd done told us. I led off 'cause I was the one wearin' moccasins, which made it easier to feel whatever was under my feet.

What we wanted to do was make note in our minds of a route that'd be safe an' sure if we come back in a mighty big hurry. Jimmy had watched them plumers till he'd no doubt they was headed for this island, an' what's more it 'peared somebody amongst 'em knowed 'bout this creek an' was leadin' 'em straight towards it. But it'd still take 'em a while to make it here an' then foller all them twists an' turns. Ought to give us plenty of time, even movin' slow like we was, to find a spot to hunker down an' lie in wait for 'em.

We wasn't just watchin' out for holes an' quicksand 'long the way. We both kept our eyes movin', from the trees an' bushes on either side to the limbs an' vines that hung overhead.

Not all the moccasins hereabouts was the ones I had on my feet.

~ 29 ~

It was like twilight under them trees, 'spite of the fact it weren't more'n a hour or two past noon. The waters of that crick we was next to looked black as pitch. An' them vines an' Spanish moss that hung down everwhere give a feller the kind of a feelin' like somethin' was goin' to reach out an' grab him all of a sudden.

The only li'l patch of sunlight we seen was on the far bank, just big enough for the two six-foot gators that was layin' there to take in the warmth. Could of been a couple logs for all the movin' they done when we passed by a half-dozen yards away. Some might of thought they didn't even know we was there. But they'd be wrong. They'd seen us an' decided we was too big to mess with for eatin' purposes. A gator don't give a lot of thought to too much else.

If we was to get up close an' act like a threat it'd be a different story. Surprisin' how fast a gator can move when it wants to, pushin' off with its tail an' grabbin' holt of somethin' in them big, tooth-filled jaws.

We kept on movin' in an' out amongst the trees till we was maybe a couple hundred yards from where we'd left Jimmy an' the boat. Then we heard voices an' the occasional slap of a paddle from somewheres further up the creek.

We held up then an' started lookin' for a place to hunker down. I seen a couple clumps of palmettos that would do to hide behind but couldn't offer much protection 'gainst bullets an' buckshot. They was also two, three good-sized cypress trees right next to the water. Weren't a whole lot else close to 'em though, which would be a problem when we wanted to leave after gettin' situated behind 'em.

What he finally settled on was this big ole deadfall some thirty feet farther on, with its roots stickin' up from the bank an' its trunk layin' off at an angle

139

from the creek. We took up places behind it, a li'l distance apart an' where we could each look out over a fair stretch of that black water. Then we waited.

We hadn't neither of us done much talkin' 'bout what it was we meant to do. But I knew Cameron took a dim view of killin' folks from ambush, an' 'spite of everthing them plumers had done, I felt the same way my ownself.

So what I figured to do was just dust 'em up a mite like I'd said, lettin' 'em feel the whip of some bullets near 'em an' maybe put a hole or three in their boats. The idea was to get 'em to slow down an' think more careful 'bout what-all could lie in front of 'em. Then maybe they wouldn't be so anxious to foller behind us too close.

'Course some mightn't be willin' to let nothin' like that discourage 'em, an' would feel obliged to do some shootin' of their own. In which case all bets was off an' they'd just have to take their chances.

Fact was, I was kind of hopin' Gator would be one of 'em.

We didn't have to wait too many minutes in back of that big ole deadfall 'fore the first of the boats 'peared 'round a bend in the creek. It were a canoe with two men in it, one of 'em up front paddlin' an' the other settin' back with a shotgun in his lap. Both was swingin' their heads side to side, tryin' to watch everthing to left an' right whilst still keepin' a eye on where they was goin'. We let 'em come on for a bit, an' pretty soon they was more boats an' men showed up behind 'em, follerin' in single file.

I waited till that canoe got close enough to where I could see the paddler's eyes underneath his hat brim. Then I took a bead on his paddle, follerin' it up an' over as he took it outen the water an' swung it to the other side. 'Bout the time he was fixin' to dip it in again I squeezed off a shot with my Winchester that smashed the bottom part to splinters. He yelped an' let go what was left of the handle like it had turned into a red-hot poker.

The man behind him shouted somethin' I wouldn't want no ladies to hear, an' lifted up his shotgun tryin' to spot where the shootin' come from. But they was down close to the water an' couldn't see too much of what was in front of 'em. So he done what a feller might do if he was too mad to use good sense. He stood up.

Soon's he got his feet under him Cameron put a couple holes in the side of the canoe right next to where he'd been settin'. He started to back up real quick an' then realized he hadn't no place to back up to. He teetered back an' forth a couple times, swingin' his arms 'round like a windmill an' lettin' go of his shotgun. Then he went over the side an' made a big splash hittin' the water.

When he done that he kicked the canoe out from under him so's it turned over an' throwed his partner into the creek with him. We watched 'em thrashin' 'round, cussin' an' spittin', whilst the canoe an' their shotguns was findin' their way down to the mud of the bottom.

They was three fellers in the boat behind 'em, close enough so's they could of poled alongside an' dragged their friends up out of the water. But they didn't do it. 'Stead they backed off kind of sudden an' fetched in next to the bank where all of 'em got out on dry land.

Somebody must of seen which side the creek we was on, 'cause the two boats behind 'em pulled over an' followed suit. I hadn't spotted Gator yet, but I figured he must be in one of 'em. Weren't much doubt he'd be bossin' the party. An' nobody else I'd seen had 'peared to be totin' a rifle.

Which were a thing me an' Cameron needed to consider. Our Winchesters had the range over shotguns an' pistols, so we'd a good chance of keepin' them others at bay for a spell till they could find 'em a way to sneak up closer. But we had to spy out Gator an' do it right quick, so's we could keep ourselves out of his line of fire whilst we went about dealin' with the others.

The first boat that follered after the canoe was still where I could see it, an' I emptied my Winchester into its waterline whilst Cameron threw some random shots into the woods just to worry them fellers an' make 'em keep their heads down. I figured that ought to fix one boat so's they'd couldn't use it to chase us too soon. They'd already lost a canoe that'd have to be pulled outen the water an' patched up 'fore they could float it, so I reckoned we'd put a li'l hitch in their pursuin' for the present.

But only if we could get back to where Jimmy an' our own boat was an' make it over to that other island without bein' shot full of lead on the way.

Everthing got kind of still whilst I went about takin' shells from my pocket an' fillin' up my Winchester again. I done it quick as I could, but I hadn't no wish to try backin' off from here with a empty rifle in my hands. Cameron kept watch in the meantime, an' I glanced 'round too off an' on. But weren't nothin' we could see.

Them two that had been in the water 'peared to of plumb disappeared. I reckon they hadn't wasted 'round none gettin' shut of the area, 'cause a couple minutes earlier I'd heard two splashes back acrost the creek that told me them gators we'd seen was now in there swimmin' with 'em.

Over towards where the other plumers was the woods that was so thick an' full of shadows we couldn't see no signs of movement. But we heard rustlin' amongst the leaves that let us know 'least some of 'em was tryin' to skulk their way closer. If they spread out a bit they'd be able to get 'round behind us 'fore too much time had passed.

Soon's my Winchester was loaded up again I looked over at Cameron an' nodded. We started to ease our way back from that fallen tree, movin' quiet an' careful in a kind of a half crouch whilst keepin' our eyes towards where we thought an' hoped the plumers was.

After maybe a dozen yards we turned an' was gettin' set to run when we heard the boom of a shotgun an' a rattle of buckshot in some palmetto fans behind us. We was too far off for 'em to do much damage even if they'd hit us. But it was a li'l disconcertin' all the same.

I swung 'round an' caught a glimpse of the feller that done the shootin' an' squeezed off a shot from the hip. It were a clean miss, but 'bout a second later Cameron scored a hit from behind a tree where he'd took cover. It weren't a killin' shot, but from the way the feller yelped an' dropped his shotgun to grab holt of his shoulder I could tell he'd caught some lead.

They was a couple more blasts of shotguns after that, but none of 'em was close enough to cause us concern. What were a sight more worrisome was the echoin' spang of a rifle that took a chunk outen the tree where Cameron was standin'.

I seen the flash an' levered three fast shots in that direction, then turned an' high-tailed it towards where we'd left Jimmy an' his skiff. I'd no idea if I'd hit anything or not, an' weren't of a mind to wait an' find out. Cameron was already in the boat by the time I reached it.

Jimmy pushed off with his pole the instant I jumped in. Cameron an' me dusted the woods behind with a couple more shots 'fore layin' our Winchesters down to take up the paddles.

I mean we flat made some time through that li'l passage in the sawgrass, expectin' any minute to hear Gator's rifle speak behind us. But it didn't. An' when we got near that other island an' chanced a look back, we didn't see nobody on the shore where we'd left from.

'Peared like we'd made a kind of impression on Gator an' his cronies. 'Leastways they wasn't near so anxious as they'd been earlier to show theirselves in the open where a feller with a rifle could see 'em.

30

THIS NEW ISLAND WHERE WE WAS WERE SOME SMALLER'N THE OTHER TWO, an' didn't have no handy creek we could run up into an' hide. Alls we could do was go 'round to the far side where they was a stand of cypress with deep shade an' a li'l water in amongst the knees that we could squeeze the boat into so's it wouldn't be easy to see.

We done that, figurin' to spend the night close by an' take our time decidin' what to do next. We'd caused some damage to them plumers' comforts an' their pride back yonder, an' prob'ly upset their plans for killin' birds durin' the next few weeks. But that weren't near all we'd in mind to do. We meant to run them fellers clean outen the country.

An' maybe a tad more if we could manage to come face to face with Gator an' the ones that put lead into Cameron, or them that burnt my cabin to the ground. Not to mention what they'd prob'ly done to that naturalist friend of his.

It took us a couple hours to reach that hidden place Jimmy recalled from his past explorin'. An' a while longer to get our boat hid an' locate some dry ground where they was room to spread out our blankets. Then Jimmy found him another tree to climb for a look-see whilst I made a hatful of fire to fix us a mite of coffee. We was far enough off by then that I weren't too worried 'bout what li'l smell of smoke they'd be, an' with all that Spanish moss an' branches overhead wasn't nobody goin' to see it.

Only trouble with the place we'd picked for our camp was that it'd be nigh onto impossible to leave out from there in a hurry. But with the shortage of boats we'd left Gator an' his crew it'd be some li'l while 'fore most of 'em could come 'round seekin' us. An' if I was them I wouldn't care to try it.

From what Jimmy told us after he come back to the ground, it 'peared like they agreed. He said he'd spotted a couple boats way off 'crost the Glades headin' towards the east, most likely comin' from that first island we'd been at. Could be somebody was goin' after supplies to replace what-all they'd lost. Or it might be that none of 'em had plans for comin' back.

Either way, they'd be out of the picture for now at least. An' the boats they was in would be out of it along with 'em.

I built the fire up a mite an' Jimmy fetched a skillet from one of our packs so's we could fry up some bacon along with a few cans of tomatoes. We ate that together with pilot bread an' coffee, an' it made for a satisfyin' dinner.

Afterwards, I put out the fire, not wantin' to risk nobody seein' it after dark, an' we spent the rest of the afternoon talkin' over plans an' ideas.

'Course whatever plans we made would depend some on what Gator an' his crowd meant to do. But we wasn't of a mind to just set back an' wait on 'em. From the very first Cameron an' me had been wantin' to take the war to them.

We asked Jimmy what he knew 'bout any other campin' places or shootin' stands in the area, an' he said he'd spotted a couple, mostly deeper into the Glades from where we was now. But none of 'em was even halfway permanent like the one we'd just set fire to. He figured they'd prob'ly got 'em a headquarters someplace, prob'ly in a part of that big wet wilderness he hadn't ever been to.

So what it looked like were a choice between goin' after 'em where they was right now, or at that first island if they headed back to it. Or else spendin' days or weeks searchin' through country even Jimmy couldn't tell us 'bout, an' where he was just nearly as liable to get lost in as us.

None of them choices sounded too appealin', an' by the time the sun was low in the west an' it were near black everwhere about us, we still hadn't reached no kind of a decision. So we figured we'd just sleep on it for now, an' see how things looked in the mornin'.

We wasn't much 'spectin' no visitors durin' the night, but that weren't no reason to take a chanct on our expectations turnin' out wrong. So Jimmy took the first watch, follered by me an' lastly Cameron. Me an' him rolled up in our blankets 'gainst the skeeters an' I didn't do no more thinkin' for another three-four hours.

When Jimmy touched me kind of careful on the shoulder I come wide awake an' took holt of the six-shooter that was layin' under my hand. But he whispered he hadn't heard nothin' a-tall but some owls an' crickets an' the woman-like scream of a painter somewheres off in the distance.

I rolled out an' put on my hat, then slipped into my moccasins after checkin' 'em for scorpions an' other critters. Time I'd stood up an' swung my gun belt 'round me that boy was already in his blankets, breathin' slow an' regular.

My turn on watch was pretty quiet an' uneventful, just like Jimmy'd said his was. Didn't hear no painters, but they was some gators gruntin' an' blowin' not far off. An' I heard some rustlin' time to time amongst the bushes closer by. Possum prob'ly, or maybe a ole raccoon.

A few hours shy of daylight I woke Cameron an' climbed back into my blankets to grab what sleep I could 'fore the sun come peekin' through the branches.

'Long about the time it did I was woke by this kind of a hissin' sound from somewheres not far off. My eyes come open all of a sudden, thinkin' 'bout snakes or I don't know what-all. But it didn't sound like no snake I'd ever heard. It were goin' "Sss . . . sss . . . sss," with a kind of a pause between the hisses.

When I got 'round to turnin' my head to look, with my six-gun in my fist, I didn't see nothin'. Cameron were somewheres out of sight, maybe huntin' more wood for the fire I seen he'd started. Jimmy's bedroll was in back of me, so I couldn't tell if he was up an' about or not.

An' then I heard the voice.

"Hello, the fire?" It were said real quiet an' didn't sound too sure of itself. Not 'zactly what a feller would call no full-blooded haloo. "Cameron? . . . Bri? . . . Is that you?"

I rolled over, turnin' my pistol to cover where the voice 'peared to be comin' from. An' at the same instant Cameron come hustlin' acrost the clearin', headed straight towards it.

"Dick?" He pushed some bushes aside an' kept on goin' smack into the middle of 'em. After a second I heard him speak again, soundin' like he couldn't believe what he seen but happy an' relieved at the same time. "Dick Summerfield!"

They was some crackin' of branches an' scufflin' of feet, an' then he come back to where I could see him with his arm 'round this old feller that were kind of saggin' up against him.

I mean that man he was supportin' looked like he'd been rode hard an' put up wet. He'd got straggly white hair an' a beard to match, coverin' most of his face. What li'l I could see of the rest looked like it might of been old enough to of wore out two-three bodies. They was twigs an' leaves scattered 'bout in the hair an' the beard, which didn't 'pear to of had a comb put to 'em in a coon's age.

His clothes was all ragged an' tattered, hangin' loose on his body like he hadn't been eatin' too regular for a right long spell. They 'peared to be what were left of the kind them Yankees wore when they set off into the woods: a khaki-colored jacket, frayed 'round the edges an' with a hole in one elbow, plus the knee-length trousers them fellers favored. Had on high laced-up boots that was all cracked an' wrinkled from bein' in an' out of the water, an' one of the heels was missin'.

Whilst I climbed out from my blankets an' got on my feet Cameron was helpin' the old man over next to the fire an' settin' him down with his back 'gainst the trunk of a tree. He fetched his canteen an' knelt to hold it so's the feller could drink. Then he rummaged 'round in one of the packs an' come up with a pint bottle of whiskey I hadn't knowed was there. He pulled the cork an' poured a healthy shot of it down the feller's throat, which made him cough an' gag but 'peared to perk him up a mite.

Time I'd come over to stand nearby he was lookin' up at me kind of bright-eyed an' curious. Cameron replaced the cork in the bottle an' got to his feet.

"Tate Barkley," he said, lookin' from one to the other of us, "allow me to present Doctor Richard Summerfield, professor emeritus of Princeton University."

Well I reckon you could of knocked me over with a feather like the feller says. I hadn't never met no university folks before, an' not too many doctors neither, come to that. But whatever it was I'd thought one of 'em ought to look like, it surely weren't this wore down ole raggedy-muffin settin' there in front of me. He 'peared more like the swamper in some second-rates saloon than no university perfesser.

"I'm very pleased to meet you," he said, smilin' like he knowed what I was thinkin'. "I'm afraid I'm not at my best just now. But you must believe that my pleasure at our meeting is more heartfelt and genuine than any I've formerly experienced!"

Cameron took up the coffee pot an' fetched another li'l one from out of our packs, handin' both to me with a nod towards the li'l spring bubblin' up amongst the cypress. "You just sit there and rest," he told the perfesser, "and before you know it we'll have hot coffee and broth to help you regain your strength." He got out some jerky an' a can of peaches, then squatted down by the fire.

Time I come back with the water Doc Summerfield was eatin' peaches outen the can an' Cameron had shaved a pile of jerky into a cup. Whilst I fixed the coffee he dumped the jerky into the other pot an' added a can of peas an' onions we'd brung with us. "A good hearty broth should be just the ticket," he told the man settin' next to him. "It's a wonder you haven't starved to death in all the weeks you've been alone out here."

"There are advantages to being a naturalist, my boy." The old man took a li'l break from his eatin'. "If a man knows what to look for and where to find it, there are many sources of food in the wilderness." He give kind of a lop-sided smile. "But never, it seems, in sufficient quantity to fully satisfy hunger."

A minute or two later Jimmy come down from the tree where he'd been keepin' watch. After bein' introduced to the perfesser, he told us they weren't a lot he could report 'bout what them plumers was doin'. Mostly they'd stayed back in the woods where we left 'em an' he'd scarcely caught a glimpse of 'em.

Leastways there weren't no sign they meant to come huntin' us any time soon. He figured they was prob'ly spendin' their time tryin' to patch their canoe an' that boat I'd filled full of holes. Afterwards they might head this direction, or they might go back to that island where their camp had been. Or maybe somewheres else.

In any case, he didn't reckon they'd goin' noplace 'fore tomorrow, though he meant to keep climbin' trees time to time to make sure.

Right now he said he was hungry, an' none of the rest of us had had no breakfast neither what with all the recent excitement. That broth Cameron was makin' had started to smell good, but Jimmy an' me had a hankerin' for a mess of bacon an' other fixin's. So we spread out the fire a mite an' put the skillet over it, then got a pound or so of sliced hog meat to sizzlin' an' poppin'.

Onct we was finished eatin' that with pilot bread an' coffee, we filled up our cups again an' sat 'round sharin' some more cans of peaches whilst we got that Princeton perfesser to tell us his story.

❧ 31 ❧

H E SAID WHEN HE FIRST COME OUT HERE HE HADN'T NO PLANS TO CHAL-lenge them plumers, nor even meet up with 'em if he could help it. 'Course he knowed 'bout them an what they was doin', an' he didn't like it a li'l bit. But right then he only wanted to study all them birds in their natural habitats an' take notes on how they was livin'.

He'd hired a feller to guide him out in the Glades, a agreeable sort that said he'd spent all his life 'round these parts, which prob'ly were true. Feller went on to say he was mad as all get-out over what he called the massacree of birds he'd been seein' since he was a young-un. Which weren't hardly the truth a-tall. Fact is, he was a sometime plumer his ownself, tryin' to pick up a li'l extry cash durin' in the slow season.

But Doc Summerfield were happy to take him at his word, figurin' he'd found what he called a kindred spirit.

They covered a good part of the Glades over the next week or so, an' the doc started noticin' things that made him right worried. He'd been keepin' a tally of the kinds of birds they seen, an' some like the snowy egret weren't hardly to be found. Same was true of some others like the spoonbill an' flamingo.

Then they come acrost a couple rookeries where the plumers had done their work. He said it were the ugliest thing he ever saw in his life. Hundreds an' thousands of dead birds was just layin' on the ground an' in amongst the bushes, their carcasses left to rot after the feathers had been pulled off. They was hundreds more li'l dead baby birds too, hangin' out from their nests an' starved to death 'cause they didn't have no mamas nor papas to feed 'em.

That's when Doc Summerfield went from just bein' worried to bein' mad. He decided somethin' had got to be done, an' he made up his mind that he was goin' to see about doin' it.

He was a knowed man up in New Jersey an' other parts of the North where he come from, an' had friends amongst the politicians an' money men there. He also knew they was others here an' there that had started to raise a ruckus over what the plumers was doin'. If he was to add his voice to what them folks was sayin', maybe they'd be able to get some laws passed that would finally put a rein on the plumin' trade. Such as taxin' it or even outlawin' all the buyin' an' sellin'.

Cameron had said he didn't think it too likely. Them rich ladies that enjoyed the way their fancy hats made 'em look weren't 'bout to give 'em up just over a bunch of dead birds they hadn't never seen or a few noisy naturalists that 'peared bound an' determined to wreck their notions of fashion. From what li'l I knew of womenfolks my ownself, I figured he were prob'ly right.

But Doc Summerfield had got to be a man with a mission now, an' would of turned a deaf ear to anybody even suggested he might be chasin' a will o' the wisp. From the way he talked settin' there by the fire, I reckoned nothin' that happened to him lately had made a awful lot of difference to his thinkin' neither. He could be a right passionate feller when it come to lookin' out for poor defenseless birds.

None of us said nothin' to try an' change his mind, not seein' much point in it an' wantin' him to go on with his story. Me, I hadn't no quarrel with what he was hopin' to do, 'long as I could still fetch me a duck or a quail now an' then for the table. Most of them water birds wasn't hardly fit to eat noways, livin' on fish like they was. An' I never did see the sense of killin' nothin' I didn't plan to eat.

Doc Summerfield went on 'bout how he'd been mad as a hornet over what he'd seen in them rookeries. An' he didn't spare no words talkin' it over with the man he'd hired as a guide. 'Course that feller was still makin' out like he agreed, though he 'peared to of got a mite quieter 'bout it.

An then the perfesser went an' made a mistake.

He'd been fumin' an' runnin' on 'bout things for the better part of a day, an' after they made camp for the night he had him a notion. He still meant to do what he'd been thinkin' to do after he got back up North, talkin' it up to everbody he could meet with an' tryin' to convince the politicians to make some new laws. But maybe, just maybe, they was somethin' he could do right here in the Glades.

'Cept for his latest passion 'bout rescuin' birds, Doc Summerfield had always been, 'cordin' to what Cameron said, a deep-thinkin' man. An' at that university where he worked 'most everbody 'round him was pretty much the same. Nobody ever made much of a decision or took no kind of action without mullin' it over for a right long spell. 'Fact Cameron said that often as not they weren't hardly no decisions made nor actions took a-tall.

Didn't sound sensible to me. Man comes after you with a gun you'd best make up your mind pretty quick whether you was goin' to high-tail it or risk a shoot-out. An' already be movin' when you did it. But Cameron said them kind of situations didn't come up too often on a university campus, an' nobody give much thought to what they'd do if it happened.

I hadn't never lived no place where life was that settled, though I'd heard tell of it time to time. Where I been, both here an' in the West, it were a whole different kind of a world. An' a world Perfesser Richard Summerfield didn't 'pear to of had no knowledge nor experience of.

Nobody'd ever told him to keep a rein on his mouth or be reachin' for a gun if he didn't. He'd never seen a man stretched out in the dust for callin' another a liar or a coward. Nor a feller dancin' at the end of a rope for makin' slightin' remarks over a decent woman. An' it didn't 'pear to of occurred to him that when a man made some kind of a threat he'd be expected to back it up with more than just words.

So when he asked that guide of his if he knew how to find the boss of the plumers an' see 'bout fixin' up a meetin' with him, even the feller he was askin' hadn't no idea what he'd in mind to be sayin'. Might of just gone on an' done what he was asked anyhow. But they was 'least a chance he'd of had some second thoughts 'bout it an' tried to keep it from happenin'.

Next day the guide left him alone in camp an' were gone for three-four hours. When he come back he said it was all set up. A feller called Gator'd be willin' to meet with him at a place he had, 'long about dark that very same day.

Now you or me could of been a mite hesitant 'bout takin' him up on that offer, 'specially if we'd any notion the sort of a man Gator was. But Doc Summerfield didn't hardly give it a thought. He was still workin' on that mad of his, an' he'd had a heap of time now to let it grow.

So when they come up to this run-down cabin in the woods with shadows all 'round an' coal oil lanterns for light, he met Gator for the first time an' a crowd of other plumers with him. 'Pears he didn't waste no time tellin' 'em what he thought of 'em all. Said the kind of low-lifes that made their livin's killin' helpless birds didn't have no right to call theirselves men. Called 'em ignorant savages an' went on to use a bunch of big university words they prob'ly couldn't understand but didn't leave no doubt 'bout what his opinion of 'em was.

Then he told 'em how he'd in mind to get some laws passed that would turn the whole lot of 'em into outlaws. Said he'd see 'em all in jail or prison 'fore a couple more years was gone, an' that he'd be right pleased to know he'd had a hand in bringin' it about.

Gator, he just sat quiet till the old gent 'peared to run out things to say. Then he smiled an' told him he 'preciated hearin' what he thought an' maybe he'd consider on it a mite. Offered him a drink from the jug that was at hand to show there weren't no hard feelin's. When the perfesser didn't take him up on it he shrugged an' told one of his men to go with 'em on the way back to their camp. So's they wouldn't get lost in the dark he said.

Now Gator had already got a earful 'bout who Doc Summerfield was from that plumer he'd hired to guide him. None of what he heard was inclined to worry him a awful lot. The perfesser was just one old man that didn't even carry a gun. Whoever he might know or whatever he might do up North was a long ways off an' weren't likely to change nothin' in the Glades for a right long spell. An' if it ever did he'd have him enough money by then to go where he pleased an' pretty much do what he wanted.

Trouble of it was, he'd called him—Gator—some mighty bad things an' threatened him into the bargain. What was worse, he'd done it in front of a bunch of the men that follered him. That were a serious matter for anybody wanted to keep bein' the boss of such men. Weren't no way he could just let it pass an' act like it didn't happen.

On the way back through the Glades it 'peared Doc Summerfield was finally startin' to realize he might of spoke out of turn. The man that come with 'em in the boat didn't hardly say nothin' an' kept lookin' at him like he was some kind of a rabbit in a trap. He were a hard-eyed feller that toted a shotgun an' had a pistol shoved down in his belt.

'Course the doc could only guess what was in Gator's mind when he left him, an' it were a far cry from any kind of thinkin' he'd run acrost before. A good part of what I just said was my readin' of how somebody like Gator would look at the matter, me havin' more'n a little experience with men of that stripe.

But they was somethin' in the way the feller with the shotgun kept lookin' at him that suggested to Doc Summerfield he'd a whole lot rather be somewheres else just then. Trouble of it was, they was all there together in this li'l boat an' he couldn't see no way to get out of it by hisself. A lantern was set up in the bow to help 'em find their way, an' it showed enough of their surroundin's to make shootin' at somethin' or somebody close by in the water easy as what folks say 'bout fish in a barrel.

He told us he was gettin' mighty worried he wouldn't be headed back to Princeton after this. Nor noplace else that was in this world neither.

An' it prob'ly would of turned out that way if it hadn't been for that feller he'd been travelin' with the last week or so. Seemed like for all that he was a plumer hisself an' didn't have no plans to give it up, the idea of killin' a man in cold blood that he'd got to know an' kind of respect were too raw for his brand of thinkin'.

So when they was gettin' close to this island where we all was now, he kind of turned his head an' nodded over towards it. The perfesser had been watchin' him along with the man totin' the shotgun, hopin' 'gainst hope they might both look away at the same time an' give him a chance at escapin'.

That didn't happen, 'cause Mister Shotgun was settin' in the back an' never took his eyes offen him. The feller that was his guide were up front doin' the polin', an' all of a sudden it seemed like his foot slipped on a wet spot where water had dripped from the pole. He was swingin' it over to t'other side of the boat right then, an' somehow or another it happened to smack into that lantern an' knock it overboard.

For once Doc Summerfield didn't waste no time mullin' over what to do next. He said he was off that boat an' into the water 'fore ole Shotgun had even started cussin' good. Took him a deep breath an' went down to the bottom, pullin' hisself along by some plants till he was able crawl up onto this island an' hide.

Them plants turned out to be sawgrass mostly, an' he said they cut his hands up considerable. But he'd found the means to doctor 'em.

"I used sphagnum moss and sap I extracted from a few pines in the area," he said, "together with juice from an aloe that made them feel better and seemed to help them heal." He shrugged an' shook his head. "I'll gladly trade a few minor cuts for what a pistol or a shotgun would do—any day and twice on Sundays!"

Well, there weren't nothin' we could find to argue with 'bout that, so we all just sat quiet for a time after he'd got done talkin'. They was prob'ly some questions we could of asked, but nobody seemed able to come up with none right then.

❧ 32 ❧

THE PERFESSER WAS PRETTY MUCH WORE TO A FRAZZLE AFTER ALL HE'D BEEN through, so Cameron fetched his bedroll an' laid it out where he could roll over on it an' catch hisself a nap. Jimmy went on down the island to find him a tree farther off that might give him a better view of what the plumers was up to.

Which left Cameron an' me with time on our hands an' not a awful lot needed to be done just now so long as nobody started showin' signs of comin' acrost to this island here. We spent awhile cleanin' our rifles an' pistols, runnin' cloths through the barrels an' wipin' each of the bullets clean of dirt an' wetness. Whilst we was doin' it, we talked over what Doc Summerfield had told us an' what we reckoned ought to be done in the future.

"Ain't much doubt that Gator's a stone-cold killer," I said, "'spite of the fact he ain't had a awful lot of success when it come to you an' the Doc."

"Yes. It wouldn't surprise me if he's killed other men in the past."

"Sendin' a feller in the boat with the Doc to murder him on the sly shows the kind of a sneakin' way he likes to do things. Could of just kilt him right there in his camp if he'd a mind to. An' done it hisself 'stead of givin' the job to somebody else. Be just as easy to lose a body in one part of the Glades as another. "

"I think it's proof that he knows not all of the men who follow him are killers by nature. You saw how a couple of them reacted a while back when we suggested the possibility of murder. He didn't want to show his hand to anybody who might raise an objection, or could possibly give testimony against him."

Well, I reckoned that were somethin' to think on. Maybe they weren't a need for a whole mess of shootin', 'long as they didn't try an' come after us again like they done the day before.

But killers or not, they was still plenty of 'em didn't 'pear to have no qualms 'bout burnin' down a feller's cabin an' leavin' him with no home. An' I weren't near ready to forgive an' forget that. Whilst I was kind of mullin' it over an' thinkin' 'bout ways to pay 'em back without killin' 'em all, Cameron spoke again.

"It appears we've whittled their numbers down a bit, both back there after we talked to a few of them and more recently when Jimmy saw others leaving. How many would you think Gator still has with him?"

I shrugged. "Less'n a dozen for sure, an' likely less. Might be some of them we seen yesterday is havin' second thoughts after they learned bullets can fly both ways. But back up the country I seen him with four or five hard cases that didn't look the sort to cut an' run."

"Six then, at least. Maybe a few others. That's still more than I'd like to face at close quarters, especially since most of them seem to be armed with shotguns."

Well, I reckoned he were right 'bout that. A load of double-ought buck from a dozen yards away beats one li'l rifle or pistol ball all hollow.

"So what we have to do," Cameron went on, "is find a place where our rifles will give us the advantage. Somewhere that we can remain concealed but where we can see out over the Glades whenever they try to cross them in open boats. Then we'd be able to try sinking the boats, or perhaps wound a few so that the others would have the trouble of taking care of them."

"Uh-huh." I reckon I sounded kind of doubtful. Cameron's idea sounded good enough, 'cept for one li'l problem. "Trouble of it is," I told him, "assumin' they ain't comin this way, onct they leave out from that island over yonder we got no idea what direction they'll be headed. They ain't no hidin' place we could find where we'd be able to cover 'em all."

"Yes." He frowned an' shook his head. "I didn't think of that. They've not much reason to go back to the camp we set fire to, especially since Jimmy said the ones who stayed behind have left now. It's possible they've guessed we're here on this other island, but after we've shown them we're willing and able to shoot they may not want to risk following us across the open Glades."

"So more'n likely they'll be goin' to some other place where they've got shelter an' supplies, thinkin' to rest up an' talk things over a mite 'fore decidin' what to do next."

"That would be my guess. And such a refuge could be anyplace at all, very possibly miles away from here."

Well, that pretty much brung a end to our plannin' confab for the time bein', without no useful results 'cept a bunch of cleaned an' reloaded shootin' irons. We'd just have to sit tight an' hope Jimmy'd come up with some news or better ideas whenever he got back from his scoutin' ex-pedition. Maybe he would an' maybe he wouldn't. I'd been realizin' his travels in the Glades hadn't took him much past these three islands here, which left some five, six hundred square miles he hadn't been in an' didn't have no better knowledge of than us that was complete strangers to it.

Cameron got up an' paced kind of restless for a bit. Then he took up his Winchester an' wandered off amongst the trees. Me, I weren't 'zactly feelin' so calm an' collected my ownself. For lack of nothin' better to do I went an' fetched some water, stirred up the fire, an' set about makin' coffee.

When that pot started bubblin' an' givin' out that strong homey smell, Doc Summerfield roused hisself up on one elbow an' took a real deep whiff of it.

"Before this morning," he said, "I haven't tasted coffee or drunk anything but water for several weeks. It's amazing how much one can miss the small everyday things when forced to forgo so many other and greater comforts of civilization!"

"I reckon that's so," I said. "Been a time or two I've run out of coffee my ownself. An' food along with it. Betwixt the two, I got to admit I'd sooner done without the grub."

I fetched a couple cups an' filled 'em whilst he got hisself up to a sittin' position. Then I squatted down alongside him an' we didn't neither of us say nothin' till we'd scalded our mouths some an' waited for the coffee to cool so's we could swallow it.

"You been hidin' out on this island ever since you got shut of them fellers in that boat," I said, mostly just makin' conversation. "Reckon you been over the best part of it."

He shrugged. "There's not much of interest to see. Trees and Spanish moss and strangler vines from one end to the other. All very much the same, though I was fortunate to find a few custard apple trees and enough nuts and berries to fend off starvation. And, also fortunately under the circumstances, no marked trails or signs of habitation."

"You didn't come acrost none of them plumers' camps or shootin' stands?"

"Not on this island. Most of the bird rookeries are farther west, and the tree cover here makes shooting them in flight difficult. Not to mention retrieving the plumes."

"But you did say you seen some of them places earlier. Must of done a fair amount of travelin' 'round an' about with that feller that was guidin' you."

"A good bit. He was very knowledgeable of the Everglades and seemed to know all the hidden channels and passages among them. He never seemed to get lost or have any doubts about where we were going."

"But in all that while you never run into none of them plumers? I mean 'fore you went off to have that meetin' with Gator?"

"No. I thought it a little curious at the time. But I accepted the fact this is an enormous stretch of wilderness and their own numbers are few." He frowned an' shook his head. "I realize now, of course, that our failure to meet them was more by design than by accident."

Plus, I thought, here lately they been off up the country drinkin' an' whorin' an' what-all. Along with burnin' down cabins.

"So with all that travelin' you done," I said, finally comin' 'round to what I'd been hopin' maybe he could tell me, "you reckon you got any ideas 'bout where it was you went whenever you seen Gator at that place of his? We found one it could of been, an' didn't leave much there but some ashes."

I told him 'bout findin' an' burnin' that camp a couple islands away, thinkin' it was prob'ly where he'd been but kind of hopin' I was wrong. 'Cause if that weren't the one it meant they had 'em another place not too awful far off where they might be headed for next.

The ole perfesser perked up an' paid close attention when I started tellin' him 'bout where we'd been the last couple days an' what-all we'd done. An' then he started askin' questions. Had me go back over everthing I could recall 'bout that landin' an' the camp we'd burned, an' the island it was on. After a bit he shook his head.

"No, I'm almost certain it's not the same place."

"Then they's some other ree-sort they've got fixed up for theirselves, near enough to this island to get there an' back in no more'n a few hours by boat. The question is," I paused an' looked at him kind of sharp, "were you payin' close 'nough attention on your way there to make some kind of a guess as to where it might be?"

"Oh, I don't need to guess." He was smilin' a li'l. "We followed the border of that first island you mentioned for some several miles and were never out of sight of it. I've no doubt the place you are asking about is located at the far end of that same piece of land!"

❦ 33 ❧

WELL, 'FORE I COULD GET MY MOUTH CLOSED AN' MAKE SOME KIND OF A sensible remark, Cameron an' Jimmy come troopin' out from the woods together. They'd done smelled the coffee from a li'l ways off, an' weren't in much mood for talkin' or listenin' till they'd fetched 'em a couple cups an' filled 'em. After I'd got some fresh for the Doc an' me, we sat 'round the fire an' everbody went to tellin' what they'd seen an' found out.

Jimmy'd stayed up in his perch amongst the tree limbs until he'd managed to catch sight of Gator an' his compadres when they started out acrost the Glades again. He said they was headed back in the direction of that island they'd come from, but 'peared to be veerin' a li'l wide of that landin' an' the camp we'd burned.

'Course me an' the Doc had expected that 'cause we'd a idea now of where they was goin'. I was fair bustin' to give out the news of what I'd just heard from him, but I held my peace an' let him tell it in his own way an' time. Rightly it was his story, since him keepin' his eyes open an' his wits about him was what give us the clue to where we could find 'em onct we went lookin'.

An' weren't no doubt in nobody's mind we was goin' to do that, 'least far as me an' Cameron an' Jimmy was concerned. The perfesser didn't offer no opinion. But he knew good as we did that ours was the only boat to hand. So he didn't have a lot of choice but to come with us 'least a part of the way. Not 'less he wanted to stay here an' hide out a while longer, which I didn't figure was much likely.

Cameron come up with a bunch of questions to ask 'bout that place where he'd met up with Gator. First he wanted to know how long it took 'em to get past that big island to where it was so's we'd have some idea of the distance. 'Peared to be six or eight miles, maybe more.

Next he had the perfesser tell everthing he could 'bout the layout of the place after they'd pulled their boat in there. The ole feller's recollections was a deal better'n I'd of expected from the citified tenderfoot I'd took him for. Seemed like he were one of them rare folks that actual seen what he was lookin' at. Cameron told me afterwards it were part an' parcel of bein' a scientist. I reckoned I hadn't never give no earlier thought to what-all that meant.

Nothin' he had to tell us sounded too different from that camp we'd put a torch to. Li'l bigger maybe, with a couple more of them shanty-like dwellin' places. An' no doubt as much or more supplies an' ammunition stored up for a long stay in the Glades.

Cameron was hopin' to get some notion of how things would 'pear to somebody come up on it from the back side through the trees. But most of what the perfesser could tell us of that weren't no better'n guesses or what he called dee-ductions.

His reason for wantin' to know was 'cause we'd already figured out that if we tried comin' up on them plumers in a boat from the open Glades we'd make just good targets as they would if tried to do it to us. Now that we'd a notion where they was it 'peared to make a heap more sense to cross over to the near end of that island they was on an' then Injun our way through the woods by foot to where they all was holed up.

From what Jimmy thought an' what we'd seen our ownselves, we believed the land over yonder was high enough to do it. Some of it rose up a good three feet above the surroundin' waters, with good-sized pines an' hardwoods coverin' the better part of it. We also figured they was likely some kind of a trail betwixt the two camps, since the fellers that showed up first after the fires started had 'peared to come from somewheres off in the woods. It weren't till later that others come 'round in boats.

After Cameron had got done squeezin' ever last drop of information he could outen Perfesser Summerfield, we set ourselves to plannin' how we meant to go 'bout gettin' ourselves over yonder past that island that lay between, an' then trekkin' through the woods to where we believed the plumers was. We figured it might take a couple days, tryin' like we'd have to not to get spotted 'long the way.

What we'd do after we got there weren't that easy to figure. We still hadn't no clear notion of how to come up on the place without some better idea of what it looked like from the back side. An' we weren't real sure how many men would be there when we did.

Jimmy said he'd counted seven makin' their way acrost from that middle island where they'd been patchin' up their boats, an' one of them was wounded. But they could be more that hadn't never left this bigger camp we'd be headed for. If so, it might be 'cause they wasn't real anxious to go huntin' after men with guns 'stead of birds that didn't have 'em. But that weren't somethin' a feller wanted to rely on.

An' we hadn't no way to guess if any of 'em might be set out to watch over them woods we planned to come at 'em through. Cameron said he didn't think it too likely, given the kind of rowdies they was. But me, I weren't of a mind to go bettin' my life on it.

Upshot was, we couldn't do much more plannin' till we'd got closer an' could take a careful look 'round. In the meantime we'd need to keep our eyes peeled an' our ears pricked all the while we was makin' our way 'crost to that big island, an' even more after we started into the woods.

By the time we'd got done with all of our talkin' the coffee'd boiled down to nothin' an' the sun had slid down past the midpoint. None of us had give no thought to fixin' a noon meal, so I went about that an' made more coffee whilst Jimmy found him another tree to climb an' Cameron an' the Doc started packin' up the rest of our goods.

It was in our minds to cross over to that closer island with the crick through the middle an' spend the night somewheres close enough to where we could get to that bigger island 'fore full daylight the followin' day. When Jimmy come back he told us he hadn't seen no signs of men nor boats any- wheres in the meantime, so we'd hopes we could make it all the way without runnin' into no difficulties.

An' sure enough that's the way it worked out. We even found us a li'l piece of dry land next to the crick where we could spread out our blankets. Which were a sizable relief since they was four of us in that boat now an' hardly room to swing a paddle without pokin' somebody in the eye.

We didn't risk no fire at that place where we lighted though. Couldn't be sure they weren't watchers somewheres acrost the way. Just made a scant supper of jerky an' hard biscuit with only water to wash it down.

Next mornin' they was a mist risin' up from the Glades that helped to hide us as we made our way over to that bigger island. Cameron an' me let the Doc an' Jimmy do the paddlin' an' polin' whilst we sat with our Win- chesters ready an' kept watch for any signs of movement or whatever else might concern us.

Weren't nothin' to be seen though, 'cept skeeter hawks skimmin' the water an' once a lone egret wheelin' overhead lookin' for his breakfast. It was real quiet that time of the mornin'. Just the gentle sounds of Jimmy's pole an' the Doc's paddle when they went in an' out of the water.

We pulled in under some low-hangin' branches a li'l ways from where them plumers' landin' had been an' found a hidin' place for our boat. Then we all climbed out an' eased up through the trees till we could have a good view of what were left of their camp. Spent a good long while there just settin' back in the shadows lookin' an' listenin'.

Looked like prob'ly they weren't nobody close by. A bunch of li'l lizards was crawlin' all over or settin' on logs enjoyin' the sun. Few grackles strutted here an' there, peckin' at the ground an' actin' like they owned the place. Them lizards 'specially would of been a sight more skittish if people was 'round an' about.

But it don't never pay to take nothin' for granted. So after a bit Cameron touched my arm an' made a sign that I should cover him whilst he went an' had a closer look. Them lizards all scurried off like their tails was on fire the minute he started movin' past 'em. But nothin' else moved or made any sound, an' pretty soon he come back an' spoke to us quiet-like.

"This place is as still and deserted as the ruin of Pompeii. Come on, let's see if we can't find a trail that leads to the far end of the island."

We started lookin' 'round the edges of that place where the burnt-up shanties had been, an' 'fore long we was able to find this narrow path leadin' off amongst the pines an' palmettos. It didn't show no signs of real recent use, 'least not in the couple days we'd been off on them other islands. But it 'peared to of been traveled a good bit 'fore that.

Weren't no way to tell if it went all the way down the island to that other settlement the plumers had. But anyhow it started out in the right direction, an' would make it a sight easier goin' if we could foller it all the way there.

Assumin' they wasn't no men with shotguns waitin' for us somewheres ahead.

We decided we'd best give it a try, 'cause otherwise we could lose our way in them thick woods awful quick. Weren't no chance of takin' directions from the sun underneath all them branches an' vines an' Spanish moss. An' even if we could keep from walkin' in circles we'd of still had to try an' locate that plumers' camp by guess an' by golly.

But we'd no thought to just traipse along all fat, dumb an' happy. We figured to have one of us lead the way some dozen feet ahead, takin' the chanct of gettin' shot at whilst havin' his back watched by the others. Leastways we wouldn't all of us be targets at the exact same time.

Cameron an' Jimmy an' me all spoke for the job. But somehow it was me that got elected. At the start anyway. We'd some miles to cover an' we expected to trade off ever so often.

Each of us had packs we'd made up with food an' cartridges in 'em that we'd fetched from out of the boat. An' whilst we was shoulderin' into 'em an' gettin' ourselves set to start out, ole Doc Summerfield come up next to us an' spoke for almost the first time since we'd set foot on the island:

"I don't suppose one of you has a firearm you could lend me?" he asked.

Cameron an' me had just almost forgot he was there. "Of course," Cameron said, a li'l embarrassed. "You'll want some form of protection in case any of those men appear while you're waiting for our return. It was careless of me not to have thought of it."

"You don't understand," the Doc told him. "I've no intention of cooling my heels here while you three go off to confront those men who meant to murder me. I've as much reason to bring them to account as any of you, and possibly a little more."

Well, we all just looked at him an' didn't say nothin' for a long couple seconds.

"I'm coming with you," he went on, just in case he hadn't made it clear. "You'll have to admit I've proven I can get by in the wilderness. And though it's been years since I've handled a weapon, I did serve with some distinction in the late war. In fact, I held the rank of Colonel while my young friend here was only a major!"

They didn't 'pear to be much use in arguin', 'specially since Cameron an' Jimmy didn't voice no objections. So after a minute I unbuckled my gun belt an' handed it over to him. Cameron had offered his own, but I'd seen how slick he was with a six-shooter an' I reckoned I could make do with my Winchester. It was a real ole friend an' I felt mighty comfortable with it. Jimmy, 'course, didn't have nothin' else but that Navy Colt he was totin'.

❧ 34 ❧

WE SET OUT INJUN FASHION, ONE AFTER T'OTHER, AN' MOSTLY IN THE footsteps of the man in front. All 'cept me o'course. Bein' in the lead, I had to watch out for places that might turn out to be quicksand or maybe even some kind of a snare or trap put out by them plumers for the sake of pure meanness. Not to mention keepin' my eyes peeled all the while for anybody could be layin' out in wait for us up ahead.

I mean it were a worrisome thing an' I took my time 'bout it, movin' forward slow an' careful with my eyes shiftin' from the vines an' branches overhead to the woods all 'round, an' then down to the next place I meant to put my feet. Them moccasins I had on was a big help, lettin' me feel what was there 'fore I put my weight on it an' not step on twigs that could break an' make a noise somebody might hear.

I didn't find no man-made traps along the way, which weren't no real surprise since I'd a hunch none of them plumers had give much thought to enemies sneakin' up on 'em from this direction. But I didn't take no chances. Like my mama always said, it's a whole heap better to be safe than sorry.

An' they was sure 'nough some leaf-covered places right near the trail with water or quicksand underneath, just waitin' for a feller to step off into 'em. I also spotted a couple them manchineel trees Jimmy'd warned me 'bout, growin' close enough to brush up 'gainst 'em.

They was snakes here an' there too. Most wasn't the poisonous kind. But they was one big fat ole moccasin lyin' on a limb up above an' lookin' down on me with a ugly gleam in his eye. An' I seen a six-foot rattler slitherin' 'long underneath a stand of palmettos we passed.

He was goin' the other direction an' that moccasin just kept layin' there without hardly stirrin'. So as hard as it was for a born an' bred Cracker like me, I decided right then were a good time to just live an' let live. Last thing we needed was for one of us to start shootin' an' tell the whole wide world where we was an' what we was doin'.

Li'l after midday we took a break to chew on some jerky an' swaller some water from out of our canteens. Nobody else'd seen nothin' I haven't already mentioned, though all of 'em was just nearly as anxious an' watchful as me.

Afterwards Cameron took over the lead with the rest of us follerin' behind. It was still slow goin'. But after three hours or so he come to a stop an' raised up a hand. He looked back an' pushed his hand down to the side, tellin' us to hunker down near some of them palmettos an' other bushes on each side of the trail.

He slipped out of sight an' was gone a good while. The rest of us just waited with our guns at the ready, tryin' to guess what it was he was seein'. Finally he showed hisself again, movin' crouched over an' silent till he'd got close enough so's he could speak in a whisper:

"This is it, gentlemen. A half dozen cabins and other shelters in a small clearing surrounded by trees a hundred yards off."

"You see any of them plumers 'round?" Them an' their shotguns was of a sight more interest to me than any shacks they was livin' in. An' we still wasn't for sure this was where we'd find 'em all, though we'd reason to hope so.

"I saw one or two men moving about. No one else was in sight. But from the sounds coming from the largest of the cabins I'm fairly certain the entire gang is there."

"A mite noisy, was they?"

"More than what I'd call a mite. And it wasn't all talking. There was loud singing and laughter too." Cameron smiled kind of grim-like. "It seems that after the trials and disappointments of the last few days they've decided they've earned a little diversion—fueled by the kind of homemade whiskey we found in their other camp."

"You mean they've got theirselves all liquored up? To where a feller might just walk in an' sort of spoil their party?"

"Up to a point perhaps. I've no doubt they're all still armed, and we can't expect everyone there to be helplessly drunk." He looked 'round at us an' shook his head. "There's another problem too."

"What's that?" I was thinkin' six or eight fellers with shotguns was liable to be problem enough without nothin' else to worry 'bout. Drunk or sober, they'd still be a caution.

"Not all of the voices I heard were male," he said. "There are women in that cabin."

Well, that were a thing to consider sure 'nough. Nobody wanted to see no woman get shot, even if it happened entirely by accident.

But I'd already made up my mind I weren't goin' to shoot nobody that I absolute didn't have to. If we could get 'em separated from their shootin' irons, I'd another idea 'bout how to take out all my mad an' cussedness over what they done to my cabin an' everthing. Could be some of 'em would wish they was dead after I got through. But I weren't goin' end their sufferin' that easy if I could help it.

Could still be a mite of lead flyin' here an' there if the plumers went to shootin' their ownselves. Then I'd just try an' keep it away from the womenfolks an' hope they'd got sense enough on their part to look out for it. I reckoned they knowed the kind of men they'd been hangin' out with. An' anybody, man or woman, that messes with the band is just liable to get hit with a horn.

I couldn't guess what Cameron was thinkin', an' whatever he chose to do was his own affair. It was him that got shot an' not me, so he might be seein' things a li'l different.

We all figured that anything we done ought to wait till nightfall, which now weren't much over a hour away. Then we'd sneak up on that cabin where the most of 'em was an' prob'ly go bustin' in there an' let whatever was goin' to happen happen.

In the meantime, I was tryin' to think of some way to keep ole Doc Summerfield clear of the fightin'. 'Spite of his army service an' the fact he was tryin' his hardest to act mean an' determined like the rest of us, what we'd in mind to do weren't liable to be his kind of a party.

When it begun to get dark we spread out amongst the trees to start Injunin' up on that cabin. An' right there in front of me I seen somethin' that got me to thinkin'. Backed up to the woods where the Doc an' me was sat this li'l slant-roofed shack that I recognized from the smell an' the beat-down path leadin' up to it. It were wide enough to be a two-holer, an' were prob'ly the only one of its kind any of them plumers had took the trouble of buildin'.

No sooner'n we'd got abreast of it I seen a couple figures step away from the cabin an' start makin' a bee-line towards it. They was enough light from the moon an' the windows to see their shapes, an' weren't no doubt them shapes was of a couple women in dresses.

I took holt of the Doc's shoulder an' pulled him back into the shadows of the trees where we wouldn't be seen. Then I bent over an' put my mouth next to his ear.

"You reckon you could sort of look after them ladies whilst the rest of us go to that cabin an' have a word with their men?" He looked at me kind of curious, but then he nodded. I knowed he were 'least as concerned as the rest of us 'bout women bein' at risk onct the fracas started. Could be these here wasn't the only ones. But 'least they was two we might arrange to keep out of it.

"All right," I told him. "Then lean your shoulder up 'gainst this wall in back here an' be almighty quiet till they get theirselves inside."

He done what I said an' I took a place next to him. Then we waited, not hardly breathin', till them women come an' opened the door to go in. They was talkin' up a blue streak but I didn't pay it no mind. I was listenin' for the sound of that door bein' closed, an' thinkin' kind of off-hand 'bout why it was that females always had to do their business together. Prob'ly all the talkin' were a part of the reason.

They was a board floor in that back house an' I heard their feet on it when they stepped inside. After a li'l scufflin' 'round, the door was pulled to an' some kind of a catch was dropped in place.

I give 'em another couple seconds to get theirselves situated. Then I spoke real sharp to the perfesser, maybe a mite louder than what I'd been plannin' on. "All right! Now push!"

We put our shoulders into it an' like I may of mentioned earlier, whatever I take a notion to move most generally moves. That back house weren't anchored to nothin' on the ground, an' after a couple seconds it fell ker-smash right over on its front. With the only door to the place underneath.

They was squeals an' some unladylike cussin' inside. Sounded like a whole passel of wildcats was trapped in there fightin' to the death. But I weren't payin' no attention. I was hot-footin' it over to that cabin so's to catch up with Cameron an' Jimmy 'fore they could start somethin' without me.

❧ 35 ❧

THEY WAS WAITIN' FOR ME THOUGH, KIND OF HUNKERED DOWN ON THAT rickety front porch an' listenin' to all the racket that was goin' on inside. It was loud enough that it near-'bout drowned out all the squealin' an' cussin' behind me. I didn't reckon nobody in there was liable to notice the troubles of their womenfolks, what with the noise an' the distance an' the drinkin'.

They was a window facin' the porch, open to the night air without no glass nor screen nor shutters. We took turns peekin' through it, holdin' off to the side out of the light from a couple coal oil lanterns. Looked to be only one good-sized room in the cabin, 'less that smaller door in the back led out to another. They was more windows in the side walls, open to the air same as this one.

I counted six men inside an' no women that I could see. Four fellers was settin' 'round a rough wood table with a clay jug on it that they was passin' 'round. One of them was Gator, slouched back in a ole wicker chair he'd got from somewheres. T'other three was usin' sawed-off logs for seats. All four of 'em was talkin' loud an' rowdy, tellin' stories an' laughin' up a storm at nothin' in partic'lar.

'Nother man was leanin' up 'gainst the wall a li'l distance off, pickin' out some kind of a tune with a ole banjo in his hands. The sixth 'peared to of had enough fun for the time bein'. He was catchin' forty winks on a lumpy mattress layed out on the floor.

They was more'n enough shootin' irons in sight. Couple shotguns was leanin' 'gainst the wall near the table an' others was layin' on the floor in reach of them settin' down. Kind of neglectful, I thought, what with all the dirt an' damp hereabouts. But I'd no doubt they was loaded. An' onct their owners was sobered up they'd prob'ly get 'round to cleanin' 'em. If they still had 'em by then an' was able to do it.

169

The man with the banjo had a pistol shoved down in his belt, an' I recalled noticin' Gator had him one too. That rifle of his was leanin' 'gainst the back of his chair where it'd be a mite awkward to twist 'round an' get holt of it.

After we'd all had a chanct to kind of look over the layout, Cameron motioned for Jimmy an' me to foller him back down the steps to where we could talk 'bout things in whispers.

"Those six may be the lot," he said. "But I think we'd better have a look around before going inside—just to be sure there are no unpleasant surprises."

He asked me to circle 'round the cabin to the left, where that back house was an' another li'l shanty sat some dozens of yards beyond it. He'd head to the right an' check out the rest of the places was there. Jimmy could go back on the porch an' keep a eye on them men in the meantime.

"From what we saw inside," he said, "I'm guessing there's a back entrance to the cabin. Not even a mouse trusts itself to only one hole and Gator is no mouse. So Tate, once you've finished looking around you go and stand by there. I'll get back here as soon as possible and then fire a shot with my rifle. That will be the signal for both of us to rush in and with luck we'll take them all by surprise. Jimmy can stay on the porch to keep anybody from leaving, or fire into the room through the window if necessary."

"Sounds like a plan," I said, figurin' he'd give me the easy part an' the one that should take the least time. He headed off 'round one corner of the cabin an' I started for the other.

I kept close to the side of the place, pickin' up my feet an' puttin' 'em down careful so's not to make a lot of noise amongst the brush an' brambles that lay about everwhere. When I come to the light from the windows I eased myself under 'em, goin' down almost on my hands an' knees.

All that took a while, but I didn't see no people out an' about. That shanty off to my front 'peared dark an' silent as the grave. When I peeked 'round the far corner of the cabin they was another li'l room there, tacked on to the back like a kind of a wart. It were 'bout eight feet on a side an' prob'ly used as a storeroom or maybe a li'l tiny sleepin' space. Had a door to it sure 'nough, hangin' a li'l crooked on rusty hinges.

When I'd got that far I glanced over towards the outhouse we'd tipped over with them women inside. They'd both quieted down a tad now, an' I could see in the light from the risen moon that Doc Summerfield 'peared to be talkin' to 'em through the wall. He was bent down with that six-shooter of mine tucked into his belt, an' weren't payin' much mind to what else was 'round him.

But a minute later he looked over towards the cabin an' must of recognized somethin' 'bout me or the ole battered hat I was wearin'. He straightened up an' lifted a hand to give me a wave. Then all of a sudden, with his hand in the air, he got stiff as a statue an' swung his head to the left.

Didn't take me no time a-tall to find what he was lookin' at. They was this big black shadow comin' towards him, movin' on cat feet the same way that I had been doin'. Couldn't 'zactly tell what it was with all them dark trees behind it. At another time an' place I might even of thought it a grizzly bear. It were that big an' mean lookin'.

But this weren't no bear. I could see moonlight reflectin' off the barrel of the pistol it were carryin'.

The Doc lowered his hand to reach for the six-shooter in his belt. But the last thing we needed right then was a shot to warn all them men in the cabin. Nor a shout from me to try an' tell him to stop.

Luckily, that man movin' towards him weren't lookin' noplace else. Prob'ly tryin' to get him a better peek at the Doc there in the shadows, wonderin' who he was an' what he was doin' by that ole outhouse that 'peared to of fallen down.

I made it over there in two shakes of a hound dog's tail, comin' from his left an' a mite behind him. Weren't the quietest I'd ever moved but could of been the quickest. He heard me comin' an' turned just in time to catch my shoulder in his belly.

I'd had my left hand out in front when I slammed into him an' took a grip on the cylinder of his pistol, clampin' down tight so's he couldn't get it to fire. He tried pullin' me loose with his free hand, but when I held him off he just let go the six-shooter an' reached to take a big Bowie knife out from its scabbard.

Well, it happened that I'd got me one of them too. But 'fore I drawed it out I let go my Winchester an' slammed the side of my hand up into his Adam's apple. Whilst he was gaggin' an' chokin', I fetched my knife.

That feller were big an' he were game an' just nearly as strong as me. We stood there sweatin' an' strainin', each with a hand 'round the other's wrist an' breathin' hard into each other's face. That last weren't no pleasure on my part. I'd sooner of put my nose to the mouth of a alligator.

But I hung in there same as he did, an' it looked like neither of us was goin' to be able to get no advantage. So after a bit I loosed my grip on his knife wrist a tad. He took it to mean I was gettin' tired an' jerked his hand free to take a swipe at my belly.

Which were what I'd expected an' hoped for. I stepped back real quick as his blade swung past an' when he seen he'd missed he let go of my own wrist so's he could turn his body to come at me from the other direction. Only he didn't make it. I blocked his arm with my left an' ducked under it to shove eight inches of my Bowie in beneath his ribs.

He went down on his knees an' let go his knife. Then when I pulled mine out he got my hand all bloody. It were more'n enough to tell me he were finished, an' he knowed it too. The feller's last words was just a couple quiet cusses.

Doc Summerfield come up an' looked down on him. Didn't say nothin' for a couple long seconds, an' when he finally did it sounded almost reverent.

"That man," he swallowed hard, "that was the one that came in the boat with us intending to kill me!"

"Meant to kill me too," I said, pullin' some Spanish moss down to clean my hand an' my blade, "Reckon he were a flat failure all 'round."

The Doc turned to me an' took in a quick breath. "You're hurt!" he said.

Well, my first thought was he'd been seein' all that blood from the other feller. But then I looked down an' my shirt was tore an' I'd this red stripe all acrost my middle. "Reckon that feller were a mite faster'n I thought," I said. "But it's no more'n just a scratch. Might look into doctorin' it later."

But the Doc wouldn't let me go till he'd fetched a clasp knife from outen his pocket an' cut off some strips of my shirt for a bandage. Then he went to a pine tree an' made a slash to get pitch he could smear on the cloth. All the while I was thinkin' 'bout Cameron an' them men in the cabin. But the perfesser could move right fast when he'd a mind to, an' it didn't take more'n a few minutes to finish what he was doin' an' tie the bandage 'round me. I thanked him an' made a bee-line for the back door of the cabin.

I hadn't gone to look in that shack that were beyond it. But I figured I'd lost enough time already. Anyhow, it looked to me from the way the feller I'd fought with had been comin' it were him that had stayed in it.

I eased up the couple steps to that back door an' pushed it open a crack with the barrel of my Winchester. Everthing in there was black as pitch. Didn't give me no easy feelin' steppin' into some place where I couldn't see what was what. But just at that moment I heard the bang of Cameron's rifle. Weren't nothin' else to do then but take a deep breath an' go on inside.

No sooner'n I'd took a couple steps than this hand reached out from the dark an' grabbed holt of my Winchester.

He were doin' his best to wrench it up an' away from me. But I'd had my right hand wrapped 'round the action an' when he started liftin' the barrel I just let it go that way an' brung the butt 'round into the side of his face. He grunted an' let loose of his hold, which give me a chanct to step back up an' give full play to my rifle. After that it were pretty much all over but the shoutin'.

I smashed him over the nose with the butt-plate an' then give him a couple hard pokes under the ribs with the barrel, twistin' it some so's the sight would break the skin.

I might of done more 'cause of the scare he'd just give me. But Cameron was prob'ly already in that big room with the others. So I stepped past where this feller were on his knees, moanin' with both arms holdin' his middle, an' yanked open the door on t'other side to go in an' join my partner.

36

IT HAD GOT REAL QUIET IN THERE ALL OF A SUDDEN. CAMERON WAS STANDIN' just to one side of the open front door, an' whilst a couple men turned their heads when they heard me come in, most of 'em was watchin' him. He'd slipped the thong off the hammer of his six-shooter but didn't have his Winchester with him no longer. Prob'ly left it with Jimmy so's he could keep watch over a bigger area, includin' the landin' with all the boats drawed up some forty yards away.

Right at the moment Cameron was talkin'.

"You men have caused a lot of trouble for people in this area. I'm not happy about what you've done to large numbers of birds either. But I'll let that pass since there's no law against it. Attempted murder and destruction of property are different matters."

He said it all real calm an' quiet-like, so I reckon they wasn't too sure how serious they'd ought to take him. Couple 'peared to be coverin' up some smiles or tryin' not to laugh. Me, I'd kind of lowered the barrel of my Winchester down towards the floor an' maybe they figured I weren't of much mind to shoot neither. Which were true far as it went, 'cause I'd got some other notions.

"Now what I think would be best for everyone," Cameron went on, still soundin' mild an' reasonable, "is if all of you left the area at your earliest convenience—say before noon tomorrow." One of them fellers at the table couldn't hold it in no longer. He near-'bout choked lettin' out a big guffaw.

Cameron didn't 'pear to notice. He took a step into the room, lookin' at Gator. "There may be one exception, though. It seems you are the only one of these men who is armed with a rifle. And a few weeks ago I was shot from ambush by someone using a rifle. The sound is very different from that of a pistol or shotgun."

He paused, an' nobody 'peared to feel like laughin' no longer. "Would you care to comment on that, Mister—Gator is it?"

Ole Gator would of dearly loved to get his hands on that rifle this second. But like I said, it were leanin' 'gainst the back of his chair an' not in easy reach. I seen he'd still got his pistol though, butt forward on the left in his belt so's it'd be handy for a cross-draw.

He smiled up at Cameron over that jug of white lightnin' that sat in front of him. "Lot of folks in these parts has rifles," he said, "for huntin' deer an' bears an' gators an' such. You reckon maybe you got your eyes on the wrong feller?"

He pushed back his chair a li'l, shrugged, an' stood up. I noticed he kept one hand down near the table where it'd be partly hid by the jug. "Might even be you got yourself shot by accident, what with hunters about an' you wanderin' 'round in places you ain't familiar with."

"It could be," Cameron said kind of slow like he were thinkin' it over. Then all of a sudden he out with his six-shooter an' put a bullet in Gator's brisket.

That pistol of Gator's was in his fist but he hadn't got it all the way out yet. When he yanked it loose an' tried to point at Cameron he got two more where the first had gone. He sat down hard in his chair an' the pistol slipped out of his fingers. Made a thump when it hit the floor.

I hadn't been worried an' weren't too much surprised. I'd already seen what that gent could do. The wonder of it was that Gator hadn't had no better sense than to try guns with a man he didn't know nor even much heard tell of. Even a dumb ole Cracker like me would of wondered how he could act so calm an' collected with six men in a room full of shotguns.

I reckon liquor were some of the reason, an' it peared to be havin' a effect on the rest of 'em's thinkin' too. 'Cause no sooner'n Gator'd been shot than all of 'em started reachin' for their shootin' irons. Never mind that they was two of us standin' there with guns in our hands. Lucky for them neither of us was in the mood for more killin'.

Some of 'em might not of felt so lucky though, after we'd done what-all was needed.

Feller closest to me was reachin' to the floor for his shotgun when I slammed the butt of my Winchester down on his hand. 'Nother got a couple fingers broke when he took up his an' Cameron shot it away from him.

Jimmy had been watchin' through the window an' didn't like bein' left out. So when that man with the banjo let it drop an' reached for the gun in his belt he got a bullet in the elbow for his trouble. Reckon he'll be hummin' his music from now on.

That man on the mattress hadn't hardly moved till Cameron started shootin'. An' then it 'peared to take him a bit longer to gather his wits about him. Time he'd finally figured out what was goin' on an' were tryin' to recall what he'd done with his shotgun, he found hisself starin' down the barrel of my Winchester. He decided to stay peaceable.

Didn't take long to get all them guns away from 'em one way or another. Cameron started gatherin' 'em up so's he could tote 'em outside an' sink 'em in the mud by the landin'. Me, I handed my Winchester through the window to Jimmy an' pulled off what were left of my shirt.

"You boys done had you a heap of fun at other folks' expense," I told them fellers, "burnin' down cabins an' shootin' up livestock an' all. Now I'm a mind to have a li'l fun of my own."

They all just sat there lookin' at me for a long minute, the ones with the hurt hands an' elbow kind of favorin' 'em an' cussin' me with their eyes.

Then one of them at the table spoke up. "What you thinkin' to do?" he asked, soundin' more curious than worried.

I took a couple steps closer. "Only this," I said, an' hit him a lick that turned him tail over teakettle. The log he'd been settin' on fell over an' rumbled off into a corner.

His pal acrost the table 'peared to be thinkin' a li'l clearer. He'd figured out they was five of them an just one of me, an' none of us was armed. He jumped to his feet, laid holt of that clay jug, an' lifted it over his head.

"Come on, boys!" he yelled. "It's open season on bird lovers tonight!" He throwed the jug at my head.

I ducked under it an' jerked my elbow into the gut of another that were tryin' to lay hands on me. It stopped him, an' 'fore he could catch his breath I follered up with a left to the head that cut open his cheek an' spattered him with blood.

He backed up an' another one took his place. By then they was all crowdin' 'round tryin' to get room to hit me. The man on the mattress was a mite slower'n the rest, an' 'fore he could get on his feet I went over an' kicked him the teeth.

After that everthing was pretty much of a blur. Them plumers was a rough lot, havin' growed up scrappin' an' fightin' like I did. I recall one or t'other of 'em jumpin' on my back time to time whilst others was comin' at me in front. Even them that was hurt earlier managed to get holt of a stick of firewood or somethin' to use against me.

But I give as good as I got, layin' about me with fists an' elbows an' ever now an' again a butt of the head.

Them boys managed to do some damage though. Time it was over I'd got a smashed ear, a raw cut on my cheek, an' one of my eyes was swole almost shut. Felt like I might of had a busted rib or two 'long with it. They was even a time there when I was wonderin' if maybe I'd bit off a mite more'n I could chew.

But 'fore long Jimmy left the Winchesters out on the porch an' come inside to help. Like I said, he weren't much for bein' left out. An' it looked like he'd learnt more'n a li'l from them sailors an' fishermen he'd been used to workin' with.

Upshot of it was that after less'n a hour all them plumers was layin' out on the floor of the cabin an' takin' a li'l snooze.

Cameron come back finally, havin' missed all the fun whilst makin' another round of the settlement to see better what-all was in them shacks an' shanties. I could of said somethin' spiteful 'bout his absence, which 'peared to of took a mite longer'n it needed to. But then it hadn't been his idea to wade into them fellers with knuckle an' skull. That were my own personal notion, an' maybe not the brightest I ever had.

All the same, it give me a right warm feelin' after I'd done it 'spite of the hurts it cost me. Figured now I could go 'bout tryin' to rebuild my home place a li'l easier in the mind.

When we got 'round to countin' up, they was six men stretched out in that cabin, not countin' Gator. I'd plumb forgot the one I'd left behind on my way inside. Sometime or another he'd got hisself up an' come in to join the fightin'.

Together with the one I'd kilt outside, Cameron 'lowed this was all that was here. Plus the two women o' course. Jimmy an' him went out to lift that back house offen 'em so's they could come an' join their menfolks.

Me, I pulled Gator's body out onto the floor an' moved his chair over to the side. Then I fetched my Winchester an' plopped myself down where I could keep a eye on them sleepin' plumers.

After that it were near-'bout all I could do not to go noddin' off my ownself.

When them women come in they went right to work cleanin' up an' patchin' up their menfolks, an' one even took the trouble to do a li'l bit for me. Neither was real pleased with the job, but they didn't go to weepin' an' wailin' like some might. Nor voice too many complaints. 'Peared like maybe this weren't the first time they'd ever had occasion to do this sort of thing.

I caught me a li'l nap finally, an' when my good eye opened again it were startin' to get light outside. The plumers was all stirrin' about now an' most of 'em was on their feet. Unlike their womenfolks, they had a-plenty of spiteful things to say together with a entire chorus of moans an' groans.

Cameron an' Jimmy was standin' over 'em with their shootin' irons handy, an' soon's all of 'em was able to walk or limp they was hustled outside an' down to the landin'. They was loaded into boats along with their women, 'thout havin' no chanct to take nothin' with 'em but what was on their backs.

I got up an' watched from the porch whilst they started polin' an' rowin' through the sawgrass an' away towards the east. Jimmy an' Cameron stood by with their guns till ever last one had plumb disappeared from sight.

We'd set aside one of their canoes, an' that afternoon Doc Summerfield an' Jimmy went off in it to fetch Jimmy's boat from that other place where we'd left it. Time they got back it were almost dark, an' me an' Cameron had been busy in the meantime.

After I'd scrounged 'round an' found a shirt that fit me we set 'bout fixin' a special meal for our last night in the Glades. Mostly we used supplies them plumers left behind. Seemed whiskey an' women wasn't the only things they'd spent their money on, 'specially that Gator.

They was cans of Cedar Keys oysters an' tinned ham an' pickled swamp cabbage—somethin' I'd never of imagined—an' a whole lot else besides. Even a couple bottles of champagne that Cameron said come all the way from France.

This time it were a real for-sure celebration.

$$\begin{array}{c} \text{37} \end{array}$$

Early next mornin', we packed up an' got ready to leave. But first they was one more li'l task we'd a mind to do, after talkin' it over with Jimmy.

Weren't no wind to speak of that time of day, an' Jimmy said if we was careful to clear brush an' such-like away from anywhere near to the Glades, them shanties an' shacks sat far enough back so he reckoned no fire in them was liable to spread. 'Sides that, he said he could feel rain in the air a-comin' later on.

So we used what was left of that white lightnin' an' everthing else we could find to set the entire place alight. Meant to burn it all right down to the ground an' leave nothin' behind but ashes.

For a good while after we'd started makin' our way back through the Glades we could see that column of black smoke risin' up to the sky. But then doggone if Jimmy hadn't been right or somebody up above were listenin'. 'Cause all of a sudden the sky opened up an' that li'l boat we was in got near-'bout swamped by a real old-fashioned frog strangler an' lighter knot soaker.

First rain of any account we'd seen in two-three weeks, an' I suppose it were needed. But I'd of been just as pleased if it'd held off for another few hours longer. We was all of us soaked to the skin time we finally climbed outen that boat an' made our way through the woods to that cabin of Miz Marcy's.

She were smilin' like her face would break as soon as she seen us, 'specially Jimmy. An' she didn't waste no time gettin' a hot fire goin' in the fireplace with chunks of fat pine. Then she hustled 'round fetchin' blankets so's we could shuck our duds an' start to dry out a mite. Whilst we was doin' that she went an' kindled another fire in the stove an' put coffee on to boil.

We all sat 'round then, takin' turns tellin' her 'bout what-all we'd been up to the last several days. She didn't have a awful lot to say herself, just asked a question now an' again. Made a li'l fuss over Doc Summerfield, though, when he got to relatin' his part of it. I reckon it were the first time in her life she'd ever met up with a real live perfesser from Princeton University.

After we finally got 'round to askin' her, she said she hadn't seen hide nor hair of no plumers anywheres about. I figured maybe they'd found 'em some other place to come out from the Glades. Miz Marcy an' me wasn't the only ones hereabouts they'd started gettin' theirselves crosswise with. Most everbody owned guns, an' 'cept maybe for that storekeeper they'd got to thinkin' whatever money them fellers had to spend weren't worth all the aggravation they caused.

Could be they decided to go back there after we was gone, but I didn't think it too likely. That fire an' the rain didn't leave 'em much to go back to.

What Cameron had to tell us next made it look even less likely.

"Do you remember Mister McCarty, the man who was buying and shipping the plumes?" He was talkin' to me, 'cause everbody else was just givin' him puzzled looks. "Well, as I came to suspect, he was working for a criminal syndicate in New England. The police in the area have had their eye on them for a long time, not because they were trading in plumes, which was only a small part of their operation. They also ran opium dens and houses of prostitution, along with shanghaiing sailors for whaling and the China trade. And while the buying and selling of plumes is perfectly legal, their methods of creating a local monopoly definitely were not."

I seen a glimmer of understandin' come into Doc Summerfield's eyes. He was noddin' his head as Cameron went on.

"Any newcomers to the area with plumes for sale were robbed of them and beaten—or worse. The makers and distributors of hats were threatened with fires and other destruction of property, along with thinly veiled warnings regarding their personal safety and that of their families.

"It was all part of a larger picture, and the police were on the verge of making a move against them without even knowing what I've just told you. But my wires gave them added ammunition, and access to a more respectable group of witnesses than most of their usual victims. I've reason to believe from the last communication I received that by now they've gone ahead with their plans, and if the syndicate isn't out of business it at least has more serious concerns than controlling the trade in plumes."

"Sadly," Doc Summerfield said with a shake of his head, "that won't make any great difference in the long run. The worldwide plume trade will continue, I'm afraid, along with the shocking destruction of birds."

"You're right of course," Cameron agreed. "Nothing is likely to stop that until or unless there's a significant change in fashion. But here in this part of Florida at least, the birds will have been given a brief respite. It will take time for other plumers to make inroads into the Glades. And perhaps some of the local citizens can persuade them to show more respect for people and property. That should make things safer here, at least for humans."

"I suppose that's something," the perfesser said with a scowl. "But there still ought to be laws to protect the rookeries. And I don't intend to rest until I can see such laws enacted!"

We didn't none of us have much to say 'bout that, though we wasn't too hopeful it would happen. They was too much money bein' made an' too many women that liked the way they looked underneath them big plumed hats.

Miz Marcy got up an' set herself to fixin' us a bait of dinner, an' by the time she'd got it ready our clothes was partly dry. We put 'em on damp rather'n set down at table in nothin' but our drawers.

They weren't a lot of talkin' whilst we ate. But after we got done an' was settin' 'round over fresh-filled cups of coffee, Cameron turned to me.

"I make it something over four weeks since I first put my proposition to you about helping with my investigation and acting as my bodyguard. Call it five weeks in round numbers. At fifty a week that comes to two hundred and fifty dollars."

Well, I hadn't hardly give a thought to that arrangement for some li'l while now. What with all them plumers done an' my own feelin's towards it, seemed almost like a sin to take pay for my part in things. But my momma didn't raise me to be scornful of cash money when it was offered. An' this here gent 'peared more'n able to afford it.

'Sides, I was goin' to need me a new cabin right soon. I'd made up my mind when I settled here that my wanderin' days was over. An' I didn't want to keep moochin' offen Miz Marcy an' her son no longer'n I absolute had to.

"I reckon that's fair," I told him. "Maybe a mite more'n fair. I'll be pleased an' grateful to have it."

"I don't have enough left in my money belt just at the moment," he said. "But I can give you part of it and write you a check for the balance."

"I ain't got no doubt any check you give me would be good as gold," I answered, a li'l hesitant. "But I ain't rightly sure how an' where I'd be able to cash it. Even that ole storekeeper in Lemon City prob'ly don't keep that much to hand. Nobody else hereabouts is liable to have more'n two-three dollars at any one time."

"Well, we'll work something out. I might arrange for money to be sent to the end of the rails. Or . . ." He thought for a second an' then grinned.

"No, I'll just come back here in several weeks and pay the debt in person! I've some other ideas I'd meant to look into and they could give me more reason to return."

We left it like that, though I were more'n a li'l curious 'bout what else he'd got in mind.

We made our beds up on the floor like we'd done a few days earlier, all 'cept ole Doc Summerfield who Marcy an' Jimmy insisted had to use his bed. Jimmy slept out in the front room with us. When me an' Cameron finally got 'round to rousin' ourselves next mornin' he'd already left the cabin.

He come back a li'l later, sayin' he'd gone an' made arrangement for a boat to carry the Doc an' Cameron an' that black horse of his 'round past the Keys an' up to Jupiter Inlet. They'd be able to catch a train from there.

We seen 'em off from the dock a tad 'fore noon, all three of us watchin' an' wavin' till they was nearly out of sight. I reckon we'd come to have a kind of a family feelin' towards them two Yankees with their funny way of talkin' an' their sometimes peculiar notions.

Weren't no way to guess if we'd ever see the perfesser again. But I knowed Cameron'd be back after a while. When that feller said a thing you could just bet your last dollar that he meant it.

🙂 38 🙂

It were three, four weeks later, an' I was workin' to put up a pole corral in back of my home place, havin' cleaned up most the mess around but not yet had a chance to start the bigger job of rebuildin'. All of a sudden Jimmy McCollum come bustin' through the woods like somebody'd set his tail on fire.

"He's back!" he shouted soon's he seen me. Then he had to pull up an' bend over with his hands on his knees to catch his breath. After a couple seconds he managed to kind of gasp, "I run all the way from the landin' in Lemon City to tell you." He stopped to swallow some more air, then straightened up with a big ole grin on his face. "An' you ought to see that boat he come down here in!"

Well, I reckoned I had a idea who he was talkin' 'bout. But I asked him anyway. "Who you mean? Who's back?"

"That Mister Major Cameron is who! He was standin' up there at the rail wearin' this blue brass-buttoned jacket with one of the short-billed captain's caps on his head. An' there next to him, holdin' onto his arm. . . . Well, you just got to come an' see her for yourself!"

"All right," I said, tryin' to sound calm so's he'd settle down a mite. I laid aside the post hole digger I'd been usin' an' went over to where I'd picketed Ole Roan an' the Cracker Horse a few yards away. "Help me saddle up an' we'll both go have a look."

Time we'd got down to the landin' Cameron had come ashore an' they was a gaggle of townsfolks gathered 'round him, includin' Miz Marcy who'd beat us there aboard that mule of hers. Everbody was tryin' to talk to onct an' gawkin' kind of open-mouthed at what they seen before 'em. A few was eyin' that low white-painted sloop pulled up alongside the dock. But most was starin' at the woman standin' next to him.

She were a real handsome lady, a li'l younger'n Cameron but maybe not so young that all that gold-red hair of hers hadn't had a touch of henna added to it. The way she was dressed fair seemed to take the breath away from ever woman in the crowd. Looked 'zactly like one of them drawin's in that Godey's Ladies' Book of Marcy's. 'Cept the big floppy hat she wore didn't have no feathers on it. Just a lot of fancy colored bows an' ribbons instead.

Folks was askin' if they'd be stayin' long in Lemon City. The place had a two-story roomin' house that called itself a ho-tel now, so sleepin' on the floor of Miz Marcy's wouldn't be a question.

Cameron said he weren't sure how long they'd be here, could be a week or so. Then one of the women asked if they'd come to a church social tomorrow, an' the lady with him smiled an' took her hand, sayin' nothin' would give 'em greater pleasure.

Jimmy an' me had dismounted an' was standin' under some trees a li'l ways back from the crowd, so it were some minutes 'fore Cameron seen us. Soon's he did, he come right up to us, leavin' his lady behind smilin' at everbody an' tryin' to fend off their questions.

"We'll want to check into the hotel and freshen up a bit," he told us. "Then Mrs. McCollum has asked us to her house for coffee and cake. We'll meet you there in an hour or so. There are a number of things I'll want to discuss."

He looked over towards the dock where a block an' tackle had been rigged to lift a good-lookin' palomino out from the boat they'd come in. "That horse will be one of them."

"You brung that black of yours too?" I asked. From what I could see of the boat it didn't look near big enough to carry two horses, 'specially not that big stallion of his.

"Oh, no. I've hired a carriage to drive around the area. My wife is a fine horsewoman, but these days she likes to travel in style."

"Well, from what I'd seen of her so far I was ready to believe that last part. She was a elegant lady, an' no mistakin'. Wondered what she'd think of that plain' an' simple cabin of Miz Marcy's.

Weren't no chance to do more talkin' right then, 'cause a black-painted two-wheeled buggy come along an' the driver got down to help Miz Cameron in it. She took the reins like she knew what they was for, but then she waited till Cameron come an' set down beside her. A colored feller that 'peared to of been on the boat with 'em brought the palomino up an' climbed into this li'l postage stamp of a saddle it had on. Then he follered 'em for the short ride to the ho-tel.

Me an' Jimmy got mounted our ownselves an' made our way out to Miz Marcy's cabin. Once again she'd managed to get there ahead of us. When we come inside after puttin' up the horses she was all in a flutter layin' out a white lacy tablecloth an' napkins, then fetchin' out her best china an' wipin' off whatever li'l bit of dust there might be on it.

Us two just backed up into a corner an' tried hard to stay outen the way. She weren't askin' no help an' looked like she might just take our heads off if we was even so bold as to offer.

When she'd got everthing fixed to her likin', with the coffee on an' a cake on the table covered by a cloth, she shooed us outside to greet our guests whilst she climbed into her best Sunday go-to-meetin' dress.

They had to park that li'l buggy with its high steppin' horse under some trees just off the road. Weren't no way to get it closer on that narrow path that went to the cabin. We met 'em out there an' pretty soon I begun to get the notion this good-lookin' wife of Cameron's weren't quite so high falutin' as she'd 'peared at first glance.

He introduced her to us as Miz Delilah Cameron an' she poked him in the ribs. "Dolly, Bri. It's just Dolly to my friends!"

Then she took a look at where we had to go an' unpinned her hat to toss it in the buggy. After that she lifted up her skirts an' proceeded to high-step it through the brush an' brambles, laughin' an' jokin' like it were the most fun she'd had in a coon's age. Weren't nothin' tony 'bout this gal.

When we'd climbed the steps she stopped for a second to brush some leaves an' twigs outen her hair. Then she let Cameron open the door an' she went inside with us three follerin' after.

Marcy were standin' at the head of the table, straight an' proud like some lady from a book by that Sir Walter Scott feller. Dolly went up to her an' and held out her hand. "I'm Dolly Cameron. You must be Marcy McCollum, and I'm very glad to meet you."

After that everbody started to relax a li'l.

Onct the coffee an' cake was served none of us menfolks had a awful lot to say. Them women took over the conversation an' 'peared to hit it off like a couple long-lost sisters. Me, I was pleased to just set back an' enjoy the feelin' of bein' amongst friends without havin' to worry 'bout some feller with a gun comin' 'long to try an' ruin my day.

Found myself kind of wishin', though, that we'd thought to bring back 'least one of them jugs of white lightnin' from out of the Glades.

Cameron let the women run on for a spell. But finally he reached over an' rapped on his plate with a spoon to get everbody's attention.

"I hate to interrupt this happy gathering, and I hope we'll have more of them in the future. But it's getting late and I still have some announcements to make."

He got up an' went to the door, openin' it to give out a loud whistle. Then he turned back to us an' grinned. "It's a few months yet until Christmas, but I thought—that is, Dolly and I thought—a few gifts were in order by way of saying thank you for all you did when I was a stranger here and needed your help. Jimmy, would you come out on the porch?"

He done it, an' the rest of us trooped along behind, curious to know what that gent was up to. Right in front of the steps stood the colored feller I'd seen earlier, holdin' the reins of that palomino horse.

"I once heard you say, Jimmy, that you'd dreamed of having a horse of your own. Well, now you do. She answers to the name of Ginger, and I think you'll find she's as fast and gentle as any horse you might have imagined."

Jimmy didn't say nothin'. He just swallowed hard an' stared for a minute. Then he turned an' grabbed Cameron's hand with both of his. 'Peared like maybe he'd got a li'l somethin' in his eye when he did it.

"Go on and get acquainted," Cameron said. "But come back inside after a little bit. We've other things to discuss." He turned to Miz Marcy. "The man who brought the horse is a friend of mine. Would you mind if he joined us inside?"

The feller had took off his cap, showin' a fringe of white hair 'round his baldin' head. Marcy looked at him an' smiled. "'Course not. Any friend of yours is a friend of ours. Come on in, Mister. I'll fetch you some coffee an' a bite of cake."

"This is Josiah Weatherford," Cameron said when we was all back inside, introducin' him 'round but lookin' mostly at me. "He is one of the finest builders and carpenters I've ever known. He has agreed, with your consent, to supervise the rebuilding of your cabin. Of course I'll be paying his salary, and for any materials he thinks are necessary."

Well, it was my turn to not have nothin' to say. 'Cept after a second or so I was able to manage, "Sure thing. Whatever you think had ought to be done. An' I'm powerful grateful to you both!"

After we'd all sat down again Dolly Cameron piped up, "We didn't forget you, Mrs. McCollum. That's a lovely frock you have on but we thought you might like something a little more recent. I've some fashion books in my luggage at the hotel, and if you'll come visit me we can look through them together and pick out an ensemble that suits you."

Like Cameron said, this were gettin' to feel more an' more like Christmas mornin'. Only I hadn't never had no Christmas like this in all my entire life. An' I don't reckon Miz Marcy nor Jimmy had neither.

'Course I'd knowed all along that gent had plenty of money. Weren't like he'd ever made a secret of it. But I guess I hadn't never pictured how much money it was. Nor what it could do, not just for him but for other folks too.

An' Cameron still weren't done. When Jimmy come in again he sat him down close by an' asked him serious-like:

"You saw that sloop that brought us to Lemon City?"

"I sure did! She's pretty as a gal young-'un an' looks like a real fine sailor too."

"She is that. How would you feel about captaining such a vessel?"

"Oh, man! With a ship like that a feller could make it to Key West an' back in just a few days. Carry passengers an' cargo betwixt 'em, maybe even go to Jupiter Inlet or far's Lake Worth. Prob'ly make a mint of money doin' it."

"That's what I've been thinking. Do you believe you'd know enough to captain her?"

"I reckon. I know these waters 'round here mighty good, an' I've been studyin' navigation with a couple of the fishin' boat captains."

"All right. Then when Dolly and I are ready to leave you can take us north along the coast to where we can make connections with Mister Flagler's railroad. After that the sloop will be yours to command. I'll split the profits with you fifty-fifty, and maybe in time we can discuss your purchasing her from me."

So that's how Miz Marcy wound up with a brand new dress, me with a brand new cabin, and Jimmy with a horse an' a business of his own. I near-'bout forgot to mention that Cameron payed me the rest of the two hundred an' fifty dollars he owed me. An' later he sent down a brand-new iron cook-stove on that boat that Jimmy was sailin'.

Who says Florida ain't the land of opportunity?!

THE END

Historical Notes

COONTIE ROOT:

What Floridians call by the Seminole name "coontie" may include several varieties of cycads with starchy root trunks. After being soaked in water to remove alkaloids, they can be ground up and used like flour. A major staple of the Indians' diet, it was gathered by early settlers and sold in the North as arrowroot.

COW HUNTERS:

In earlier times, free-ranging Cracker cattle had to be hunted out of the woods and swamps before they could be branded or driven to market. The Western word "cowboy" was not used in Florida. There are old-timers who like to point out that it was a job that took men to do it; no "boys" need apply.

THE EVERGLADES:

A vast "River of Grass" as described by Marjorie Stoneman Douglas. It is a miles-wide freshwater river that flows from the vicinity of Lake Okeechobee to the Gulf of Mexico and Florida Bay. Most of the "grass" is sawgrass, razor-sharp blades that rise from the water and create the impression of a prairie.

Much larger in the late nineteenth century when this story takes place, it reached to within a mile or so of Fort Lauderdale and was no more than five or six miles from Lemon City (see below) and what would become Biscayne Boulevard in present-day Miami.

The Everglades isn't all just sawgrass and water, however. It contains a number of low-lying tree islands filled with cypress, bay, strangler vines, and more exotic trees such as gumbo-limbo and the manchineel (see below). These provide homes for abundant wildlife, much of it surviving now due to the establishment of a national park in the south part of the Glades. Deer, panthers, bears, raccoons, and many species of water fowl share their habitat with alligators, snakes, and crocodiles—along with the ever-present mosquitoes.

HENRY FLAGLER, HIS RAILROAD, AND HOTELS:
Flagler was the partner of John D. Rockefeller in Standard Oil of New Jersey and rivaled him in wealth during what is known as the Gilded Age. He chose to spend the bulk of his fortune creating resorts in Florida for the very rich. After a visit to St. Augustine with his wife in 1883, he decided the ancient city should and could become what he called "the American Riviera." He opened the Ponce de Leon and Alcazar hotels there in the 1880s, and established the Florida East Coast Railroad with its luxurious Pullman cars to import his moneyed clientèle.

When those began to tire of St. Augustine's limited attractions, he extended his line south to Ormond Beach, Palm Beach, and Miami, with grand hotels at every stop. Despite the doubts of many, including the cow hunters in the novel, he capped his career by completing an "overseas railroad" to Key West in 1912, one year before his death. Twenty-seven years later it was destroyed by a hurricane and its roadbed formed the foundation for the "overseas highway" that still exists today.

LEMON CITY:
An early settlement on Biscayne Bay that predated Miami and was roughly contemporary with Coconut Grove. Both communities have since been absorbed into the sprawling City of Miami but are still recalled by local residents. The location of Lemon City was in the general area of Miami's Northeast 65th Street.

"LIGHTER KNOT SOAKER":
A "lighter knot" is a resin-filled knot of fat pine, used to start fires and is so dense and brick-like that it is virtually impossible for it to absorb water. The colloquial term, of course, is an exaggeration.

"MAMMYING UP":
In open range country (which Florida was until 1947), when it was time for new calves to be rounded up and branded, their ownership had to be determined by pairing the calf with its already-identified mother. This was not easy to do after the animals had been running free for several months, and required a special kind of expertise on the part of cow hunters.

MANCHINEEL:
Hippomane mancinella is a tropical tree that may grow to fifteen feet in height and is notable for its bright white sap that can produce burn-like skin sores on contact. One of many reasons for caution and alertness in the Everglades.

ORANGE GROVES AND FREEZES:

Oranges have existed in Florida since the earliest Spanish explorers. Like the British, Spanish explorers were well aware of the value of citrus in preventing scurvy. But rather than carry casks of lime juice aboard ship, they brought cuttings from orange trees, planting them wherever they made landfall. (Oranges had been introduced into Spain centuries earlier by the Arabs who ruled it.)

The trees thrived in Florida, with its sandy soil and abundant rainfall. But it wasn't until the railroads arrived that the delicate fruit could profitably be shipped to market in northern cities. After that, anyone who could get their hands on a few acres in Florida wasted no time investing in the lucrative business. It took just a few years for the trees to bear fruit, and groves were established all the way from Jacksonville to Sanford. Fortunes were made almost overnight.

Unfortunately, during the winters of 1893 and 1895 fortunes were also lost—literally overnight. Devastating freezes in those years wiped out the orange crop in the north of the state and left the owners gazing out over bleak and barren vistas of dead trees and fallen, worthless fruit. Many had borrowed heavily to expand their holdings, and were left with no recourse but to forfeit their property to creditors and move on in the hope of starting a new life somewhere else.

PAINTER:

Cracker term for the Florida panther.

PHOSPHATE:

An ore rich in nitrates that was a valuable source of fertilizer in the late nineteenth century—particularly in Germany, where local sources of nitrate were appropriated for the manufacture of munitions.

Although phosphate deposits had been found earlier in the Peace River valley, it was the discovery of hard-rock phosphate near Dunnellon in 1889 that set off a "boom" resulting in hundreds of open-pit mines, well-paid miners (two dollars a day instead of the usual one dollar), boom towns, gunfights, and high living. The inevitable "bust" came when World War I cut off the German market.

PLUME HUNTING:

Beginning in the early 1870s, the height of fashion for ladies included wide-brimmed "picture hats" adorned with the plumes of egrets, spoonbills, flamingos, and other tropical birds. (Sometimes these featured the stuffed bodies of the birds themselves!) The demand for plumes became so great that by the turn of the century the price for them in northern cities exceeded that of gold by weight—upwards of one hundred dollars an ounce!

Needless to say there was no shortage of those willing and able to fill the demand. "Plumers" in the Florida Everglades and other parts of the southern United States shot and killed millions of birds a year, taking only the showiest feathers and leaving the carcasses to rot. There was a real danger of extinction for many species, especially the snowy egret.

Opposition to the practice was sporadic at first, limited to ornithological societies and a few outspoken critics. But by the turn of the century, as the extent of the carnage became more widely known (and fashions began to change), efforts were made enact laws to curb such wanton killing. Florida was the first to pass such a law. In 1901 (several years after the time of the novel), it made the hunting of nongame birds a crime. Two years later, in 1903, President Theodore Roosevelt issued an executive order that established bird sanctuaries on federal lands.

None of this was likely to have made much difference, had not the end of the Gilded Age and the onset of World War I introduced new austerities. The result was much as it was a century earlier, when men began wearing silk top-hats and finally brought an end to the thriving trade in beaver pelts.